THE *Jeweler*

BECK ANDERSON

OMNIFIC PUBLISHING
LOS ANGELES

Omnific Publishing
1901 Avenue of the Stars, 2nd floor
Los Angeles, CA 90067
www.omnificpublishing.com

First Omnific eBook edition, October 2014
First Omnific trade paperback edition, October 2014

The characters and events in this book are fictitious.
Any similarity to real persons, living or dead,
is coincidental and not intended by the author.

Library of Congress Cataloguing-in-Publication Data

Anderson, Beck.
    The Jeweler / Beck Anderson – 1st ed.
    ISBN: 978-1-623421-43-4
    1. Contemporary Romance — Fiction. 2. Idaho — Fiction.
    3. Jeweler — Fiction. 4. Grief — Fiction. I. Title

10 9 8 7 6 5 4 3 2 1

Cover Design by Micha Stone and Amy Brokaw
Interior Book Design by Coreen Montagna

Printed in the United States of America

*To my boys and to my Chix,
for always having my back when I swing for the fences.*

Chapter One

"I just don't know, Jimmy. How come there aren't any canaries?" The frosted tips of her bangs rested against the glass counter.

"Naomi, honey, I've told you: you aren't getting a yellow diamond. It's too flashy. And he'd have to ship it in from San Francisco. Isn't that right?" Jimmy looked across the counter.

Fender Barnes stared out the window at the bustle of the Friday traffic. Downtown was busy as everyone tried to get out of town early for the long Labor Day weekend. People stood at the crosswalk, waiting for the light to change. He squinted as the sun bounced off the windshield of a passing car. "My usual supplier is in San Francisco, but I guess I could call around to the other stores in town."

That didn't seem to be the response Jimmy was looking for. He turned from the counter and took big strides around the shop. "I just think…" He let out an exasperated sigh.

Naomi picked her head up and looked at him. "When you said you'd do anything for me, I believed you. Now you're hemming and hawing." She paused before letting the last words fly. "This is about Veronica, isn't it?"

Jimmy stiffened. "I divorced Veronica to be with you. How can it be about her?"

Awkwardly, Fender shifted from foot to foot behind the counter. *I should charge counseling fees. Jesus.* He'd agreed to go into the jewelry business because of the design, not the sales—and definitely not because of the people. Why, *why* people thought a piece of jewelry would fix a relationship, or prove that they loved someone, was beyond him. Rings were beautiful hunks of rock wrapped in metal. Fender never bought into the "symbolism." Diamonds weren't forever—they were little pieces of carbon that had the random luck to get squashed deep below ground for centuries. If that was supposed to symbolize marriage, then okay—trapped and squashed. *That's glamour, all right.*

Naomi stared at Jimmy, lips set in a hard line. Fender looked at the pair. *Jimmy's not gettin' any tonight.*

"Fender, call around. Damn it, Naomi." He handed Fender a business card. "Call me when you find a canary diamond."

Naomi's lips released into a wide, toothy grin. She looked like the cat that ate the canary diamond, for chrissakes. She strode out of the shop with a despondent-looking Jimmy in tow. *Yeah, marriage. What a fabulous institution.* Fender grabbed the phone and began his search for a yellow rock.

After several hours of silence, when the shop's door jingled, he cringed. He'd been looking forward to closing time. Dealing with customers like Jimmy and Naomi hurt his brain, and he wanted out of the shop. But sure enough, at five minutes to five, in waltzed Prince Charming looking all pleased with himself.

Oh, God, Fender thought. *He's a bird.*

A lovebird. The kind of guy he could sell a crappy diamond to. The kind who wouldn't have a clue the diamond was crappy but would keep insisting on "the best for his girl." And then Fender would see the guy alone at the bar six months later, crying into his beer about being wronged. People were total idiots when left to their own devices. And, sadly, his business capitalized on that. He had too much pride to scam a lovebird, but if he'd wanted to, he surely could have. Love made people stupid.

"Can I help you find something?" Fender tried to sound patient. He probably sounded annoyed.

The blond man blinked a few times and flashed a set of impossibly white teeth. "It's actually an important purchase." He remained too pleased with himself.

Oh, gee, you're in a jewelry shop. What could it be? Is it a—a—ring? Fender bit his tongue to keep the words in his mouth.

"I'm buying a ring for my girlfriend. I'm proposing to her."

"Wonderful. Let me show you a few choices, and you can get ideas. What's your price range?" Fender looked for the keys to the display case. *I won't be out of here before six thirty. This sucks.*

Ginger sat at the bottom of the stoop. The pavement was buckled. It was old concrete, grainy under her toes. Brad was late again. She watched the guys in the park across the street play Ultimate Frisbee. They were probably her age, mid-twenties, but still in the "restless waiter" mode. These guys were not career-driven; they were at the park playing too often to be working serious jobs. They came every sunny summer afternoon. She liked the easy athleticism of their game. It appealed to her, made them fun to watch.

Her eyes followed one of the Frisbee players, hat turned around backward, as he reached to make a catch. Brad wouldn't wear a baseball cap. She'd bought him one when she'd visited Boston, gone back East to see friends from college. She liked the Red Sox, and she thought he might wear it if it was from her. But he'd placed it in his closet, and it never saw the light of day again.

Why this was a litmus test for her, she didn't know. If anything, a ball cap was the uniform of frat boys — immature, selfish, spoiled little boys. When she was at UConn, some guys even wore them with a coat and tie to the football games.

The Ultimate boys had now stripped to the waist and were playing with renewed effort. *You'd think these guys were defusing bombs.* But she liked their lithe, tan arms. They looked so uncomplicated. And so beautiful.

She turned her attention away from the park and went inside to find the nail polish. She opened the wood screen door and pushed past the Husky standing in the doorway. "What does it mean when you don't mind that he's not home yet?" she asked out loud.

The dog looked up at her.

"Can't be a good sign, can it?" The dog didn't answer. She was talking to herself again. *Mental note: no more talking out loud.* She fished the nail polish out of the bathroom drawer.

Twenty-five minutes later, she looked at her shimmery toenails. Now Brad was really late, and she'd started to feel restless.

Brad used to make her feel calm. They'd met her first fall in Boise, two years ago, at a dinner party. He was friendly, and he was attentive. They chatted a bit. The big smile on his face was the first thing she'd noticed. They sat next to each other at dinner. Then they'd parted ways.

Months later, Ginger drove out to the pound and got herself a dog. She'd been lonely, worried she might not meet someone in her new hometown, so she got herself a Siberian Husky that shed way too much and chewed on or ate everything. When Zoë ate fishing line, Ginger put the big dog in the car and drove to the nearest vet.

Who happened to be Brad. Zoë sat in the corner of the examination room, a trail of plastic line dangling out of her drooly mouth. Brad strode into the room and smiled at the dog. Then he looked up at Ginger and smiled, with a hint of recognition. He looked pleased to see her again.

He'd asked her out two days after he'd opened Zoë up to get the tangle of fishing line out of her gut. Ginger had said yes. Then he'd come by her house after that first date and had asked her out again. Simple as that.

She stood up and whistled for the dog. "Let's go on a walk," she called as Zoë came trotting. Restlessness didn't sit well with her. *I could train Zoë to catch a Frisbee.* Then all of her interest in the guys across the street would be for professional purposes. *Yeah. No one's going to buy that for a second.* She slipped on her flip-flops and grabbed a leash.

Fender's patience was running out. It was five thirty. The man, the lovebird, was still looking. Not even buying yet. Looking, looking some more, sighing, looking again. Fender hadn't even pulled out a velvet tray with rings on it yet. The blond man would stare into the glass case, eyes fixed on a ring, and Fender would think, *Okay, let's go. Let's sell you that ring.* But then the man would shake his head and sigh again.

"Not to be rude, but maybe if you told me what you were looking for?" Fender let the sentence hang there.

The man straightened. "Well, I don't know what I'm looking for. I was hoping it would just call out to me. It just has to be perfect; that's all I know."

"From experience, whatever you give her, she'll love." Fender lied through his teeth, but it was five forty-five and he wanted—no, needed—a beer. No woman was ever satisfied with what she got from his experiences. He'd seen women try to exchange engagement rings. They'd come into the shop to get their rings appraised. Fender remembered a woman in a snit because her husband-to-be wasn't willing to shell out three months' pay for a rock. This apparently spoke to his view of the bride-to-be's worth as a human being.

"Maybe if I told you a little bit about her, you could help me pick something," the man said.

"Well, sir—"

"Please, call me Brad." The blond man shook Fender's hand. Even his hand was good-looking. Strong and tan. Fender had a moment of hand envy.

"Well, Brad, I might be able to steer you in the direction of something. Did you have a price range in mind?" *Something ridiculously expensive for keeping me here after five o'clock?*

Brad ignored the last question. "Great. So, this girl, my girl. What do I say about her? I think she's a kind of winsome beauty."

Fender didn't know whether Mr. Lovebird was intentionally confusing him or just attention-challenged. "Now you've lost me, Brad."

"Too vague?" The blond man arched a perfectly groomed eyebrow. *Jesus, now I'm admiring his eyebrows. This man is too pretty.*

"I was thinking about how much jewelry she wears. Does she prefer gold or silver? Is she active? You know…"

Brad was still for a moment. "She loves animals. She has a great big Husky dog. You should see her with that animal; she babies her like—"

"Off track again, Brad," Fender said, cutting him short.

"Sorry. I can't help it, I guess. Everything about this girl makes me want to take care of her and kiss her wonderful freckled lips, and well, I could go on forever."

"Does she wear a lot of *jewelry*, Brad?" Fender clenched his teeth into a smile, to keep from chewing his own leg off. This was a coyote trap of customer service.

Brad was startled. "No, no, she doesn't."

"Okay, this is a start. Does she wear earrings?"

"You know, she has one little pair of dolphins she always wears. They've got little chips of lapis lazuli. One time she lost one when we were on the beach in Yachats. She was so cute. She made me get down on my knees and look with her, and she actually found it."

"Pretty cute. Are they gold or silver?"

"Silver."

"Here's the feeling I'm getting," Fender crinkled his eyes as if he were receiving a transmission from the heavens. *Here comes the pitch, Brad. Hold on to your socks, Mr. Lovebird.*

"What? What do you think?"

"Platinum setting. Silver is cheap, and white gold's too soft. She's active, right?"

"She likes to ski."

"Platinum, definitely. Now, someone with classic, simple tastes needs a classic ring, so I'm thinking a solitaire. And the shape should evoke the little girl inside of her—something to show how that cute side of her can come popping out any ol' minute! So, that makes me feel…pear-shaped."

"Really? That doesn't strike me as little-girlish."

Fender snorted. "No. Your future wife isn't going to want to look like a little girl. We're evoking the little girl side of her with a nod to tradition. You see?"

"Sounds great."

"Hang on. I think—you know, this could be a crazy coincidence." Fender disappeared into a back office. He rattled drawers and grabbed the diamond ring Old Lady Harriman had ordered and never come back for.

Emerging, he smiled as widely as he could stomach. "I knew I remembered a diamond like this. What a wonderful coincidence! Fate's kooky, isn't it?" He plucked the ring out of its box and let it sparkle under the counter lights.

"It's exactly what we were talking about! Where did it come from?" Brad's impossibly white teeth gleamed again.

Brad was sold, Fender could tell. Fender Barnes, boy genius jeweler, would be unloading a pricey ring nobody wanted and having a beer by six thirty, tops.

After a few more minutes, Fender handed the ring box with its precious cargo to Brad. Fender looked at the sales slip again and lined it up neatly with the check Brad had given him on the counter. He smiled and waited for the guy to leave.

"Take care now, Brad. Pleasure doing business with you." Fender fingered the front door key in his pocket. Even unloading a ring he'd thought he was taking as a loss could not stanch his desire to leave. *Walk out the door so I can lock it, you moron.*

"Thanks so much. She's gonna love it. I can't wait to give it to her." Brad swung around and hurried out the door.

Fender shut the door behind him. He flipped the *Open* sign over to *Closed* and got out his keys to bolt the door so he could finish cleaning up. Just then a blue car swerved toward the store at a crazy angle. Brakes squealed, and the sound of shattering glass followed the pop of light metal and fiberglass.

Fender instinctively took two steps back from the door. The blue sedan's front tires lurched up onto the sidewalk, and the car jerked to a stop against a light pole. Fender ran out the door to see. A man in a business suit jumped out and shook himself off. Then he turned and sprinted to the center of the street. Fender thought it strange that the man didn't come around the front of the car to check the damage.

That's when he saw the person. Actually, all he could see was a person's foot. It poked out from behind the tire of a red station wagon, which was turned sideways behind the blue car. A crowd of people hid the rest of the person.

Then Fender spotted something else. Under the chassis of the wagon was an object, amid the broken glass. It was small. It was a box. It looked like a ring box. It looked like the ring box he'd placed in Brad's hands less than two minutes ago.

Fender walked to the station wagon and got to his knees. Reaching an arm under the car, he felt for the fuzzy ring box. He closed his fingers around it, careful to avoid the shards of glass. He stood up and looked at the box in his hand as an ambulance arrived, and the paramedics loaded the injured person inside. When it left, the ambulance pulled away slowly, with no sirens or lights. The crowd of onlookers was silent. Fender turned and walked back into the shop, past the wrecked car on the sidewalk. A feeling pressed down on his chest. It felt like dread.

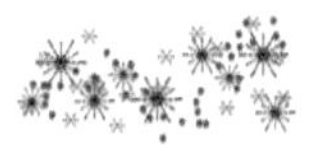

Zoë made a beeline for her water bowl as Ginger dropped the leash on a chair. The phone had rung three times before she could get it. When she did, a man spoke on the other end of the phone.

"Mrs. Janson?" The connection was crackly.

"No, what can I help you with?" *Salesman,* she thought.

"Is this the home of Brad Janson?"

"Yes, it is. What can I do for you?"

"Ma'am, Mr. Janson has been involved in an accident. Does he have family I can contact?"

"Not here. His parents live in Florida."

"We're transporting him to St. Mark's. You should contact his next-of-kin as soon as possible."

*Next-of-kin. They say that when…*Ginger grabbed her car keys. "I'm going to the hospital now. Thank you for calling."

"Good-bye, ma'am." The line went dead.

In the car, she clutched the steering wheel and tried to breathe. *Just get there; just get there,* she told herself. Every light turned red as she approached. The parking lot of the hospital was full. By the time she made it to the reception desk, her heart felt taut with adrenaline.

The nurse took her name, wrote down Brad's information, and left to find out his status.

The waiting area faced a covered drive with ambulances parked under the canopy. Two young men, paramedics, put a stretcher back into the one parked closest to her. She wondered if Brad had come to the hospital with them. No one else sat in the dingy chairs. She watched other people walk to the bank of elevators. Some looked relaxed; others had a worn look about them. She felt sick. She kept her focus on these people who did not seem surprised or shocked to find themselves here.

The magazines in front of her were all outdated copies of *Reader's Digest.* She absently flipped through them. She kept trying to figure out how to handle this and what was happening, anyway. Nothing came to her. But her hands wouldn't stop shaking.

The nurse came over, looking grim. She took one of Ginger's shaky hands in hers.

"Hon, I'm going to have you follow me."

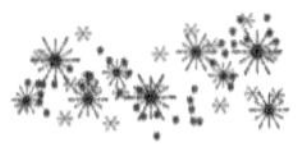

Fender locked the shop door and headed down the street with the ring box in his coat pocket. He wasn't sure what to do. After a moment, he looked up and found himself in front of the chrome door of the Rendezvous Bar. He nodded. *Pop will know what to do.*

He stepped inside. This thing was going to gnaw at him. *Really, how are you supposed to react when the guy who just bought an engagement ring from you becomes road pizza?* He had no idea. If someone else had found it, they would've kept it. That thought chapped Fender. *I worked hard on that sucker, it's worth a good chunk of money, and some dumbass off the street could've just picked it up.* So at least he had the ring. And he had the check Brad had given him. Now what? Now that he had the ring back, was it was stealing to keep the money? Maybe if he got rid of the ring, he could keep the money. But how was he supposed to know who to give it to?

"Sonny!" Fender knew that voice: Pop.

Fender's dad had retired five years ago and left his son the family business. Fender'd taken it on grudgingly. He was awfully young to be saddled with so much responsibility, and it was a forever kind of responsibility. He liked the finer points of owning a jewelry shop: designing stuff, flexible hours (Fender took a whole lot of license with the word *flexible*), and sometimes it was even a good conversation starter with a girl who caught his eye. But it was a job, and it was the family "legacy," and he was Fender Barnes, king of screwing shit up. He certainly couldn't take on Barnes and Son and then sell it to a schmuck off the street if things didn't go well. That would kill his pop. And he worried a lot that he'd lose the business. That would definitely kill Pop. *And he's been so happy lately, killing him with my ineptitude just wouldn't be fair.* Pop's occupation now was holding court in a booth in the back of the Rendezvous. He dispensed advice and opinions to anyone who stumbled into the bar on weekday afternoons. He especially liked to give advice to his son.

Fender made his way to the vinyl booth and scooted in opposite his father. "Hi, Pop."

Fender got the up and down once-over. "How are you? You look like you're worried."

"I'm okay." Fender paused.

Pop was eating an unusually greasy Rueben. He stopped mid-bite. "Fender, out with it. You're mulling. It's enough to give me heartburn."

"You get heartburn all the time. Look at what you eat, for crying out loud."

Pop set the sandwich down. "Are we going to chat like librarians at tea or are you going to tell me what you're here for? I know my son. Cut to the chase."

Fender shifted, and the vinyl creaked noisily. "This guy bought an engagement ring from me."

Pop huffed. "You'll have that in a jewelry store, my son. I'm beginning to wonder if putting you in charge was such a good idea."

Fender grew annoyed. Pop was right—time to cut to the chase. "He wouldn't shut up about the girl, and then he walked out in the street and got hit by a car. He dropped the ring, and I picked it up. So, now what do I do with it?"

"Take it to him in the hospital."

"I think he died, Pop. The way the ambulance took him away, I'm pretty sure…" His voice trailed off.

"Oh. Who's the girl?" His father focused intently on him.

"What girl?"

"Who was he going to give the ring to?"

"I have no idea." Fender wished for a second that he'd paid more attention to the love-struck man. *What was her name? Did he say it?*

"No worries, Sonny. This is what you do. Take the ring to his funeral; they'll say where it is in the paper. Look around for the saddest girl. That's the girlfriend. Give her the ring."

"I don't know, Pop, this—"

"Fender, this girl, this woman, she needs to know about that ring. This man was thinking of her in his last moments. She should know that, know that he wanted to marry her."

Fender felt a bad mood creeping up on him. "Maybe she'll be glad she's off the hook." He motioned to a figure behind the bar. He'd take that beer now.

Chapter Two

When Pop had called five days later, Fender hadn't even gotten out of bed yet.

"Found it for you, Sonny."

"What?" Fender had tried to clear his voice. He and two of the goldsmiths from up north had been out late the night before. He felt a little hung over. Maybe a lot hung over.

"The funeral. Of the guy. It's in the paper this morning. Now you can go find this woman. It's today out at Dry Creek. Four p.m."

"Thanks, Pop."

"Well?"

"Well, what?"

"You're going, aren't you?"

"*Yes*, Pop, I'll go."

"Grouchy! You ought to get more sleep. Bye, Sonny."

So, just a few hours later, there he was, at the funeral of a person he didn't even know. But he had to admit, the whole thing had been bugging him. He'd taken the ring home. The little box sat on his dresser and reminded him of the accident each time he reached in his drawer for socks.

He'd dug his one suit out of the back of the closet. He'd even taken a dishrag to the dust that had settled on the shoulders.

The sad fact was that people didn't even dress up for funerals anymore. He stood at the edge of the crowd and felt stupid in a dark wool suit. Beads of sweat raced from his armpits down to his waistband inside the shirt. What a stupid idea. What the hell was he doing here?

Then the priest started. *Well, shit. Now I can't go anywhere.* Who ever heard of somebody leaving a funeral early?

The priest really did say a lot of nice things about Brad, though. Sounded like he knew him personally. *That's nice. Jesus, no one'll probably even realize I'm dead until the stench is so bad from my condo, the neighbors call the cops.* Fender shook himself out of it. *I'm supposed to find the girlfriend. Concentrate.* The ring box pressed against his chest pocket urgently. *Find the girl, Fender.*

He looked around. *Okay. She's the girlfriend, so probably near the casket. Not right next to it.* He stepped left to get a better view of the chairs under the awning. There were only two. *Gotta be Mom and Dad.* Sure looked like it. A gray-headed man in a suit had his arm around the woman. She had dark hair, a Nancy Reagan suit, and bony, old-looking hands. She kept her eyes focused on the ground in front of her. A handkerchief was permanently at her mouth in one of the bony hands, stifling sobs.

Behind them. It had to be her. She looked around at the other people. She looked bewildered, almost. She had long, reddish-blond hair. Part of it was pulled into a barrette at the top of her head, and some had fallen into her face.

Her eyes darted around again and rested on him briefly. They were a very deep green. They were wet with tears. She shifted, and he noticed how the hem of her dress floated up with the breeze.

Hmm… This had to be her. *Oh, God, I cannot talk to this woman. She is…she's like…* Fender turned around and headed for the car, certain he was the first person in history ever to bail in the middle of a funeral.

Ginger stood still and felt the wind play at the hem of her dress as she looked out over the town. The streets had a haze of brownish smog over them. She could barely make out the cars. She had a strong sense that, for the rest of the city, time moved forward and an ordinary day was in full swing.

But for her, time had paused here, in this green square perched on a dusty foothill. The arch of the cemetery gate signaled a time-out from the regular world. It'd been five days since she had gotten the awful phone call. Ginger felt loss, but it still seemed Brad had gone away, that he was alive somewhere, just not here.

So, she tried to talk herself into it. She focused on the glossy lid of the coffin and reminded herself that he was in there. She wondered if people who witnessed a death were the only ones who really believed the dead person wasn't just away.

Ginger had never seen someone die. Only once had she seen someone almost die. It'd been terrifying. A man had collapsed at a football game when she was in college. He'd been walking on the track, coming toward her, holding a Coke and a bag of popcorn. It'd been a humidly oppressive day. She'd been looking at him because she was bored and because he was in front of her.

And then it happened. His personality disappeared. He'd had a distinctive walk — a swagger almost — as if he'd been conscious of walking in front of the crowd. But in an instant, his face was expressionless, his eyes not focused anywhere. He fell forward, and his hands did not come up to break his fall.

The paramedics, rushing from the sideline of the field, had descended on him and rolled him over. He'd already become a person again, only a person in pain and distress. His face was bleeding, but the emotion and expression had returned.

What stayed with her was the impression that his personality had evaporated in the afternoon sun. She remembered feeling scared and bewildered as she witnessed his body shutting down.

Maybe if she'd seen Brad's face just at that moment when he was gone…then maybe she could stand here and realize the void opening in her life. Right now she just felt numb.

The green awning over the grave creaked a bit in the wind, and Ginger looked around at the other people in attendance. Some were visibly upset. Others looked more concerned with finding a good vantage point. She stood at the edge of the Astroturf that lined the gaping hole in front of her. Brad's parents sat in front of her.

Ginger hadn't made much of an effort to talk with them. She felt out of place after the hospital. She'd made the awful calls and picked up his parents at the airport the next morning, but afterward there had been a strange stillness to her life. Brad's folks handled the details of the funeral, and they didn't seem to care to have her involved. Ever since she and Brad had moved in together, she hadn't worked during the summer — Brad's practice was successful, and with her off in the summer, it had given them flexibility to travel. So now she had nothing to do. Even her friend Molly had cooked dinner for her and picked out the navy dress she wore for the funeral.

She'd skipped the open house Brad's family held and made a brief appearance at the wake. Brad's mother had come by the house to pick out a suit for him to be buried in and a photograph to place on the casket at the graveside service. But she didn't touch anything else, and she hadn't lingered. Brad hadn't made his family very happy when he'd decided to move out west. He hadn't really gone home to visit, and they hadn't come out to see him, at least not since he and Ginger had been together. She simply didn't know his mom well enough to have anything but brief apologies and sympathies to say to her during her short time at the house. And then Ginger had been left alone.

It was a relief to go to the funeral, really. Facing the prospect of cleaning the house or packing up his things was unthinkable. What would she do with his clothes?

The house was filled with his things, their things together. What upset her was looking at all the mundane stuff. Toothbrush. Who cared about his toothbrush? How could she get rid of it, though? A person accumulated stuff, never figuring he wouldn't be around to tie up the loose ends. Brad had arrogant, unfinished stuff, like half-drunk Gatorade bottles in the fridge.

And his office. Who'd take his patients? Who'd take care of Zoë? It all washed over her, and she felt powerless against the details. This was her grief, and she had a feeling this was how she would realize the cold fact of it: Brad was dead, and he was not coming back. And people would probably deal with that, eventually. The details would be tied up, his affairs settled, and some other vet would treat Zoë when the dog was sick.

Ginger felt nauseated. A vague uneasiness worked its way up into her consciousness. She couldn't put a finger on it, and exploring what this was about felt evil and rumbled in her gut. She didn't poke at it. She let the strange awareness stay under her shock and sorrow.

People crowded around, and she marveled at the variety. Some of Brad's buddies wore khakis and golf shirts. Older friends of Brad's parents had flown in and wore dark suits. Women's attire ran the gamut. Only in the West would casual attire be okay at a funeral. No place was too fancy or too somber for shorts. She thought Brad might have liked that.

It occurred to her, looking around, that she shared no friends with Brad. He had his mountain biking buddies, his fellow veterinarians, his fishing buddies—she knew none of these men except in passing. She had no one to speak to at his funeral, really. That struck an odd chord, and she tried not to dwell on it.

The priest seemed to be wrapping up his homily, so Ginger tried to quiet her mind and listen. He was a client of Brad's. His golden retrievers were longtime customers, and it was comforting to know this man in black could say something about Brad from experience. She decided she needed to get to know clergy. If she were gone tomorrow, it'd be an anonymous service some holy man would have to give.

That would be horrible. Brad was different, though. So many people could think of him fondly and tell good stories about him. *Life is not fair.*

Chapter Three

After the funeral, Ginger retreated to her mother's house in Washington State. Her parents had divorced some time before, and Mom had chosen to make her home in the wet forests of the Northwest. In the woods, Ginger took long walks in the ever-present drizzle and stared out of the window a lot. At night, she turned on the TV for distraction and did not think of sleep until the sky had edges of pink in the east. She gathered her mother's Corgi dogs and Zoë's big Husky fluffiness around her on the bed as the dawn came. Then she fell into the deep sleep of melancholy. Whenever she awoke, she felt as though she was entering a hazy world she wasn't connected to. And by then, her mother had gone off to work, and she was alone.

What should've been a few weeks' stay turned into two months. Then—suddenly it seemed—autumn crept into the forest. On a typically wet day, Ginger smelled fall in the air as she walked along the path to the house. She kicked at the fallen leaves and pine needles under her feet, and the dogs all bobbed along the trail in front of her. As she approached the house, Ginger saw her mother sitting on the porch in one of the lawn chairs. She had a thick coat pulled up around her chin. Ginger sat down next to her. The dogs continued to circle the porch, sniffing twigs and rocks for clues. Ginger watched the dogs and avoided her mom's gaze.

"Ginger, it's time to go back."

Ginger looked up at her. Her eyes seemed soft, but Ginger knew she'd be firm. So, she packed up and took one last walk with Zoë and the little squat dogs through the mist. Then she headed back to life.

When she opened the door to the house, she shuddered. Tied to the habit of unlocking the door was the expectation of Brad's voice greeting her from the kitchen. But the house held its tongue, and loneliness settled over her. Zoë seemed to sense the tension of the moment and flew past her into the living room, skidding across the hardwood floor, butt first.

Ginger could not think. She carefully brought her bags into the house, unpacked them, brushed her teeth, put on pajamas, and climbed into bed. She held the grief and thoughts and worries and avalanche of emotion behind a wall inside of her, and lay very still. It was the only way she could figure to function. She could survive and hold on, and maybe later she could handle something more than that.

A few mornings after her return, the dry November air in Boise smelled like snow, and Ginger actually felt an enthusiasm creeping up on her. The season was about to begin, and she could lose herself in the work on the mountain. She would zipper up her winter coat and be surrounded by little girls and boys demanding her attention and love. Teaching them to ski meant distraction, and maybe even smiles.

And it was true. Snow dumped on the resort the week before Thanksgiving, and she went back to the mountain. In the bustle of a new season, it was easy to work and to forget. The one thing that tugged her back to her memories felt a whole lot like guilt. She noticed men. She'd be riding the chairlift and look down to see a strong figure cutting long, lazy curves in the snow. She'd gaze down at the man and wonder about his life. Wonder what kind of woman lay in bed next to him at night, or if he was alone—alone like she was.

And as soon as she remembered her loneliness, she remembered the reason. Then her stomach would turn at the sight of the man. Out of guilt, or fear, or remembering, she didn't know, but Ginger's body recoiled, whatever it was.

At night, she did sometimes sleep, mostly because of the sheer physical exhaustion of lifting little kids up from the snow all day. But many nights stretched into day, and Ginger would stare at the ceiling, turning what had happened over and over in her head.

She was torn about the house. Brad, ever the responsible one, owned it outright and had left it to her in his will. She'd never even considered a will, but Brad had his veterinary practice, he owned things, he had things to leave to people. She owned a dog. And a bike her mom had given her when she graduated high school. She could leave a nice set of luggage to someone—her grandpa had bought it for her when she turned sixteen.

Nights passed. She lay in this house that was hers now and stared at its ceiling. She couldn't imagine selling it, but it felt suffocating. Sometimes it felt safe, but sometimes it was a reminder of so much, it felt like that ceiling would collapse in on her. It was loaded down with so many memories. All of this would tumble through her brain for most of the night, on most nights. If she were lucky, she'd fall asleep in short spurts, waking fitfully and often drenched in sweat. And then she'd drag herself out of bed and go to teach on the mountain.

She wondered when it would all feel okay again.

Chapter Four

Fender didn't tell Pop the truth. When he'd returned to the bar the night of the funeral, Pop had asked if it went well, and he'd just said yes and left it at that.

Maybe his father knew he was lying, but Pop didn't press the issue. He was grateful for that. In fact, Pop hadn't mentioned the girl again.

Not that Fender forgot about her. He could close his eyes and see her on that hillside—the green eyes wet with tears, the bewildered look, the long reddish-blond hair—all of it would come back to him. Then he'd shrug it off, because it reminded him that he'd turned so abruptly and headed for the car. In the middle of a funeral, no less. To him it was yet another sign that he was morally bankrupt and probably going to hell.

Because his train of thought about the girl usually ended in a picture of him frying for all eternity, he tried not to think about her. *Tried* being the operative word. There was the ring, after all. Every night he passed the ring box on his dresser as he went to brush his teeth. Some nights he'd open the box just to check that the ring was still in there. And it would be, the pear-shaped diamond reflecting up at him like a cat's eye in a dim room, sparkling.

After some months, as the weather turned cool, it was easier to walk past without picking it up. But it was still there, and it still summoned the vision of that lovely young woman, dress fluttering in the breeze, standing under the burden of her loss.

A realization struck him one night in bed, and the force of it sat him straight up out of a deepening sleep. As he'd been dozing, the sickening pop of metal and glass echoed somewhere in his memory, and he saw the flash of a slow ambulance pulling away. Then the dry, sunny day at the cemetery flickered in his drowsy mind. Hell or no hell, it was right to give her the ring. Find her and give her the ring. Even if his mad dash to the car the day of the funeral had doomed him, *she* gave him the resolve to find her. It certainly wasn't his moral fortitude. No, it was the girl herself who asked him to do this for her. Or at least that's how it seemed as he sat up in bed one night.

So, he did some detective work. He looked at Brad's address on the sales slip, and then spent at least a good month talking himself into it first. In fact, all the soul-searching took Fender into the autumn months.

When he went to the house in November, there was a chill in the air. The tips of the mountains were already piled with snow, and flurries had been threatening the valley on a regular basis. The weather matched the house's mood; it was quiet, and in the gathering dark of a fall evening, it seemed to hold no promise of the girl. *Maybe she moved after he died, genius. She may never even have lived here with him.* Fender hated his own stupidity sometimes.

He sat in his car for at least half an hour, contemplating the sad face of the house. He realized it was not within his power to get out of the car. He just watched the sycamore in front of the house let its leaves drift to the sidewalk.

He was still sitting there when the car pulled up—a little white hatchback. It zipped into a parking space in front of the house, just down from Fender's car. The car's lights winked off, and the driver's door swung open. There was snow on the bumper and at the base of the windshield.

Fender held his breath. She got out of the car. It was the girlfriend, no question. The long hair was swept up in a sloppy ponytail, her slim form outlined in a black turtleneck and black leggings. From where he was parked and in the increasing darkness, he couldn't see her face very well. Oh, but it was her. Then he realized he should breathe again and gasped noisily.

She began to take something out of the hatchback of her car. A clue to her life. What would it be?

She hauled out a pair of skis and a big black parka with the words *Blackwolf Ski Resort* across the back. She was a skier. *Of course she is*, Fender remembered. Brad had told him she was. He felt an idea forming in the crevices of his brain. A skier. Maybe he could track her down at the resort.

He'd been sitting here long enough. He started the car and turned in the seat to back out of the space. His elbow leaned against the steering wheel, and his heart jumped as the horn blared into the night. *Sweet Jesus!* Fender peeled out, flying past the little white car and its owner.

Ginger jumped when she heard the car's horn. She turned around as its engine revved too high and the black sedan peeled out.

That was weird. She tucked her parka under her arm. She'd forgotten to turn on the porch light this morning, and it was getting dark quickly. The faded two-story house sat quietly under its bare sycamore tree. She still wasn't sure how she felt about the house. Sometimes it was a familiar friend. Sometimes it just reminded her of Brad and what had happened to him. She'd resolved to worry about staying or selling it after some time had passed, at the very least after ski season was over.

Because she didn't want to think about that now. Tonight she was going to start living her life again, no matter how hollow it made her feel.

After he'd hounded her for weeks, Ginger had decided she'd go out with Bode, a ski patroller. She said hello to him every day at the top of the Deercreek lift, where he manned the patrol lookout. He was a little younger than she was, but he was always very sweet and had been especially nice to her since the word got out about Brad. This season, when he saw her, he'd always ski along with her for a few feet and ask how things were going. This little routine had been going on for three weeks when, one day, Bode touched her elbow and stopped her from heading down the cat track.

"Ginger?"

"Yeah?" She looked into his scruffy face.

"Hey, can I ask you something?" He shifted on his skis and stabbed at the snow with the tip of his pole.

"Sure." She looked past him at the eight-year-olds she was supposed to be teaching. They pummeled each other with snowballs. "You better ask me quick, though—the natives are getting restless."

"Yeah, those little guys are cute. I think it's great how you teach 'em to ski. Really great." He smiled at her. They just stood there, smiling at each other.

"Bode, what were you going to ask me?"

"Huh? Oh, okay. Hey, I was thinking you could go out with me. We could go have pizza, or if you don't like pizza we could have Chinese, and it would be casual—not serious 'cause I know how you felt about Brad and all—geez, I didn't mean to remind you about that—but anyway, do you want to sometime?"

"I don't know."

"Hey, you know, you're so pretty, and you seem so sad, and I thought you might deserve a nice night out." He smiled really wide again, and his sun-streaked hair hung in front of his eyes.

The Ultimate boys. He's just like one of the Ultimate Frisbee boys in the park during the summer. "That sounds good. When do you want to go?" Ginger breathed in deeply.

So, now she was hustling into her house to get ready for a date. They were going to Peking, the Chinese restaurant downtown, and she was terrified. A couple times today, as she'd gotten off Deercreek lift, she'd thought about canceling. It was too soon. Brad would've thought it was too soon.

But then she'd seen Bode, and it seemed like it wasn't the worst idea in the world. He'd been tossing pistachios into another patroller's mouth in front of the patrol shack. That'd reminded her again of the Frisbee boys. Some part of her thought it might not be too bad to go.

She pulled on her jeans and tried to ignore the terrible feeling clutching at her heart. She felt as if she were drifting. No routine, no regular way to handle this. She'd relied on familiarity, patterns, to keep her life on track. A date with another person had never been part of the routine while Brad was…*Oh, Brad.* She blew off the tight feeling in her chest. *Screw this. I've got to go out, and that's it. It's time to be alive again.*

A car pulled up in the drive. It was Bode. She grabbed her keys and got the hell out of the gloomy house.

"I'm a snake." Bode announced sixty-eight minutes later as they dug into the General's chicken. Ginger paused mid-chew. Had she misheard him?

"What did you say?"

He swallowed a very full bite. "I'm a snake."

She wondered if she was supposed to protest. He'd seemed nice enough this evening. "Okay…"

"What are you?" He smiled at her and stabbed his chopsticks into a big pile of lo mein.

"Excuse me?"

He shook his head. "You have no idea what I'm talking about. Chinese zodiac. What sign are you?" He pointed a chopstick at the placemat on the table, the animals of the Chinese zodiac pictured in an illustrated wheel.

She took a minute and looked. "Dragon."

"That's cooler than a snake. I sound like I'm not a good guy." He chewed and thought about it for a minute.

"Are you?" Ginger wondered what he might say.

Bode had already moved on. "Am I what?"

She smiled. *Frisbee boy.* "Nothing. You're pretty quick with the chopsticks."

He nodded and launched into a story, waving his chopsticks around aimlessly. "I'm the youngest of three brothers. Back when I was little, if I wasn't fast, I'd end up with no food on my plate." He shoveled another mouthful of rice into his mouth with the sticks sideways. She listened and watched him eat and talk. He seemed only vaguely aware that she was there. He'd probably talk and eat like this with or without someone across the table.

Snake or no, he was definitely entertaining.

Three hours passed with a lot less pain than Ginger had expected. As Bode parked his car in front of her house, she felt pretty good. She'd even stopped checking the time on her phone after the main course. He'd kept the conversation moving through dinner, and they never once touched on the subject of Brad.

"Do you want to come in for a second?" She heard it come out of her mouth.

After some glasses of red wine in the living room, Ginger found herself on the couch with Bode. Now he was definitely paying attention to her. Definitely knew she was there. Things felt increasingly intimate. The conversation had stalled, and he touched her arm. He rubbed her shoulder in light circles with his fingers. She tried to think of something funny or witty to say to distract him, or her, from the fact that he was working up to something.

Ginger could see where this was heading. She felt a twinge of dread.

He was still for a moment and looked into her eyes. "You've got a stray hair." He brushed the hair off of her cheek. Then he leaned close to her and kissed her.

"You're a really beautiful gal." Bode rubbed her back. He said it again. "You're so beautiful."

If he kept talking, he was going to ruin it. Who says *gal?* She hated the word *gal.* The hair move was a little cheesy, too. Everything that came out of his mouth now sounded tired and well-practiced. He was a player—that's what everyone on the mountain said. Maybe he really was a snake.

She couldn't quiet her brain. How many women had he used these lines on? She started to feel a little claustrophobic.

At that moment, there was an awful shredding sound from the center of the room. It sounded like the seams being torn out of something.

"What the hell was that?" Bode sat up on the couch.

Ginger reached behind her and turned on the light. Zoë stood in the center of the rug with Bode's red Patagonia parka in her teeth. The zipper had been torn completely out.

"Hey, dog! That's my coat!" He leapt off the couch and tried to wrench the shreds out of Zoë's mouth.

"God, I'm sorry. She's being protective, I guess." Ginger left off there.

"I think I'm going to go."

"Okay." Ginger didn't put up much of a fight. It wasn't time to try this yet.

Chapter Five

In the weeks after his potentially humiliating experience on her street, Fender tried to forget the girlfriend. He hoped she hadn't noticed the black car fly by her, but he knew it was unavoidable. Even he could smell burned rubber after the peel-out. *How cool was that? So suave.*

He still had the diamond. He didn't have the guts to walk up to the door of her house and ring the doorbell. He kept trying to picture it: "Hi, you don't know me, but I've held onto a ring your dead boyfriend bought from me three months ago, and I thought you might like it. Oh yeah, and I picked it up off the street after he got flattened out front of my store." Yes, that would be truly the best introduction to a woman he'd ever make.

Actually, it'd probably just skip a lot of the steps Fender usually went through with a woman, before they got to the part where she slapped him or slammed the door on his toe and burned his underwear in a pile on the street. He never did seem to get along with women very well.

Maybe it was because he and Pop had lived alone for so long. After Fender's mother had passed on, it was up to Pop to run the jewelry store and the house and make sure Fender didn't end up in the penitentiary. Pop always said that considering the circumstances, he felt Fender had a halfway normal childhood. Fender didn't know about normal. But then again, he figured he could have grown up with Ward and June, and his true warped self would have shone through (or turned up like a persistent fungus—it kind of depended on how Fender was appreciating his personality that day).

During Fender's youth, Pop and he had spent lots of quality time over blue topazes and platinum settings in the store—and having heart to hearts on the way home from the police station.

Fender's memories of the time right after Mom died were dim. Lots of tears, rooms too quiet, and sometimes Pop in the bedroom with the door closed and sounds of crying. Fender tried to be good, to stay out of the way and under the radar. But later, after he survived his grammar school years and emerged as a teen, Fender had found he just didn't give a shit what other people thought. One night he got arrested for releasing the parking brakes on all the cars parked on Sherman Hill in the east end of town. That was pretty damn fun to watch: the cars slowly cruising, driverless, down to the bottom of the road, rolling right into the barrow pit at the end of the lane.

Another time, after he'd passed through that phase, Fender had tried to talk to Pop about his mom over a tray of amethysts set in fourteen-carat gold.

"Pop?"

"Yes, Sonny?"

"What did Mom love about me? Do you remember?"

Pop had stopped placing the rings in the tray and looked out the plate glass windows, staring at something far, far in the distance. "Your mom loved the future in you."

"What do you mean?"

"She loved talking about what you were going to be like when you grew up, that's all." Pop made a snorting noise, pulled out a blue handkerchief, and blew his nose, hard.

Fender felt his hands go clammy. "We don't have to talk about it anymore, Pop."

Pop shook his head. "No, it's fine, Sonny. She would've liked you here with me. I know that. She loved it when we had Kowalski re-do the lettering on the storefront to read 'Barnes and Son' when you were born. That made her year when we did that. She gave me a hard time about it, said I was 'predetermining destiny,' but she really loved the idea of it." He cleared his throat and tucked his handkerchief back in his pants pocket. "And she'd love it that you're learning about the business. Take these amethysts, for instance. If you grab a loop, I'll show you why this one here is ten times the ring that other one is."

And the moment was over, just like that.

Poor Pop. Fender looked back on his "wasted youth" and didn't feel regret; he just felt sorry for his dad. Oh, to have a son who excelled in mediocrity, with a side of troublemaking. This was yet another reason to never have children; they might inherit his juvenile delinquency. And another reason not to get married. But Fender was constantly reminded why he despised marriage, regardless. Every time he'd craft a delicate setting with a pale, clear diamond, and it went on the hand of a crass, selfish gold digger, or some cheating, sweaty lout gave a necklace of blood red rubies to his unsuspecting, hard-working wife, Fender remembered how he felt about the sacred institution.

And so today, Fender stood behind the counter at the store, trying to decide which bar to end up at after he closed. Downtown was busy with holiday shoppers, and Fender was worn out. Business was good, but it was tiring, actually selling jewelry instead of goofing off.

And then he saw it: an unmistakably huge frizz of blond-streaked hair. *Oh, Jesus. Naomi. Jimmy's Naomi. As in get-me-a-canary-diamond-or-I-will-tie-your-balls-in-a-knot Naomi.* God, he'd called all over town to get a yellow diamond for ol' Jimmy. Fender remembered the pained tone of Jimmy's voice after he'd told the poor guy how much it'd cost to get the one he'd found in Portland. But Jimmy had spent the money, all in the name of love, marriage, and the American dream.

"Excuse me."

The hair was hovering in front of him. *Oh Lord, she said something.* "Can I help you?"

"Do you remember me? I came in here with Jimmy."

"Yes, I remember you. Naomi, wasn't it?" Fender felt a headache coming on.

"Let me tell you what I'm here for, and you tell me if you can help me."

"Okay."

"How much is the ring worth?" She took it off her finger and chucked it on the counter. Fender cringed as it clattered against the glass of the display.

"Well, now, that's not totally easy to say. It's a custom ring, you know."

"Look, just tell me what it's worth. I want to know what Jimmy was willing to spend on his second wife. You know, the runner-up, the second-best choice, the consolation prize." Here she sucked in her breath, like she was going to discuss some horrible atrocity. "His trophy wife." Her voice was sour, like lemon squeezed into a weak drink.

You're one hell of a trophy to win. "Well, Jimmy bought it as a gift. I don't think he intended for you to know what it cost. It kind of spoils the sentiment, doesn't it?"

"What it does is tighten his hold over me. That's what my therapist says. She says no woman should be bought for a shiny piece of glass. She says Jimmy wants me to think I can be bought or sold like property, that he owns me. Like our wedding gave him power over me."

Fender realized he was in the wrong profession, obviously. He should be blowing smoke up somebody's ass for a hundred bucks an hour.

He took a deep breath and looked the stupid bitch straight in the eye. "Jimmy doesn't strike me as a tyrant. In fact, he seems like a really nice guy. He bought you a very expensive diamond because you wanted it. Now you come in here and want to know what it's worth? He only bought it because you wanted it, and you think he was trying to buy you? I think that's damn sad."

Her blond head quivered under all that hair. "Fine." She picked up the ring and walked out.

Well, now, that was fun. Jimmy is a poor bastard. Fender decided a beer at the Corral was definitely in order—in honor of Jimmy, the husband wedded to the wife from hell.

It was quiet at the Corral. Most normal people didn't frequent it until they'd consumed a good number of drinks in some other more-respectable establishment. That was one reason Fender came here early. He could rest assured there would be no hipster nonsense or collegiate crap for another couple hours.

He felt kind of bad for avoiding the Rendezvous, but he just didn't want to see Pop tonight. His father always had to reign supreme over the crowd in there and act like being a regular endeared him to all the customers. Most of the time Fender could deal with Pop's unrelenting friendliness and hospitality, but tonight he wasn't in the mood.

He also didn't want to discuss the dead guy's ring or girlfriend with Pop. He could talk about it with Sam. He hadn't seen Sam in a long time, and maybe he could understand why this ring thing bugged him so much. And if Sam didn't understand, hell — they could just get tanked.

He stepped outside to call him. The phone rang twice before someone answered it.

"*What?*"

"Hey, Sam, it's Fender."

"Oh geez, sorry. Sears Credit's called nine times in the last two hours, and I'm gettin' sick of it. I keep telling 'em I'm not paying for a flat screen that was stolen ten months ago, you know?"

"Let it go to voice mail, then."

"That's too easy. This is war, my friend."

Fender loved Sam, if only because his life was more screwed up than his own. Sam actually took satisfaction in defying every logical life lesson he could. After a degree from a culinary school in California, he'd returned home to take on a very prestigious position as a short order cook at the Morning Bird Restaurant. He also tried to smoke more weed than the rest of the town combined and prided himself on living in a house that was on the verge of being condemned.

"Come down and meet me at the Corral."

"Okay." The line went dead. The other thing Fender loved about Sam? Never had to twist his arm about going out.

<h1 style="text-align:center">Chapter Six</h1>

A dog is the perfect companion.

Take Zoë: she always cuddled close on a winter night, and she smiled at things like squeaky rubber newspapers, burned dinners, and toilet seats left up for a drink. She barked at things that went bump in the night. Chased squirrels out of the yard, too.

Zoë also bailed her owner out of potentially embarrassing situations. Zoë's penchant for impromptu chew toys had saved Ginger from a possible mistake of the century with Bode last month, which probably would've made news at every patrol lookout on the mountain before the lifts opened the next day. But because of Zoë, it hadn't.

Zoë also didn't look at her owner twice when she ate a pint of Ben & Jerry's Phish Food in one sitting. Didn't look down her pink nose at the movies Ginger watched on the Hallmark Channel. Didn't question her commitment to the relationship if she let the laundry pile up, or the house plants die, or one or two — okay, ten — checks bounce at the bank. Zoë was perfectly fine with all of that.

Brad wouldn't have liked that Zoë sat in bed with Ginger now, watching those movies and eating the ice cream. Hell, Zoë and Ginger even used the same spoon, though not on purpose. But Ginger was disappointed in herself, too. Where were her standards? Did she have no shame? Did she plan on being a poor ski instructor who went home to her dog every night and spent her paltry income on frozen novelty food?

She told herself it was a stage, and she was content to let it run its course. So far, its course had lasted some four months—into January—but that seemed appropriate. Her mom, the on-the-phone advisor, told her it was depression and she needed to see a counselor and experiment with medication. But Ginger believed she was still basically functional. She got up every morning, showered, put her hair in a ponytail, and went to work. Granted, sometimes she sobbed all the way, especially if she heard some song that reminded her of Brad. But by the time she arrived at Blackwolf, she'd pulled herself together. She'd slip on her trusty Oakleys to hide the wet, red eyes, and head out to teach.

The only real side effect of her current lifestyle was the white and black dog hair liberally covering every piece of clothing she wore. And that her ski pants were tighter than they should be.

But there were days in this life that were good. As she drove to the ski hill today in her little car, for instance, it felt like this might be one of those days.

In midwinter, the sun rose later in the morning. As she made one of the last turns before the road slipped into the trees, the orange ball popped up over the pavement. She squinted, turned the visor down, and watched as the snow crystallized and shone.

On January days like this, by the time she got to the parking lot, the sky was a stiff bright blue, sometimes with bits of cloud edging the bowl of mountains. She parked in the upper lot. The area was quiet yet. On weekdays, the lifts started running at ten, and she made it in time for the nine fifteen meeting.

As she walked down to the ski school building, it was nearly silent. In the bright sunshine, she squinted hard to find her footing down the slope from the parking lot. The reader board mounted above the lodge made clicking noises like the shuffling of cards.

"Ginger! Ginger!"

She'd made her way down to the flats and turned to see two women behind her. She'd forgotten it was Wednesday. This was the day a group of older skiers descended upon the mountain. The Silver Skiers group had only one membership requirement: sixty years of age, minimum. And Rose and Miriam were two of them. The loudest two.

"Hi, ladies. How are you?"

Rose always spoke first. She had faintly blue hair that today peeked out from under a cap with a huge pom-pom on the top. She was at least seventy, as she'd been skiing with the Silver Skiers for more than ten years. "We're ready to cut up some powder, my dear. And we've rented you for the day. Just us gals. Are you ready?" Miriam wore a purple jumpsuit, which accentuated all the strange bumps and lumps a woman past sixty begins to acquire.

Ginger smiled. These two were supposed to ski with the rest of the older women, but they always bought an all-day lesson and "ditched the slow girls," to quote Miriam.

Miriam spoke to Rose. "I love the way you say 'rented.' You make it sound trashy." The ladies giggled, and Rose gave Ginger a big wink.

"I need to check in with my supervisor and get my gear on. After that, I'm all yours. Meet me at the bottom of Chair Two?" Ginger turned toward the ski school room to boot up.

"We'll get in some warm-up runs on Lulu. Wouldn't want to get cold before we get to the backside!"

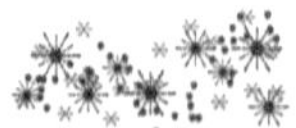

At the Corral last night, Fender had told Sam his story, and Sam came up with a fabulous plan: Fender was going skiing. If this mystery girlfriend had a Blackwolf parka, Sam surmised, she was an employee. It couldn't be too hard to track her down.

He'd also advised that Fender rid himself of the ring and the whole mess and move on. Sam, never big on guilt or conscience, suggested handing her the ring with a one-sentence accompaniment like, "Your boyfriend wanted you to have this," and scooting off, never to be seen again. End of discussion.

With more than a few tequilas under his belt, Fender had decided this was a good idea. But now, the next morning, driving up an icy, narrow road, he wasn't so sure. He'd left a note on the shop door: *Gone Skiing*, instead of *Gone Fishing*, so at least they'd know where to look for his body when he didn't turn up the next day.

In high school, he'd been up to the resort once, on a field trip. He'd taken one lesson. He knew how to stop, using the "pizza wedge." The wedge, or snow plow, involved turning the two planks on his feet in toward each other in a V-shape that looked like, as the bouncy instructor told him that high school day, "a piece of pizza, 'kay?" That was all he'd learned from perky ski girl.

On that trip, it had served him just fine. His friends dragged him up the rope tow and across some terrain to a stand of trees. They'd spent the rest of the day smoking pot while hidden from view. Then he'd wedged down the slope and stumbled out of his skis and onto a bus for the ride home. That's about all he remembered.

As he parked the car, he realized the first thing he'd forgotten: it is cold in a place that has snow. His attire probably wasn't going to cut it. There was a light breeze, and it sneaked through the sweater he'd put on, chilling his skin.

But all he had to do was spot this girl and dispose of the ring. *The ring. Damn it.* He'd left it on his dresser in its place of infamy. Well, what the hell was the point of his trip up here, then? He started back to the car. Of course, he could do reconnaissance. He'd screwed this all up already. Maybe some careful spying could improve his position and finish the mess more quickly. So, like any good intelligence man, he turned and pressed on.

The first building he came to, he entered. He thought his search for this girl should be systematic. That, and he was just cold. *Going inside is good.*

His first sensation was a stink. An odor. Oh, God, it was bad. Feet, and probably — judging from the horde of people — hundreds of pairs of feet, stinking together in perfect harmony. A young bearded boy thwarted Fender's retreat, taking him by the arm to a table in the corner.

"Fill this out. Sign at the bottom on the reverse, and don't leave out your shoe size or weight." The bearded boy stuck a pen in his hand and moved to the next victim.

Fender could've struggled. Yet the cloud of odor had penetrated his mind, and in this foot fog, he completed the form. He walked toward the counter. *The girl might work in here. Keep your eyes open,* he told himself.

In looking for the girl, he was carried along an involuntary current of efficiency. He found himself putting his feet into a pair of the reeky ski boots. Bearded boy had materialized again and now buckled the buckles and Velcroed the Velcro of the boots.

"There. Now, next time you come up, even if it's sunny, I wouldn't wear jeans. See how hard it is to even get the cuffs over the boot? It'll feel a little uncomfortable with your jeans pushed up around your shins, too. And try not to spend much time down on the snow, or you'll get wet."

Fender realized this wave of activity was going to culminate in a pair of skis on his feet. This was not good. He had to put a stop to it now. *Vigilance has its limits.*

Bearded boy hadn't paused for comment from Fender, who now found himself in the back room, waiting for another scruffy-looking boy to hand over a pair of skis. There were hundreds, thousands of pairs, suspended behind the teen. He would summarily take the form out of each customer's hand. Looking at the paper, he'd scrunch up his features in thought, jot something at the bottom of the form, and turn and reach for a pair of hanging sticks. Every pair was red with yellow lettering. The word *Rossignol* was screened on the thick plastic in a slant and made the skis look fast.

Fender imagined all these skis hung up when they were new, and it probably looked quite advanced and technical. But the thing was, these skis were rentals. They'd seen their fair share of abuse. Most of the skis had large scratches, and some had chunks of their metal edges missing.

The little skis the scruffy man brought down for the young girl in front of Fender looked rough. These tiny, shrunken versions of the bigger skis hanging in front of him had come from farther down the aisle of swaying skis. Now he realized what the hanging skis reminded him of: sides of beef. Like the ones Rocky punched while training in the slaughterhouse. Or was it a meat locker? He couldn't remember.

The little girl stepped into the skis, and everyone around her clucked and shook their heads and scurried around to take them off of her feet. A woman, probably her mother, patted her hand and said, "No, silly, you put them on outside. Now just carry them, honey. You can't walk around inside with them on. What a silly goose!" She led the girl out the door and cast an apologetic, even sheepish, smile to the young man behind the ski counter.

All Fender could think was that he was glad the little girl did it before he had the chance to screw up. And he needed to see was where the ski return was, so he could get these god-awful things away from him before someone was killed. *Just take the skis, walk out the door, walk to the return, and dump them.* He could handle that. That way no one would be maimed.

The guy was saying something about his binding setting and ski number, but Fender just nodded, grabbed the skis, and headed for the same door through which the little girl had escaped.

He was blinded. He literally could see nothing but piercing white light. Something was wrong with his legs. He couldn't flex his ankles. *Oh my God, I'm going to fall down a flight of stairs, in ski boots, and knock myself unconscious.* He stumbled and tripped, skis in hand.

It was two or three steps. His hip landed on cold, hard ground. And then he felt wet: snow. *Oh joy.*

He stood up, found his sunglasses on his head, and put them over his eyes. First, he looked around to see who'd witnessed his plunge. Few seemed to have noticed. Then he picked up the skis. Their sharp edges hurt the skin of his palms. His hip and his butt were wet, and his jeans had a big, navy blue wet spot spreading around to the front of the pant legs. He was cold again. *Ditch the skis. Ditch the ski boots. Escape!* Fender felt an urge to run screaming to the car.

"Hey, my friend, need some help?"

Fender turned around. *Sam. The bastard.* He'd remembered their Corral conversation and come up to revel in Fender's failings.

"Sam, Jesus Christ. They made me get this stuff. Help me return it, huh? I want to leave."

"They *made* you rent. Wow, I had no idea they forced people to ski. Wow." Sam took Fender by the arm and straightened him up. "Look at you, you're a regular ski bunny! Oh, I knew I had to come up today. I knew this was going to be good." Sam chuckled, and his double chin bobbed over his neck scarf.

In fact, Fender had to laugh too as he admired Sam from head to toe. A cigarette hung from his lips. He wore a black polar fleece scarf paired with an old grease-smeared pair of Carhartt coveralls. Sam was fat, and the flannel-lined, tan work suit made him thicker than ever. The beauty of it was, Sam didn't care.

"Jesus, Fender —" he coughed through his cigarette " — were you planning on wearing that to ski?"

"I wasn't planning on skiing, Sam. I was just going to look for the girl and leave. Now, I just want to leave. I'm wet."

Sam shook his head. "You're a sad sonofabitch. A sweater will not keep you dry. Jeans will not keep you dry. Plus, you can't bend in jeans, and you can't keep the family jewels warm in jeans. Why didn't you call me this morning? I could've lent you my other Carhartts."

"Sam, you don't get the point, do you? I'm leaving now. *Now.* Going away."

But then Fender saw something. Somebody. The girl. The sad girl at the cemetery. The girl under the drooping sycamore in the deepening dusk. It was her. It had to be her. And she was circling around the end of a line of people, following a pair of old ladies. Heading to a chair lift. Getting away.

He popped Sam on the arm. "Hey, that's her—over there—that's the girl!"

Sam swiveled on his skis. "Who, her?" He pointed at her with a gloved hand lengthened by a very long ski pole.

"Stop it! She's going to see you pointing at her. That's her, and she's going to that thing, the lift." Fender realized he sounded frantic.

"Okay. Stay calm. I'm going to follow her. She's going up Chair Two. Chances are she'll come down a trail that leads her back to here. You, go to the ticket office. Get a ticket. And ask for a garbage bag."

"Garbage bag?"

"Don't ask me now; she's getting away! She's getting away, remember? I must pursue your mystery girl! Farewell, I follow her!" He turned with a flourish and skated off to the lift, Olympic-figure-skater style. He looked like an elephant in a tutu.

Fender obeyed Sam's command and dragged himself and the two skis to a ticket office window.

"I need a ticket to ride that lift and a garbage bag." He stared into the glass in front of him. The girl behind the glass arched an eyebrow at his request. She set her paperback down and stared at him.

"You can't buy a ticket to ride just one lift. It'll be forty-two dollars."

"Excuse me?" Fender dug into his wallet and mumbled several inappropriate expletives. He slid the money under the glass partition and out came a ticket on backing, a wire mini-coat hanger, and a big, black, glossy garbage bag.

He scraped the tails of the skis along the brick patio and found a bench. Plunking down, he looked around for Sam.

As he waited, he peeled the ticket off and stuck it to his sweater. He had no idea what the little wire thing was for, so he tossed that on the ground. He put the skis on the ground in front of him and realized he was actually thinking of skiing. How stupid. But if he could get close to the girl, talk to her…*About what?* He didn't have the ring with him, so Sam's idea of dumping the ring and escaping was useless. Plus, how was he going to "scoot off" if he had a pair of giant Popsicle sticks on his feet?

"Fender."

He turned around. "Yeah?" It was Sam. He was wheezing, and his face glowed with sweat.

"Oh, what did you do with the ticket? That's not how you wear it. You look like you're marked down for quick sale." Sam leaned over Fender and peeled the ticket off his sweater. Picking the lint off the back of the ticket, he took the wire on the ground and slid it through a belt loop on Fender's jeans. Then he folded the ticket over the ends of the wire. "This is a wicket. You put the ticket on it like this. Gimme the garbage bag." Fender complied. Sam punched a hole at the top and two on the sides.

"Come here, Fender. Stick out your arms."

"Oh, no, no, nonono! Sam, I'll look like a black vinyl Teletubbie. God, this was an incredibly stupid idea!"

"Fender, come here and stop complaining. The garbage bag'll keep you from getting so wet. Now, the girl's apparently a ski instructor. She took one run and caught up with the two old ladies. She was talking with them about halfway down Lulu. You can ski as good as two antiques, trust me. We'll go to the top of the lift, ski down the run, and catch up with them."

"Sam, the last time we went skiing, all I had to do was ski sideways and sit in the trees for four hours. I don't even remember how to stop. I'll just wait here for her to come back down."

"They might not be back down this way. You can get to two other lifts from where they are. Step into your skis. Hold onto my arms and step into them, toe first. Push down with your heel till they click."

Fender did as he was told. The big plastic boots slid over the tops of the skis. He felt as if he had huge weights on his ankles.

"Just hold your feet steady over the bindings and push, Fender. Here, hold onto my elbows." Sam stood in front of him. The boots clicked, and now he was attached. *This must be how a condemned man feels.*

"I want you to shuffle your feet, Fender. Don't try to go anywhere, just scoot your feet back and forth in place. Feel that? Okay, now I want you to act like you're wearing skates, like when we were in hockey. Push like you're skating."

The shuffle thing felt fine. The hockey skating thing did not. "Sam, I sucked at hockey. This isn't going to work!"

Sam turned his back on him, then stuck a ski pole back. "Just grab hold with both hands and hang on. You're such a baby." Fender grabbed hold and was tugged as Sam took off, skating on his skis. As Sam pushed his fat body from side to side, Fender saw the chair lift looming ahead of him. The part in front of him now was like a two-story house with an overhang. From under the blue roof dangled metal chairs, following one after the other, looping the house. As the chairs were about to emerge from under the house's eaves, people scooted up in front of them and plunked down. Then the chairs would accelerate and whiz up the mountain, disappearing over the first rise. The speed thing worried Fender.

"What if I miss the chair? What if I don't sit down on it right?"

Sam looked over his shoulder, wheezing from the tugboat job he'd undertaken. "You won't miss. See, the chair detaches from the main cable and slows down. That's just for morons such as yourself, so you can take extra time to sit. Anyway, if you miss it, the lift operator is supposed to catch the chair so it won't clobber you. Although I did see this girl get clocked once. Man, I forgot about that. Boy, it came around the bullwheel — you know, at the back of the terminal — came up, and rang her bell!" Sam yelled over his shoulder now. He'd kind of hit a stride and was pushing with less effort. Fender bobbed along behind him like a rubber duck.

"I didn't need to hear that."

"That's nothing. It's so funny to watch people get off up on top. This one time, I thought I might bust a gasket, it was so damn funny. This guy was trying to get off, but his coat was caught on the back of the chair. So he slid off, but then he kind of got picked up. The liftie stopped the chair, but this guy was already like ten feet off the ground and almost headed back down the mountain, hanging from the lift by the back of his coat!" Sam hee-hawed, laughing as he tried to catch his breath.

"You're not helping."

Now they were in the line, scooting toward the loading area. Fender's legs were numb, and his hands hurt from white-knuckling the ski pole. People filled in behind him and edged forward as a new chair came, picked up its victims, and then launched up the side of the mountain. Fender had a moment of painful self-awareness. He was a grown man wearing a garbage bag. A very big man held him by the arm and dragged him along each time the line moved at all.

I'll never be able to look another human being in the face again. I'm officially the biggest girly-man I know. I need a drink. Maybe if I pray hard enough, God will strike this large metal house with lightning, and I'll die now before things get worse.

"Let's go." Sam grabbed him and yanked him forward into the path of the next chair. Fender didn't know what was happening until the chair bumped him in the back of the knees, and the attendant said, "Sit down. Keep your tips up." But the voice was quickly behind him. Sam sat next to him, and they dangled over the snow, hurtling up the mountain.

It didn't seem too terrible. He had a passing thought about the weight of the skis on his feet dragging him off the chair. He looked at the snow, some twenty feet below him, and wondered if it was soft enough to cushion a fall.

"Fender, it's better to sit back. Don't tempt the fates, my friend. You're still in one piece; let's try to keep it that way." Sam said this as he reached into his Carhartts and produced a pack of Marlboros. He pulled one of his gloves off with his teeth and lit the cigarette. "Now, let's talk about getting off."

Apprehension struck Fender. "Why—what's so hard about getting off?"

"It's not that hard; you just have to know something about this particular chair. It's got a really short turnaround before it makes the bullwheel and heads back down the mountain."

"So?"

"So, if you don't get out of the way fast enough, it'll clock you in the back of the head. For you, the best thing would probably be to just tuck and slide. Pretend you're going to do the YMCA fishes dive—you know, where you crouch over and tuck your head to your chest. Do that. If you fall, don't get up. I'll drag you clear of the chair."

"Remind me again why I'm doing this."

"Fender, you've suddenly grown some sense of a conscience. I, for one, am heartily surprised. Plus, I just like to see you squirm. Oh, and when you're getting off, scoot your butt to the edge of the chair. We're almost at the last tower. Try not to drop a ski pole either, okay?"

Fender didn't think it was possible to sweat in the middle of winter, but he was downright soaking. *Excellent—pit stains to add to my overall attractiveness. How come I'm still single?*

The end of his ride came and went quickly. He felt the ground under his skis, and as Sam stood up, so did he. When his butt and the rest of his body started to slide backward, he grabbed Sam's arm.

"Tuck, Fender! Remember the fishes. Dive like the fishes!" Sam was ahead of him, and he dragged Fender along behind. The rubber ducky image came to Fender again.

They slid to a stop, and Fender realized the altitude they'd gained. It was even kind of pretty up here.

"Fender, stop gawking. Let's get out of the way and go find that girl."

The hill receded in front of them gently. It narrowed into a thin trail.

Sam flicked his cigarette into the brush by the side of the trail. "Well, amigo, let's see if you remember your death wedge."

"Death wedge?" Fender was just trying to stay upright. Now he had to move? It was so unfair.

"Please tell me you at least remember making a wedge. Point the tips of your skis together and push the tails out. God, we didn't smoke that much pot the time we were up here in high school."

"Speak for yourself, Mr. Clean."

Sam wiped his nose on the sleeve of his Carhartts and chuckled. "Oh, the piercing wit returns. You must be feeling less terrified. Don't forget, my scrawny friend, that I'm your one hope of getting off this mountain alive."

"Okay." Fender tried the pizza move. "And what is this wedge going to help me do?"

"Stop. The advanced stage is to push harder with one leg than the other. Then you can turn. But let's take one thing at a time. Stopping's a good thing."

"Just aim me where she went. We need to get this over with." Fender stood a little taller, straightening the garbage bag and smoothing it over him. *Dignity. There must've been a time when I had some dignity.* Right now, he couldn't recall when that was.

Then they were moving down the trail. He slid slowly forward. Whenever he felt himself gaining any kind of speed, Fender leaned back and pushed his skis out as hard as he could. Sam began to get out ahead of him.

"Fender, you're doing fine. Don't stand too wide; you'll tear yourself in half doing the splits." Sam looked at Fender for a minute and then turned to face the downhill again. His shoulders were kind of shaking.

"Sam? Are you laughing at me?"

He wouldn't turn back around. "I can't help it, man. You look so funny." Sam was now stopped ahead of him, bent over, hee-hawing so loudly soft snow fell from the pines above.

Fender caught up to Sam, now standing tall again, wiping tears of laughter away from his eyes. Suddenly he focused down the ever-broadening trail.

He looks kind of like a German shorthair going on point. "What?"

"I can't believe it. They're still right down here! What's she doing?" Sam moved forward. "Oh, it looks like the old broad's buckle broke on her boot. This is perfect. Maybe this is your destiny, Fender—God must want you to redeem your poor corrupt life, 'cause she's still here."

"What're you going to do?" Fender wedged behind, trying to use Sam's large body for cover.

"Well, I can go up and offer to help out with the old biddy's buckle. Then you come up and tell the instructor girl your story. Give her the ring, and we'll ski off."

"I didn't bring it." Fender felt sheepish.

"What? What the hell are we doing, then? For the love of Mike. Where is it?"

"I forgot it at home. I meant to bring it, really." Fender followed so close on the trail behind Sam, he brushed into him.

"Okay. Geez, Fender! Is it your intention to crawl up my ass? Back up. You're going to take me out at the knees. Okay. All's not lost. Same plan. Just tell her you'll drop the ring off in her mailbox or something. Let's go, they're right there."

You can't leave a ring like that in a mailbox! I'd have ditched it months ago if it were that simple. Fender had no time to tell Sam this, though. Sam had pushed ahead a little and was now gliding toward the three women stopped by a stand of trees. They were about a hundred feet down the trail now, on a wide strip of open snow. Instead of traversing along the slope of the hill, the trail turned straight down it. Fender wondered if his braking could withstand this much gravity.

He got his answer. Following Sam, Fender tentatively edged down the slope. He started to pick up speed. He leaned back into his wedge, but it seemed to do little good. He felt the air moving past him more quickly, and his skis made a crunchy noise. *I'm going to crash into her. Her, and Sam, and two old ladies. Then trees. Trees.* He felt a life-and-death panic rising in his bowels. *Trees are not good.*

Sam's voice was in his head again. What was it he'd said? *Lean harder on one ski and you'll turn.* He wanted to turn left. *I want to turn left. I need to turn left. Please, Lord, help me in this turning left. Trees are bad. Turn! Turn! Turn!*

At the end of her shift, Ginger drove down the mountain, listening to the radio and the grumbling of her stomach. *Kind of a weird day, today.*

There wasn't anything weird about the lesson. The day had been clear, the snow powder, and Miriam and Rose had skied beautifully.

What was weird was the interlude on Lulu. Ginger had stopped to help Miriam fix her buckle, as it must not have been wrenched down correctly. It was being kind of stubborn, so Ginger had stood up to take her gloves off before trying again to fix it. She and the women chatted. She'd been appreciating what a pretty day it was.

Then she'd spotted two men coming toward them. The first was very fat and dressed like a car mechanic. He had a wide smile on his face. *He wants to help out*, she'd thought.

But the one behind was more noticeable. Clad in a garbage bag, he hunched over his skis and held his arms like he was steering a car. He was wedging like there was no tomorrow but was pointed straight downhill at them. As he started to pick up speed, Ginger could barely make out a face contorting in sheer panic. She looked at Miriam and Rose. *He's going to make bowling pins out of all of us.* The fat man must have realized her concern, and he turned around. He began to wave his arms wildly. They were all bracing for a collision, when suddenly the garbage bag man leaned over and turned left, riding his outer ski like it was on a rail. Then he was pointed down the hill in the opposite direction and began to pick up speed again. Ginger could hear him yelling. Actually, it sounded more like a high shriek of terror.

His friend, who'd stopped in front of them, maybe in an effort to break the impact, looked at Ginger. He held up his hands. "Beginner.

What can I say?" Then he turned to pursue the wailing creature down the rest of Lulu.

The ladies thought it was wonderful. They regarded the whole episode as something of an adventure and had talked about it for the rest of the day. Ginger was glad no one got hurt. They'd skied down to the bottom of Lulu, and she'd half-expected to find ski patrol with a sled, carting the poor soul off. But the two men had vanished.

Later, after finishing the day with Miriam and Rose, Ginger had gone to the lodge. She'd walked through the tables and even the bar area. The fat man would've been easy to spot. The other man had been kind of a blur, but he'd seemed strangely familiar. The dark hair, or something. From somewhere before.

But they hadn't been in the lodge. And even now, driving down the mountain, she couldn't put her finger on it.

She stopped thinking so hard and laughed. *That boy needs a lesson.* She could add this to her long list of stories from teaching skiing.

Rocket, for instance. Rocket's real name had been John. He was a three-year-old in the ski school program, and he was a terror. He knew no fear. He would gather his little self up and tuck, roaring down the steepest run. Rocket could take terrible spills and stand up from the wreckage not even shaken. On one sunny morning, Ginger and Rocket had sat and chatted on the chairlift. They'd talked about what you can talk about with a three-year-old: his dog, his preschool teacher, his mommy.

It was about the time Ginger was asking Rocket about his dog that he interrupted her.

"Miss Ginger?"

"Yes, Rocket?"

"I'm going to jump off, 'kay?"

"*Huh?*"

And then he'd pitched forward. They were three towers away from the top of the chair and about twenty feet off the ground. Her heart leaped into her mouth, and she grabbed at him reflexively. He was tipped down, falling out of the chair already, and she went for the handle on his vest. Then she had him, and she was staring at the red letters *MOGUL MOUSE* on his little yellow back. Rocket screamed bloody murder and demanded to be let down so he could "jump in the fluffies." At the top, Ginger had managed to drag him off the chair and ski down to the ski school building, basically carrying him all the way because she hadn't wanted to let him go. Ever since then, she'd maintained an iron grip on the little ones as they rode up the chair.

Part of teaching was caretaking. Of course, it was obvious with the little ones. The three-to-five-year-olds came in at eleven forty-five for a break. They had lunch and then watched videos and hopefully napped. These littlest learners were the Mogul Mice. Some of them could actually ski moguls, too. Or anything else thrown at them, Ginger figured. Though most were more cautious than Rocket, they really did not possess a fearful bone in their bodies. Unless she'd taught it to them. Since Brad's accident, Ginger had felt the need to be careful. She was always thinking the worst. Protecting when protection wasn't needed. Hovering.

Even in the Mouse House, the carpeted room where they penned the children for lunch, she hovered. The other instructors ate their lunches and kept one eye on the kids, but Ginger was in the thick of the Mice. She kept so close that the kids even noticed.

One day, a splinter group of Mice decided watching movies was for "babies" and dragged out their skis. They made a game of placing an empty boot in the bindings, clicking it down, and then popping the release, sending the boot flying. Ginger swooped down on them and took the ski and boot away. Rocket was one of the instigators, and he piped up in protest.

"We're not babies, Miss Ginger. We can do it. Go away."

Ginger knew Rocket was right, but it didn't melt the knot in her stomach. She wished for the impossible: control over the uncontrollable.

Of course, then Rocket would pull a stunt like the attempted swan dive from the chair, and Ginger would be glad she tried to protect them.

"It wasn't that bad, Fender." Sam sucked a little of the foam from the top of his mug.

"Who are you kidding? I don't even want to talk about it. I thought I already made that very clear." Fender stared at the oversized deco mirror behind the bar, stenciled with *The 'Vous* in red and white paint.

"What are we talking about?" Pop slid into the booth next to Fender. The red vinyl squeaked.

Fender looked at Pop. He'd never been very tall, and now age made him basically little. He'd boxed in San Francisco during high school and college—in featherweight classes, Fender assumed. He'd been wiry, but age had worn that away, too. If Fender didn't know Pop, he'd think he might be helpless. But he wasn't. He could be belligerent and overbearing. Women loved him, though. They thought he was "cute" or "adorable." And Pop adored them. He loved women's attention, which is why he came to the Rendezvous so often to hold court. The waitresses would flirt with him, bring him sandwiches ("Do you feed him?" they'd ask Fender), and play songs on the jukebox for him.

Two years ago, once he officially gave the business over to Fender, Pop took on a number of other hobbies. He'd eat breakfast with the cook at the Rendezvous and walk over to the Statehouse, if it was in session. He'd sit up in the gallery and read the newspaper, listening to roll calls or filibusters. He also liked to walk down to the library and read in the rust-colored chairs of the reference section. Sometimes Fender could tell when Pop had been to the library by the rusty lint on his clothes. Pop probably took more naps than read books, but the librarians didn't seem to care.

Pop's questioning gray eyes were still trained on Fender, and his sparse mustache twitched with curiosity. "Tell me, Sonny. What'd you do today?"

"Nothing." The day had been humiliating enough. He didn't want to his dad to know on top of it all.

"Jerry, he was in fine form." Sam sat across the table from them, out of Fender's striking distance.

Fender tilted his head and shot his most withering look at Sam. "I went skiing."

"No, no, it's better than that. We went after this girl, and Fender learned how to ski all over again. He also tried to use two old ladies as bowling pins." Sam's shoulders were shaking again.

As per usual, Pop focused on the woman in the conversation. "Fender went after a girl? Really? Does this mean little Sandy didn't make you swear off women forever?"

Sam brightened. "I'd almost forgotten about Sandy. Isn't she the one that wrote *I HATE YOU* with weed killer on your front lawn?"

Sam sat back and stretched his arms out on the top of the booth, relaxed and apparently prepared for a stroll down Fender's memory lane of exes.

Fender shifted uncomfortably. All of this attention was too much. He also felt his back stiffening. *I wonder if I can still stand up.* The skiing thing had just about killed him.

Pop waited for a response.

"Okay. I went up the mountain looking for the girlfriend. Remember the big diamond? And the guy? When I went to the funeral?"

Pop loved stories. He loved stories he was a part of, especially. "The man I found for you in the obituaries? Yes, yes, I remember. I thought you found her at the funeral."

This is why I don't talk to my father. It always turns into a discussion of what I didn't do right. Or what I didn't do, period.

Sam chimed in. "Yeah, how come you didn't give it to her then? Or when you saw her at her house?"

Pop pursed his lips. "You know, don't you, Fender, that this state has stalking laws?"

"Both of you stop. I'm not going to discuss this with you if you're not going to let me finish." Fender signaled to the waitress. He definitely wanted a Dewar's. "Neither of you has really seen her."

"I saw her. Today. After you almost killed her. Yep, that was definitely her I was apologizing to, if I recall correctly. She's actually kind of good-looking, if you go for the outdoorsy, crunchy-granola kind of girl."

"What the hell did you just call her? Are you calling her cereal? She's not whatever you just said. You didn't see her at the funeral. She's… lost, or something. It's in her eyes. I have to do this right."

Pop and Sam sat back and smiled broadly. Sam spoke first.

"I'm not sure there's ever been a documented case of Fender wanting to do something right. Are you aware of one, Jerry?"

Pop slapped Fender on the back, sloshing the Dewar's now in Fender's hand. "Let's give him a break. I sense something. Call it father's intuition. Let him do this, Sam. Who knows, maybe the young lady needs a shoulder to cry on in her time of need?"

"You're disgusting, Pop. That's not what I'm talking about. I could just keep the ring, but she deserves it. I don't know why, but I know she deserves better than what I usually give. Now if you'll excuse me,

I'm going to go home and cover myself with Bengay." Fender tried to make a grand exit, but Pop had to climb out of the booth first. And then he was too sore to really stomp out.

What am I thinking? This whole ring thing was ridiculous. He was going to go home and toss the thing. Screw the girl. She'd probably forgotten the dead guy anyway. He breezed through the bar toward the front.

He came out of the door and onto the street. And she stood in front of him. Fender choked at the sight of her. Her hair was down, framing her face and those eyes. She wore a brown jacket over a purplish dress with brown boots. She seemed to recognize him, and he tried to fight the impulse to run. Who was he kidding? He was so sore he could barely walk. He could not flee.

"Hey, the guy from Lulu. You're still in one piece?" She stood in front of him as another woman walked up the sidewalk to meet her.

"Sorry." He stared at her.

She dug into her purse and handed him a card. "See you later." She and her friend walked past him into the Greek restaurant next to the Rendezvous.

He stood on the sidewalk. *Sorry? I see her, and all I can say is sorry?* Fender marveled at his stupidity.

He looked at the card in his hand.

GINGER STEVENS
PROFESSIONAL SKI INSTRUCTOR
BLACKWOLF SKI RESORT
LESSONS@BLACKWOLF.COM
888-555-0101

Ginger. Now he knew her name.

Chapter Seven

A few days later, with a little Dewar's in his stomach in place of resolve, he'd dialed the number on the card and spoken to the Blackwolf Resort Ski and Snowboard School. He hadn't been sure of his plan or what he wanted to say, but he'd picked up the phone anyway.

A nice saleslady had answered. She sold him a private lesson with Ginger Stevens, the girlfriend, she of the green eyes, for later that very day. So here he was, driving up the mountain. This time, he'd brought the ring. It was in its velvety box, tucked in the glove compartment.

His big plan at this moment was to take the lesson, strike up a conversation, and find a gentle way to give the ring back to her. Maybe she'd mention the dead boyfriend.

Fender stopped thinking about it. When he explored the train of thought too far, it didn't make any sense, and he had to stop. *I am going to throw up. If I don't figure this out, I will throw up or drive off the road or something.*

Which is when Fender decided not to think about it anymore.

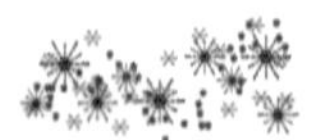

Ginger picked up her lesson slips in the office after the morning meeting. It was mid-January, but on Sundays, things had begun to slow down a bit. She had a lesson at nine with the Davises, a brother and sister who'd learned to ski with her last year. But then she had a request for a private lesson with a Fender Barnes at two. This did not ring a bell. Usually requests were people she'd taught in lessons before.

There was one possibility, and she dismissed it almost as soon as it occurred to her: the Lulu guy. She'd run into him downtown when she and Molly went for Greek food a couple days ago. It was pretty weird, running into him. She'd looked for him and his friend in the lodge, but to see him downtown the same night was quite a coincidence. It had also made for fun dinner conversation with Molly. The story made her smile even now. What a crazy guy.

And maybe that crazy guy was this Fender Barnes. Her two o'clock. She shrugged and went to boot up for the Davis kids.

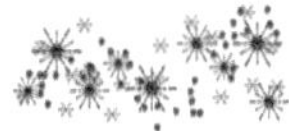

Fender almost felt like an old pro as he made his way through the rental shop. Now when the little kid in front of him tried to put the skis on inside, Fender shared a knowing laugh with the kid's dad. When Fender stepped outside of the shop, he remembered to step down. He bought a ticket and put it on the right way. It took him two tries to step into his skis, but so what? *Maybe this skiing thing isn't so bad after all.*

The lady on the phone had told him to look for a little bench in front of the lodge, to the right of the ticket window. He saw it now. Above the brown bench was a sign: PRIVATE LESSONS. He shuffled over and plopped down.

Then Fender looked at his watch. It was one thirty. He had half an hour to wait. The old feelings of panic and inadequacy raced back into his brain. *Someone'll notice me sitting here for that long. Jesus, I'll probably get arrested for loitering.*

He came up with a plan to look purposeful. *If I look like I'm supposed to be sitting here, then I'm fine. Look like you belong on this bench. Own the bench, Fender. Be one with the bench.*

So he sat. At about fifteen till, a red-haired young boy shuffled up to him. He was dragging a pale blue snowboard behind him, tied with black cord to his ankle.

"Can I sit here?" The boy moved to the end of the bench and began to sit down.

"No, no, you can't. I'm waiting for someone." Fender spread his arms out on either side of him, taking up most of the room.

This didn't deter the boy. He detached the board from his leg and stood staring at Fender.

"Didn't you hear me, Red? I'm waiting for someone. The bench's taken. Move along."

"Let me sit down, mister."

"Are you going to take a private lesson?" Fender was on the attack now. *I've got logic on my side.*

"No."

Fender sat up straighter in his righteousness. "If you noticed the sign, this bench's clearly the meeting spot for private lessons. You're not in a private lesson, so you cannot sit on this bench. Now move along, mouth-breather."

Defeated, the red-haired boy put the cord to his board around his ankle again and scooted off.

Then Fender saw her. She glided toward him on skis, her hair tucked up in a knitted cap. She had the Blackwolf parka on and a pair of black ski pants. She smiled broadly. In front of the bench, she turned and stopped hockey-style, kicking up a puff of snow.

"Hi. You're Fender, right?"

"Yeah." He stood and almost fell right over. "That's me. I have a private lesson with you."

"I'm Ginger. Well, let's go see what you can learn today."

She didn't mention the Lulu incident. *Does she recognize me? Of course she does. She's being polite. She's a nice person. Nice people don't remind losers of their humiliating moments.*

Fender followed in an awkward shuffle behind her. She guided him to a flat area in front of a lift and reviewed the wedge turn. She showed him how to get up if he fell. He liked watching her smile and the way the corners of her mouth turned up when she talked.

"I think we should try the lift."

She was talking to him. He nodded. *Whatever.* He noticed that he felt good around her. He wondered if she was still sad.

He was still wondering about this when he realized they were in line to go up the mountain. All the horror of the other day came to him at once.

"Are you ready, Fender? I think we should go up this lift and try the beginner terrain. You'll find it's a little more forgiving than where you were the other day."

I guess she does recognize me. She's nice. Of course she's nice. He thought her eyes were probably very pretty right now, except that she was wearing sunglasses.

They waited in line for the lift. Another person in a Blackwolf parka skied up. Behind him were three small children. They all had bright yellow vests on over their coats.

"Hey, Justin." Ginger waved at him. Justin's lesson kids slowly shuffled up behind him.

"Is this your private?" Justin pushed his goggles up on his forehead to get a closer look at Fender. Fender noticed the little kids were eyeing him as well. He suddenly felt very stupid.

"Yep. Are you guys going up the chair too?"

"I was waiting for someone else to ride up with one of my guys. I can only ride two on the triple. But no one's shown up, and we really need to get going. This is the last week, and I want these guys to ride up the chair a lot today." Justin motioned behind him to the three kids. Fender noticed one had plopped down and was eating snow.

"We can ride one up to the top."

"I'd appreciate it. Thanks, Ginger." Justin picked the snow-eater up off the ground and shoved him up to where Ginger and Fender were in line. "This is Wylie. Say hi to Ginger." Wylie chewed on one of his gloves now. He looked up at Ginger and then at Fender.

"I want to ride next to him." Wylie pointed directly at Fender.

Ginger pulled Wylie into line next to her. "Well, Fender's learning just like you, so you have to sit next to me, Wylie." She lowered her voice and looked at Fender. "I'm sorry about this. Usually we have chair riders to take the little ones up. They can't ride alone. We're just really short-handed today."

She's apologizing to me. She's sweet. Fender shook himself out of his reverie. "It's okay. Totally. Don't worry about it." He tried to smile as broadly as he could. *Totally? What am I now, a Valley Girl?* He marveled at how lame he could be.

Wylie was growing impatient. "I said I want to ride with him!" He again pointed at Fender.

Ginger picked Wylie up and put him between her and Fender. "How's that, Wylie? Now you can ride next to both of us." The little boy grabbed Fender's hand.

Getting on the chair was actually okay. Fender just tried with every fiber of his being not to get in the way of the little kid or Ginger. As the chair swung around behind them, Ginger lifted Wylie up and put him on the chair between them.

It was quiet for a minute. Ginger had an arm looped around Wylie's waist. She seemed to have a tight grip on him. Wylie turned to look at Fender. He stared. *I should say something to the kid. I don't want to look like a jerk.*

"So, do you have any brothers or sisters?" Seemed like a safe question.

"I have a sister. She's a black Lab. I like to kiss her." Fender tried to keep up with the three-year-old train of thought. "Not here." Wylie pointed to his nose. "Here." He lifted up his upper lip and pointed to the gum beneath. "The pink part. You think it's wet, but it's not. It's dry." Wylie smiled. Fender tried not to shudder. Ginger just shook her head.

"That's a pretty nice dog to let you kiss her like that," Ginger said to Wylie.

"She's my favorite friend. And she can catch the Frisbee, too."

Ginger was still giggling a little as they neared the top of the lift, but she hazarded a glance over at her student. He wore a yellow coat, and his head was bare. He had a nice head of black hair — a little shaggy — plus a smaller nose, fair skin, blue eyes. And he currently looked like he might throw up.

At the top of the lift, she delivered Wylie to Justin.

"Ask Wylie about his sister, Justin." She turned to Fender and smiled.

Justin seemed puzzled. "I thought you didn't have any brothers or sisters, Wylie."

"Let him tell you about it. See you later." Ginger turned around to face her student. He smiled. He had a nice smile.

"Let's teach you to ski, Fender. Are you ready?"

"I guess."

He stood next to her at the top of a smooth, curving run. It was broad and open. He'd been brave to come back up here, Ginger knew. Most grown men wouldn't suffer the embarrassment of the other day and admit to needing a lesson.

"Look down the run for me, Fender." He did as he was told. "See how much more gentle this run is? This is where your friend should have taken you the other day."

"Yeah, but Sam may or may not be sane. I'd be short a couple of limbs if I left more stuff up to him. When we were eight, he was the one who convinced me that a burning pool of gasoline on the driveway would look awesome."

"But you were the one who listened." Ginger smiled.

"Point taken. In his defense…" He paused. "I'm amazed I'm defending him—he should be here to witness this. In his defense, the other day on Lulu was my idea, kind of."

"Really?" she said.

"Well, I wanted to meet you. I saw you at the bottom of the mountain, and I made him follow you." He'd been looking at the ground. Now he looked up quickly with a wide grin for her.

This guy's downright charming.

I'm charming her. I think I'm actually acting halfway normal. And I've almost maneuvered the conversation to the dead boyfriend ring thing.

But Fender retreated from it as soon as he had the thought. *I don't want to spoil this. She's smiling. Hey, I'm smiling. I probably won't even kill Sam when I get home.* He looked at her. She leaned forward on her ski poles, sliding her skis back and forth in a little subconscious dance. *She's really cute. It's been a while since I've been with a cute girl. A nice girl.*

Fender thought about his standard choice in women. Besides their fondness for burning his underwear in effigy, most of his dates were high maintenance: hard to please, with expensive tastes and big hair. *Oh, face it,* Fender told himself, *you usually dig bitches. I'm surprised you didn't try to wrestle Naomi away from Jimmy.*

Well, this girl was not a bitch. Did he dig her? No, that was too predatory a word. And anyway, that wasn't the point of this whole thing.

"So, let's review a little before we head down this run."

She was talking to him. *Oh, yes. Skiing.* Fender tensed up. How could he forget?

"Fender, don't panic. You're going to be fine. Remember to put your weight over the center of the skis. Ease the heels away from each other to make your wedge. Try that right now."

Fender obeyed.

"Good. Now, how do we manage our speed?"

"By turning."

"Yes, by turning. Often." She smiled a little. "To make those turns, take your wedge and put more weight on one foot than the other. Pressure the ski, and you'll turn." She positioned herself to face down the slope. "Let's do that now. Follow me, and turn when I turn."

They made their way down the run in long, deliberate loops. Fender's brow was wet from concentration. At the bottom, she turned back around and congratulated him.

"That's how skiing works. Nice job. I think you're ready for Cougar Forest."

"You know, this is working. I haven't injured anyone. Why ruin it?" Fender had been thinking more about a celebratory beer in the lodge.

"You can do this. And besides, you need to see more of the mountain than one run. Cougar Forest is just a cat track through some stands of trees. It's still gentle. It's a little narrower, but I think you're up to the challenge. It's off of this same lift."

"Okay."

So he found himself on the chair again with Ginger. He sat quietly while she reminded him about the wedge and the pressure on the ski and all the other skiing crap. But it wasn't bad to just listen to her talk, really. He nodded a lot and then got off the lift when she told him to.

They began the slow, exaggerated turning again. Things seemed to be going fine. They passed through a stand of trees. The slope was mild, but the trail was skinnier than the last one. Ginger stayed in front of him, modeling the big turns. They neared a bend in the track.

"I forgot to mention one thing about this trail."

"What?" And things had been going so well.

"It's no big deal. It's just that up ahead there're gonna be some big cutout animals." Ginger had turned around on her skis like they were ballet slippers and now skied backward, facing him. He was astonished by her grace.

"Cutouts?"

"You know, like the ones you stick your head through for pictures at the fair. These don't have holes to put your head through, but they're like that."

"Why?"

"We take a lot of little kids down this trail. It gives them something to turn around. We make up games and races and stuff using them. It's no big deal. I just wanted you to know about them. We'll just make our big turns around them like we've been doing."

They rounded the turn, and he saw them. As promised, there were three human-sized animals in the middle of the trail. There was a badly painted bunny Fender assumed was supposed to be the March Hare; a turtle who'd been left out in the weather too long, with peeling lime green paint punctuated by splotches of bare plywood; and a gigantic mouse wearing a yellow vest just like the one Wylie had worn.

"Look, an R.O.U.S.," Fender said out loud.

"What?"

"A Rodent of Unusual Size. It's from *The Princess Bride*. A movie. Never mind."

Ginger had pulled far out ahead of him. She was talking, but he couldn't hear very well. *I shouldn't be this far behind.* He skipped a turn to try to catch up.

Then they appeared. Little kids in lessons, the Mogul Mice. The kids in Justin's ski class. They'd skied onto the cat track from an adjoining trail. They were between Ginger and Fender.

He looked past the Mice, and he realized he'd stopped turning and was picking up speed. *A lot of speed for such a mild trail.* He was coming up behind the bunch of kids.

"Excuse me. Coming through, on your left. Watch it." He zoomed past two of the little ones and the instructor, Justin. He needed to catch up to Ginger.

Ahead, instead of a clear trail to his instructor, Fender saw terrible, terrible calamity.

Actually, he saw this: three plywood animals looming large and one kid. The kid sat in the middle of the trail, eating snow. It was Wylie the dog-kisser.

Fender did the only thing he could. He wedged for all the money he was worth and managed to avoid Wylie, but it was at the expense of the March Hare. There was a loud splitting of wood and pain. Then a moment of eerie silence.

Then, pleasantly enough, shrieks of small children pierced the air.

"You killed Mr. Bunny! You killed Mr. Bunny!" Wylie led the charge down the trail, and then small, mittened fists pummeled him.

Justin picked children off of him, but they were like little hornets. Fender saw Ginger approaching, skating back up the trail from where she'd stood, waiting for him to catch up. She broke up the swarm.

"Everybody calm down. Mr. Bunny is fixable. Look at poor Mr. Barnes—you guys are being so mean to him." She helped Fender to his feet and picked up his skis, which had come off in the tangle with the rabbit.

Justin picked the plywood up off the ground and tried to right it. It stood for a moment and toppled again. The Mogul Mice let out a painful collective gasp. Justin, the young ski instructor, looked at Fender.

"Dude. You took out the bunny. Cool."

Ginger smiled at Fender and declared the lesson done for the day.

That night, Ginger stared at the ceiling for a long time.

There was a really interesting grayish spot on the far left corner, just short of the molding. She wondered for a long time if it was a leak from the roof, darkening the drywall from above.

Insomnia: Never a problem for her before Brad died, now a familiar companion.

Zoë snored. The hairy stinker had no problem sleeping whatsoever.

Ginger sighed. At least tomorrow was her day off. She'd tried all sorts of remedies and tricks to get to sleep. Molly had lent her a white noise machine, she'd bought a little fountain for her bedroom, she exercised in the morning instead of at night, she listened to guided meditation, she took melatonin. None of it had worked so far.

She did finally drift off. She felt herself falling into sleep and wondered how late it was, how long it would last.

Then she woke up. The nape of her neck and her stomach were wet with sweat, and she'd kicked the covers to the floor at some point.

She was sitting up in bed. Her heart raced. She grabbed the pillow from Brad's side of the bed and held it tight.

Fingers of pink streaked the sky. *I might as well get up.* She looked at the clock and figured she'd had about four hours of sleep.

And it was her day off. The irony of complete wakefulness when she could sleep in was just sad at this point.

She got up, took a hot shower, and got dressed in her ski clothes. *If you can't beat 'em, join 'em. I'll get first tracks at least.* She drove the road up to the ski resort as the morning lightened. If she parked at the upper lodge, she could get her first run in just before the lifts opened. Then she could ride the chair to the back side and ski hard.

In the parking lot, she poured a cup of coffee from her thermos and sat in the car for a minute before booting up. Brad never would've gone along with this kind of impromptu ski day. He'd liked things planned. Ginger shook her head. *Who am I kidding? He liked things planned when he was the one doing the planning. He liked things planned* his *way. Spur of the moment is my thing.*

She got to the top of the run from the parking lot, slipped in her earbuds, and turned the music on loud. She pushed off down the run and felt the crunch of the snow under her skis.

It felt good. She kept her turns tight, then lengthened them out, feeling the edges of her skis curve and cut into the newly groomed run. Not another soul in sight.

At the bottom of the run, the lift operator stood, watching the chairs slowly gather speed and head up the mountain. The lift had just been fired up. The liftie looked for glitches, anything off balance or hung up.

As she glided up to the load board, she heard someone behind her.

"Ginger!"

Bode. He slid in next to her and smiled.

She was trapped. The next chair was there, and she would be riding it all the way up to the top of the mountain with Bode. *Why, why? What am I going to say to him?*

"I know what you're thinking." Bode tucked his poles under his leg, pulled his goggles up so he could look her in the eye.

"Do you?" *God, I hope not.*

"You're wondering if I'm still mad about the coat."

"I wasn't, but I hope you aren't." She counted lift towers till the top of the mountain. Too many. And she was too high off the ground to pull a Rocket and jump. Though it was starting to sound like a tempting option.

"Naw. How are you?" He smiled at her.

"Fine, I guess."

"You're not working today?"

"Nope. Couldn't sleep last night, so I figured I'd try skiing till I dropped."

"I've got some time. We could get in a couple runs on the backside. I'm supposed to check out the upper left side of War Eagle. Snow's gettin' a little thin. One of the patrollers thought there might be a hazard I need to mark if they used the winch cat last night—there's that one big slab of rock they might've exposed."

"Race you to it." *Brilliant, Ginger. I'm proud of you. There's no chit chat in racing somewhere.*

Bode took the challenge. "Loser buys beers in the lodge."

"You're on."

They crested the top of the mountain, and a fierce wind greeted them, kicking up a fine mist of blown snow, thrown high into the bright morning sky.

Ginger pushed off the chair and made a sharp turn, cutting across a sketchy patch of ungroomed snow to hit the top of War Eagle.

"Cheater!" Bode yelled after her. He'd taken the gentler slope off the front of the ramp, the way skiers were supposed to exit the chair.

She couldn't hear anything else from behind her after that.

She looked down the run and picked her line. War Eagle hadn't been groomed the night before, so the hazard Bode was supposed to look for was still hidden under the snow. She didn't see a sign of it anywhere. No rocks scraped bare by a winch cat here—just ungroomed chop and moguls.

It was icy in patches, and the moguls were uneven. Spring skiing made most of the runs unpredictable. She opened it up. Her thighs burned, and she felt her body warming up as she pushed her skis through the chop.

The speed felt good. She felt light. She picked her way across the run and chose a line through the mogul field, letting her skis come up and piston down in a satisfying rhythm.

She never skied this well when she skied with Brad. This was Ginger, pure and untempered. No holding back, no checking for her partner, no worrying about leaving him behind or choosing a run he wouldn't like.

Just me. Just me, and it feels good. It feels okay.

She finished up the run and kicked up a huge puff of snow, hockey-stopping at the bottom. Bode was quickly behind her.

"You won on a technicality—we were supposed to race to the hazard. I think cheater buys," he announced.

"No winch cat, no bare hazards, you obviously race to the bottom."

"Whatever. You're buying tonight, no matter what." He pulled a glove off and offered a handshake.

She shook on it. "I may have to rain check that. I'm betting I'll be too tired to last the whole day."

He smiled. "If you ski like that, I agree. You're a bad ass."

No one had ever told her that before. She liked it. "Thanks."

"I've got to go. Check-in at the top of Chair One in twenty, you know." Bode had a patrollers' morning meeting to attend. He skated off to the lift.

Ginger stood alone and breathed in the air, smelling the fresh pine and clean snow of the mountains. She thought about her lesson yesterday. She thought about the guy in her lesson yesterday, the beat-down he'd gotten from the little Mogul Mice. *Fender.* It made her smile to think about him.

Maybe things are going to be okay. I've got bluebird days to ski, lessons to teach. Maybe I can do this.

It sure felt better to focus on those things, and she needed a way to move forward, not dwell in the past. Maybe this was the way.

For the next two months, she kept telling herself that.

Chapter Eight

Fender could hear Sam messing around in the office at the back of the shop. He was sitting at the jeweler's bench, playing with the grinder. Anything he could find nearby, he was grinding down to a nub — pencils, old keys, anything.

"Fender, what about teeth? Could I grind my teeth down on this? You know, into vampire points?"

Fender worked out front by one of the display cases. "Feel free to try it, and let me know how it goes." He pulled one of the velvet trays out from the display case. He reached into his pants pocket and retrieved a ring box. *The* ring box. It was starting to look a little worn. And no wonder: Fender had toted it around with him for two months now, and the gray velvet had rubbed smooth at the corners. He cracked the box. There it was. The ring had ridden along in Fender's glove box as he went to his lessons with Ginger. It never made it out of the glove box, but it had logged some mileage.

Ginger. He thought about her. He stopped thinking about her. Back to the matter at hand: putting the ring back in the store. Time to let sleeping dogs lie. Things were going well with Ginger. He'd had two more lessons with her: one right after the bunny disaster, and then as soon as he could after that, in early February. But then the weather had turned subzero, and even he had limits. And anyway there had never seemed to be an opportunity to tell her the truth.

He didn't have the guts to take things beyond the slopes. He was a heel. And she was too good. Telling her about the ring and the proposed proposal by Dead Boyfriend would complicate matters. Fender liked how uncomplicated everything felt right now. And that made him want another ski lesson.

A loud screeching of metal broke the Zen moment. Sam stood, and Fender could see him through the office window. In an instant, Sam was at the door to the office. "It's handled! I'm all right. Everything's under control." He came up to the counter and stood next to Fender. "What are you doing out here?"

"Putting something away." Fender held the ring up to look at it again. It was a platinum band, smooth and free of decoration. A simple prong setting held the diamond. It was pear-shaped and big, a little shy of two carats. It was beautiful. *Dead Boyfriend had good taste; I'll give him that. Actually, Old Lady Harriman was the one with great taste. I just convinced him to take it off my hands*, Fender remembered. A ring with no owner. First Harriman, then Ginger's boyfriend.

"God, that's huge. What's that from?" Sam hadn't noticed the ring box, which Fender now slipped back into his pocket.

"An estate sale. Somebody died." Fender ignored the tweak he felt in his gut and tucked the ring into one of the slots on the tray.

Chapter Nine

On the day of Fender's fourth scheduled lesson, it rained. Ginger checked in at the office, expecting a cancellation. But there were no messages for her. *He's really getting into skiing. I'm surprised.*

She smiled. Fender Barnes. This student definitely won the prize for perseverance. Even she would have given up on skiing after his run-in with Wylie and Mr. Bunny, his plywood nemesis. One person could take only so much. But to her surprise, he'd called the next weekend and requested her again. She'd seen him once more in February, and that whole lesson he'd just seemed to smile a lot. Then a couple of rotten weeks of cold, miserable weather had passed, and she'd thought maybe he'd given up on skiing entirely.

But now, almost two months after his inaugural lesson, he was back. And bless his heart, despite the additional lessons she'd given him since then, he still wasn't really catching on. After three lessons, he had the wedge turn down, but that was about it. Typically, Ginger had adults on intermediate terrain by three lessons.

But there wasn't much about Fender that was typical. He'd graduated to wearing a coat rather than a garbage bag. When she was teaching, though, she had the feeling that sometimes he was just looking at her, that not much of anything was really sinking in. She'd ask if she was making sense, and he'd just grin and nod.

It wasn't a lot of skin off her nose if he just liked taking lessons. She'd keep teaching as long as he kept signing up. When it rained, though, even Ginger didn't have much fun skiing, and she considered herself a diehard.

Rain wasn't totally unusual as the season drew to a close. The weather had warmed up and become more unpredictable. She'd skied in March and April in snow, sleet, fog, rain, and lightning. Today was March third, so she was ready for anything.

It was a slow morning. Most of the instructors sat in the ski school locker room. They played cards or tuned their skis.

At ten minutes to eleven, Ginger began to get her gear on. A couple of the other instructors patted her on the back in pity. It was pouring rain outside. There was a puddle of water standing on the snow in front of the door to the locker room. It was grim. Ginger resigned herself to getting completely soaked. She thought ahead to a hot bath and warm bed with Zoë curled up at the end of it. *I can do this. If Fender can take it, I can take it.*

She walked out to the private lesson bench in the rain. *Why am I doing this? I'm doing this because it's my job, and because I like Fender.* She slowed a little. She liked him. *I like Fender, and I like the way he makes me laugh.*

She spotted him as soon as she walked up to the meeting area. Fender sat on the bench, holding an umbrella. She bit her lip to keep from laughing.

"Hi. I didn't know if you'd come." His pants were already soaked through.

"You buy, I fly, my brave friend. But I have bad news for you, Fender. You can't ski with an umbrella."

"I was trying to save the total soaking for the lesson."

Ginger turned and headed for Chair Two. "Follow me."

They got on the lift. Ginger liked riding the lift with Fender. She usually looked at him and watched the expressions on his face and the crinkle to his eyes. Today it was raining so dang hard, she just tried to pick out the next tower through the sheets of water. But it still was nice to have him sitting next to her.

"This is interesting." Fender shifted his shoulders a little. "I didn't know it was possible to have small tributaries of water running into your underwear. And they're icy. How pleasant." He sat up a little straighter and pointed off into the rain. "What's that?"

Ginger followed the path of his finger to Summit Lodge. Or at least in the general direction of it. It was a restaurant at the top of Chair Two. Earlier in the season it was busy, but today it'd be dead.

"It's Summit Lodge. What're you thinking about?"

"If I've paid for the lesson, does it matter what we actually do in the lesson?"

Ginger smiled. "Usually I'm supposed to teach you how to ski."

"But what if I'm a pain in the ass and throw a temper tantrum? Would you have to appease me?"

"If it was in the name of total quality guest service, I guess I'd have to make you happy, yeah." Ginger saw the last tower emerging out of the rain.

"Okay. So here's the plan. We go into Summit Lodge and wait until it stops raining. And if anyone questions you, tell them I insisted. I'm well-known for being a first-class jackass, so it'll be believable."

"First class, huh?"

"Ask anyone. I am Grade A jack." The chair deposited them at the top of the lift, and they turned toward the lodge.

After checking their equipment, they found a table inside. The Summit Lodge was big, with bare log beams, antler chandeliers, and high ceilings. But today it was quiet and even seemed cozy. Fender plunked down at a table by the fireplace.

"I'm going to have an Irish coffee. What do you want?" He waved to a waitress at the bar.

"I'm still on the job. I'll have a regular coffee, though. With lots of cream." She stood. "Will you order that for me? I'm going to go towel off. I'm drenched through. You may have witnessed a record, Fender. I don't remember it ever pouring this badly." She excused herself to the bathroom.

In the ladies' room, she peeled off successive sopping layers. She ran the hand dryer and stuck her head under it. Every time she looked in the mirror, she caught herself grinning. Perma-grin. *God, I haven't smiled this way about a man in a long time.* She didn't stop herself this time; she let herself go there. *Not even with Brad did I smile like this. Not even with Brad.* She paused for a moment and took stock: how did admitting that feel? She wrung out her fleece. It felt okay. She hadn't been struck down for thinking it.

Fender sipped his coffee when she returned. He had his boots and socks off. "Because you are a nice girl, I'll only have one drink."

"Do you usually have more?"

"Well, you see, I have really bad judgment when it comes to women. They usually warrant drinking until I can't hear the screeching. Or I hear it, but I don't care."

"Tell me a bad judgment story." Ginger sipped her coffee and felt her body warm up.

"Well, there was Sandy. And Sandy's parakeet. I don't know if I should tell you that one. It makes me out to be a bird killer. Oh, but there's Emilia. She was a hoot. I don't know if she thought I was much fun, but oh well. See, I own a jewelry shop—"

Ginger interrupted. "You do? That's really cool. Which one?"

"It's not so cool. Barnes and Son, downtown. I'm the son. The prodigal son to boot. But we don't have time for that sad tale. So, Emilia was from Massachusetts. I think she was even a debutante at one point in her life. I don't remember how she found her way out west. I think she was a programmer or something.

"I met her down at the Rendezvous one day when I was hanging out with Pop. She was gorgeous, so I asked her out. I think I suggested something original like dinner and a movie. So, we go out, and we talk about our jobs. When I said I was a jeweler, her eyes lit up. I don't know what it is with chicks and shiny stuff. They're as bad as crows with aluminum foil, I tell you what." He paused and looked at her. "Except you. I'm sure you're not that way. Oh, Jesus. If I say anything that offends you, just ignore me. Chalk it up to hypothermic insanity or something."

Ginger looked across the table at him and smiled. "I like your stories. You're fine."

"You could hit me when I start to say something that pisses you off. Wouldn't be the first time a girl decked me, either."

"Your track record sounds amazing."

"You know, my charms are boundless. But have you ever had a student as entertaining?" He sat back and looked straight at her.

I like his eyes. I like his smile. Ginger felt warm. *I don't feel cold anymore.*

"Hello?" He touched her fingertips, and she jumped, almost knocked over her coffee.

"What were we talking about?"

He looked at her, and Ginger realized he was on to her. *He can tell, can't he, that I was thinking about him?* He raised an eyebrow. "I think we were talking about how much you like me."

She wasn't ready. She changed the direction of the conversation.

"No, I'm pretty sure we were talking about other crazy students I've had. I'll tell you about Rocket. He gives you a run for your money."

He nodded, giving her the point. "Okay. Tell me about Rocket."

They chatted and laughed, and Ginger watched his eyes and face and just generally enjoyed him, forgetting herself.

Until she saw the clock on the wall behind him. "Our lesson time's about up. I need to go check in at the ski school pretty soon. I've got about fifteen minutes to get down the front side to the office."

He sat up in alarm. "I don't want to get you in trouble. Just leave me here. I'm not going out again."

"Thanks for the coffee. If you want, call me. We'll schedule a make-up time to ski on our own. No charge, just to make up for the lousy weather today."

He stood up and handed Ginger her scarf. "Actually, I'm not entirely thrilled about the whole skiing thing anyway. I do want to ask you something, though."

"What?"

"Would you have dinner with me one night? Maybe go see a movie?"

"Yeah. I'd like that."

Ginger skied back down to the office, but she didn't notice the rain. All she could feel was the wide grin on her face.

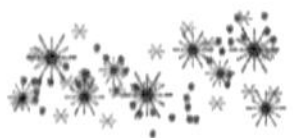

Only when he was in the car, driving down the mountain, did Fender realize he had set a date for the same old thing: dinner and a movie.

Who am I to be inventive at this point? Of course, there was a reason for this kind of date. It limited the amount of talking he'd be doing, which was never a bad thing. Talking was usually how he got into trouble.

Actually, as he thought about it, it seemed that as soon as women got to know him a little better…well, that was usually the thing that ended the relationship for him. *Hell, the more I know myself, the less I like me.*

Oh, but there were so many other ways to screw this one up. Like, for instance, the fact that he was already keeping secrets from her. He hadn't even slept with her yet, and he was already lying. *I may have broken my own record on that one.*

He was sure there'd be a time to tell her Dead Boyfriend had wanted to give the ring to her and propose. That he, Fender, had been given the opportunity to tell her all about it months ago and didn't. That her new date now was trying to sell the ring again to get rid of it. Oh, and that he still had the check Brad had written him for it in the top drawer of the desk in the back office of the shop.

Yes, this was a recipe for success if he knew one. But he didn't care. He loved the way she made him feel. She made him feel like he could even figure a way out of all of this, eventually. She made him feel handsome and clever. And a little less like a total asshole.

So, one night the next week, he found himself standing in front of the display cases, looking at his reflection. He was going to the house to pick her up for their first date.

He'd been smart enough to remember to ask for directions, even though he already knew where she lived. *Stalkers never get a second date*, he reminded himself. The bells above the front door tinkled.

He didn't turn around. "We just closed. Come back tomorrow."

The customer responded by slapping him on the back, hard. "God love you, quality is job zero around here." It was Sam. "What're you doing? I came to see if you wanted to go have a beer." Sam was always up for a beer.

"I've got plans." *This isn't going to be easy. Sam is the Jedi Master of secrets.* He could always tell when Fender had one.

"No, no, no, you're not getting off that easy." Sam closed in on Fender, circling like a buzzard in the desert. "You even smell good. Who is she? What's up with the CIA action?"

"It's no big deal."

"It must be a big deal; I think you're even wearing clean socks!" Sam leaned back against the counter.

"I just don't want to jinx it. And you're getting huge palm prints on the case." Fender started looking for his keys. Sam took a step away from the counter and smoothed the glass with the hem of his T-shirt. Fender could practically see the little gears turning in his brain.

"You haven't met anybody lately—oh my God!" Sam chased Fender behind the counter. "I know exactly who it is. You haven't met any chicks lately except one: the ski girl! Dead Boyfriend's girl!

You asked her out? You dog! Well, how'd she take the news about roadkill and the ring?"

The jig was up. He couldn't lie to Sam. Fender just looked at him.

Sam's smile was as wide as the Rio Grande. "You didn't tell her. I knew the new-and-improved Fender would be short-lived. You didn't tell her, and now you're hornin' in on the dead guy's territory."

Fender tried to be sanctimonious. "You almost look pleased that I haven't told her."

Sam laughed. "I am pleased! You're a never-ending source of entertainment for me, Fender. I love you, but God, you do stupid things sometimes. So, how's this going to work? Will you bed her and slip the ring into the eggs the morning after? Or with a note tucked under the pillow?"

Fender really did feel a little hurt. "It's not like that, Sam. I know I usually don't go for the long-term thing with women…" He paused because Sam was clearly trying not to laugh. "I know it usually doesn't work out after a while, but I want it to be different with her. Don't tell me another thing because I've already thought about all of it."

"All right, studmuffin. You know what? If you think this is a chance for happiness, I'm not going to lecture you. I just don't remember big fatty lies being the cornerstone of a great relationship."

"Excuse me, oh Honest Sam. I recall someone in this room calling the cable company to bitch about the cable being out before remembering that he'd hot-wired the cable from his neighbor's cable box in the first place. Ring any bells?"

"Well, go on your date and have fun. I'm proud of you, too, for bathing. That lets a girl know she's special." Sam got out of the shop door before Fender could retaliate.

Ginger cried in the car all the way down the mountain.

It'd just been a horrific day. She'd had lessons back to back on a miserable, wet March Tuesday. All morning long she'd looked forward to changing her socks at lunch and having a warm cup of soup. When she'd trudged back to the instructors' room, however, she'd found another slip of paper for her, pegged with a golf tee on the big assignment board. Another lesson. A lunch lesson. She could've cried. But she'd turned around and marched out to the flats again, wet socks, cold toes, and all.

She never said no. She wanted the work, and she worried that if she turned one lesson down, no others would come her way.

So, she'd gone to teach another lesson. Followed by another, and then another. At the end of the day, she'd been bone tired and cold.

Her last lesson had been a kid of nine or ten. Colby was his name. The mother had wanted to stand on the snow next to them and watch. That'd been Ginger's first hint of trouble.

Colby was a brat. A spoiled mama's boy. He was also hopelessly uncoordinated. By the end of the hour, Ginger had been ready to strangle him. But she'd kept at it, trying to get him to wedge turn, or stop, or even just get up by himself.

When they had ten minutes left in the lesson, Colby had fallen and wouldn't get up. Ginger had tried everything, but he was planted. So, she'd sat down in the snow next to him, resolved to wait until he decided he wanted to get up.

Which was when the mother had stormed up to them.

"What's going on here?" Colby had seen his mother's approach and began to wail.

Before Ginger could utter any kind of explanation, the mother had scooped her son up off the snow and lit into Ginger with relish.

"I'll see to it that your boss knows about this negligence. I'm appalled. I left my son in your care, and this is what I come back to find? You obviously can think of no one but yourself. You aren't competent. Do you know that?" The mother had actually seemed to expect a reply.

Now Ginger couldn't even remember what she'd said to the woman, but it had been apologetic. Ginger was furious with herself. She hadn't said one word in her own defense. What was worse, a tiny nagging part of her said the woman was right.

She wiped her nose on the cuff of her jacket. This sucked. It made her want to eat lots of brownies and curl up under the covers. It made her miss Brad.

Brad had fallen in love with her when she hadn't even been trying her hardest. She'd really loved that about him, because inside somewhere she realized someone could love her just as she was, not only on her best behavior.

She'd been so thrilled to have someone, someone who loved her. She'd cleaned the house and done his laundry even before they were living together. She'd bought him presents. She was uber-woman, hear her roar.

But when she began teaching again the following season, she'd discovered — actually Brad had discovered — she couldn't keep up the pace of super-housekeeper and also work at the resort. One Monday, she remembered, she'd been in bed, waiting for Brad to finish in the bathroom so she could get up.

Brad had gotten up before six, showering and getting ready to go in for an early surgery at the vet clinic. He came out of the bathroom and began to open and close all of his drawers, open and close the closet door.

She shook herself out of sleep. "What's up? You can't find something?"

She knew the answer before he even said it. "Where's that one shirt? The one with the blue collar and the white stripes?"

She fought the urge to throw something at him. "You wore it Saturday."

"It's not clean?" He opened and closed another drawer for effect.

"I'm sorry, hon, I didn't get to the washing. I was so beat when I got off the mountain yesterday."

"It's fine. I'll wear whatever." And he stomped out of the room.

Of course, he'd known exactly where the shirt was: in the dirty laundry, right where he'd tossed it. But he wanted her admission, as if it were a piece of ammunition he would save for later arguments.

Little things like that, she let slide. But she'd let other stuff slide, too, that maybe she shouldn't have. Like asking for what she wanted.

She'd wanted things she hadn't had the guts to ask for. She liked compliments; she liked flowers. But he never did these things for her because she'd never asked. And more than that, they never occurred to him on his own.

When the little things started to seem not so little, that was when Ginger had begun to watch the Frisbee players in the park. And then it didn't matter.

This thought launched Ginger into another sob. "We never got to see what was next. I never got to see if it would have worked."

She realized she was talking to herself. The car filled with her voice above the turning of the tires on the road. It soothed her to hear herself talk, even though it was the first sign of insanity. "You know what else would be soothing? A long bath and a plate of brownies."

And then she remembered: *Oh my God, I have a date!* She didn't want to go. This made her want to sob all over again. It was with Fender, her student. This was a full-scale emergency.

She drove down the rest of the road as quickly as she could. Maybe he'd forget. She didn't know what to do, but she knew she didn't want to go. She just wanted to crawl into bed, warm up, and sleep. Or try to sleep. She tried to remember where she'd put his phone number.

She parked in front of her house, leaving her skis in the back of her car. She got the door open and walked inside, already scanning the living room for the scrap of paper with his number on it.

It was no use. She looked high and low and couldn't find it anywhere. Zoë followed her from room to room and whined with concern. Ginger spouted a long string of curses and self-pitying remarks, which seemed to disturb the big dog.

She plopped down on the couch. Giving up, she peeled off her jacket and fleece and stooped down to unlace her boots. It was six forty-five. He'd be here in fifteen minutes. *Screw it. I'm going to take off my wet socks and make a cup of hot chocolate. When he comes to the door, I'll tell him the truth: I'm having a nervous breakdown, and you'll have to come back another day to take me out. That's what I'll do.*

And then Zoë puked. It was a sudden, all-at-once kind of hurl. The dog bent her fluffy head down in an arch, splayed her front paws, and let go in the middle of the living room rug. And then the doorbell rang. Ginger let out a cry of pain; *it's official. I have entered the first level of hell.* She felt tears welling up in her eyes, and the doorbell rang again.

Fender heard a kind of strangled cry when he rang the doorbell. *Well, that's always a sign of a good date to come.* He rang the doorbell again. For a moment, nothing happened. He was going to look pretty silly if she didn't open the door soon.

Then the door swung open, slowly, like in a horror movie. Ginger stood a few steps back from the threshold. She was a sight to behold.

And not in a good way. Between her legs was a large Husky dog who'd apparently just vomited all over the carpet. This was evidenced by a pile of partially digested Alpo chunks, smack in the middle of the living room rug, not far behind the woman and dog. Ginger's hair was falling out of a ponytail, and her eyes and nose were red.

"Um, hi." This was the best he could do.

"Hi." Ginger said this in a wavering voice. He noticed she was biting her lip, and he realized she was on the verge of crying. He hated it when women cried.

"You know, this doesn't look like a good time, maybe I'll call you." This is what he usually would've said. Instead, he heard this come out of his mouth: "Why don't you sit down on the couch? I'll find something to clean up the puke." He came inside and walked toward the back of the house, careful to avoid the toxic dog vomit.

He liked her kitchen. It had old white wooden cabinets, a comfortable feel. He grabbed a dishrag.

As he came back into the living room, Ginger tried to say something. "I just want…It's been…She ate…" She plopped down on the couch with the most defeated look on her face Fender had ever seen.

"Shitty day, huh?"

She nodded vehemently. He knelt over the puke. It was acid-yellow and steamed a little. *Oh baby, now this is a turn-on.* The dishrag was not going to cut it. He stood again, trying not to gag, to look for a more suitable tool. "You just sit there and hold that dog. Don't worry about anything."

In the kitchen, Fender looked around and decided on a soup ladle and the trash can. He hurried back into the living room. It was a nasty business. He found if he held his breath while over the toxic mess, he could get the puke into the trash with minimal gagging on his part. Soon, he'd ladled all the vomit into the trash can. Then he used the dishrag to mop the spot left on the carpet.

Ginger seemed to sink a little more comfortably into the couch. "I think she knew I was going out. I don't know what the hell she ate to make that, though."

"Perhaps we need a priest. I saw very similar puke in *The Exorcist*. Has her head spun around yet?" He saw Ginger smile a little. He felt brave. "You know what? Why don't we bag the movie idea?"

She wiped her nose on the sleeve of her black fleece. "That sounds really good."

"I'll just run down to the store and get us something to eat. Do you want me to rent a movie?"

She shook her head. "I don't know if I can last for the two hours. Dinner here would be good, though." She hunkered down on the couch. As she talked to him, she pulled the rubber band out of her hair. A thick tangle of strawberry blond fell down around her shoulders. Then she swept it all back up again and refastened the band. *She's beautiful, honest-to-God beautiful.*

She went to the bathroom to blow her nose, and he hopped in his car and drove to the store. He got to the closest market and went inside. It was the natural foods grocery store. He felt lost. His idea of dinner at home was a can of SpaghettiOs mixed with chili. He ate a lot down at the Rendezvous or at Pop's house.

Now Fender scanned the aisles. There were organic veggie snacks and cookies called "frookies" because of some scary ingredient they had. He walked to the meat case and things weren't much better: free-range chicken, hormone-free beef, fish caught in the nets of disenfranchised Native American lesbians, that kind of stuff. Fender didn't really get into the whole environmental thing, and he had enough self-awareness to know he lived so far away from political correctness he'd need a map to get there.

Finally, he got what looked like a relatively safe choice: a frozen pizza. He knew how to cook those. Sure, it was an organic, wheat-crusted pizza with pine nuts and sun-dried tomatoes, but it was pizza. He picked up a couple sparkling juices to go with it and headed back to her house.

He was helping her, even taking care of her a little. It felt good.

She'd left the door open for him, and he went inside. She had the TV on and had curled up into a little ball in one corner of the couch. A purple and blue afghan was tucked around her, and the dog was piled on top of the corner of that.

"Hi. What'd you find?" Just her head and the fingers on one hand showed above the afghan.

"Pizza. I'll go take care of it."

"Fender?"

"Uh-huh?"

"Thanks. This is really good of you. I feel a lot better."

"I'm glad I could help."

"I didn't even want to see you tonight; I was in such a bad mood. But I'm glad you came over."

Fender felt a weird tingle in his ribcage. "I just want to repay you for all the stuff you taught me in lessons." He stood there, not quite sure what to do next.

There was a knock at the door. Ginger sat up, popping out of the cocoon of her afghan. "That's really weird." She got up and went to the door.

The door was barely open a crack when a petite, dark-haired woman squeezed herself through. She wore a plaid shirt, black horn-rimmed glasses, and a little pleated skirt. Fender inwardly groaned. This girl was so hipster it hurt.

"Molly! What's going on?" Ginger gave the girl a hug.

"I was over at Dragonfly." Molly eyed Fender suspiciously. "I saw this fern incense, and it reminded me of you. So, here I am, bearing gifts." She handed Ginger a bundle of what looked like twigs.

Ginger turned to Fender. "Fender, this is my friend Molly. She works in the ticket office."

Fender took a step forward and shook Molly's extended hand. As she clasped his fingers, she closed her eyes and breathed in deeply, like she was smelling him. Fender decided then and there that he didn't like her. *What the hell was that?* Was she trained as a bomb-sniffing dog alternate? He smiled weakly. She was going to ruin everything.

When Ginger thought about it a little while later, the date had kind of been the date that wasn't. As soon as Fender got back from the store, Molly had knocked on the door. She was a good friend. Sure, she was flaky as all get out, but that was kind of fun. Molly always had a new cause. Lately, she was petitioning Jell-O to stop making, well, Jell-O, because it was made from animal parts. Anyone who could get behind such a futile cause had to be a good person. Not altogether with it, but a good person.

Molly'd been there for Ginger when she needed her, too. After the funeral, when Ginger came home from her self-imposed exile at her mom's, it'd seemed there was a dark space waiting to consume her. It waited on the other side of the doors in her life; she dreaded it when she entered the house or walked through the doorway to the kitchen. The dark space was there, just on the other side of that door, in the next room. It was the void that had consumed Brad and left her alone.

But Molly'd been the first person to show up at the house when she returned. Ginger was still grateful for that. Molly had dragged her out to dinner, to the movies, to the grocery store. She'd helped go through the house and "de-Brad" it: his lawn mowing shoes, the razor in the shower, gloves and hats and scarves in the front hall closet. Even now, despite the months that had passed, just thinking about these things gave Ginger a queasy knot in her stomach.

But Molly had gathered up all of these little pieces of Brad that had paralyzed Ginger with grief. She'd tidied up Ginger's life, made it bearable without him.

"Just take up space for now, you know? If you can just live in the house and occupy the space and breathe the air, you're doing great," Molly had said.

At that point, Molly's view of the world had given Ginger a lot of comfort. Ginger didn't have her own sense of anything after this world. It seemed like the back of a picture. The living saw the side with the image, and the reverse was empty. The border between life and the empty space behind it had seemed very slim.

Molly, on the other hand, thought the reverse side of life was a huge expanse of wonder and beauty. She would talk of the worlds she would one day get to explore, and she always sounded sure of their existence. It wasn't a leap of faith for her; it was a given. Something about that confidence rubbed off on Ginger. She'd started to buoy herself with Molly's steadfast beliefs. Brad was okay, she'd told herself. He was somewhere else, and it was a really interesting place to be.

Molly had painted a picture of heaven for Ginger so lush and intriguing that it had felt better to let Brad slip into the corners of her mind. Now he only surfaced on occasion, when she called forth his memory on purpose or when something surprised her with a memory, like the smell of rosemary and chicken baking.

Molly had helped her begin to let go, and she appreciated that. So, whenever Molly dropped by, she was welcome. Although tonight, she'd knocked on the door just as Fender seemed like he'd begun to relax.

The dog puking hadn't seemed to faze him very much, and she'd been looking forward to having him here with her. She'd hoped he would sit on the couch next to her. But when Molly showed up, something in Fender's posture had changed. Stiffened. Kind of like a cat arching its back at a dog.

"I just realized I left a door to my shop unlocked," he'd said. Then he'd scooted out the door Molly left open.

Molly seemed odd, too. "What a weird guy," she said, peering after him.

Too much weirdness. So, Ginger had begged out of hanging with Molly and sent her on her way just a few minutes after Fender. She'd had a day.

She shook her head and settled in on the couch, alone once again, and thinking sleep sounded good to her right now. Another strange and brief encounter with Fender Barnes.

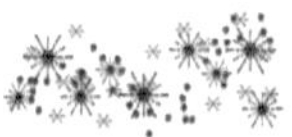

He drove home to his apartment—and not by way of the shop; he didn't have to. There wasn't an unlocked door. He'd lied. Not that it was a new thing for him to lie. No, it seemed to be par for the course in this relationship.

He coughed involuntarily. *Did I just say relationship? Oh, good God.*

He did feel really bad, though. But when Ginger's friend had shown up, the house felt tiny, and he needed to get out of there. It was a deep urge for escape. Primal. *It was the sign that I'm not meant for human interaction.* So he'd made up an excuse, and fled.

He parked in front of his building and went up the stairs to the door. The stone façade looked shoddy and crumbly. He hadn't remembered it looking like that.

Inside his condo, all was quiet. Fender had no pets. It was probably more humane that way. He might forget to feed them. Also, they shed everywhere, and he hated the smell of cat piss. He didn't even have a plant.

It was quiet.

This wasn't a big deal. Cleaning up dog puke tonight reminded him why he was better off alone.

He went to the fridge and dug out the spaghetti Pop had sent home with him the last time he was over for dinner. Pop had always cooked, even when Mom was alive, and Fender thought he was good at it. He made mostly the basics, but he knew them well. When Fender had lived at home, one of the things he'd liked most was the schedule. He could always count on tacos on Monday, spaghetti on Tuesdays, and "breakfast anytime" on Sundays, when they ate waffles and eggs and bacon for dinner.

After eating at the kitchen table, Fender turned on the TV, as he usually did when he was home. It masked any noise the neighbors might make, and it filled up the space of the condo.

There was nothing on, and it was too early to go to bed. He didn't feel like getting on the computer. He called Sam, but his friend wasn't home. *What the hell is my problem?* He felt aimless. It was too quiet. The carpet sucked up all the sound, like a sponge.

He decided to take a shower. He turned the water on hot, really hot. As he stood there, suddenly he felt very irritated. There were hairs all over the floor of the tub. The shower curtain had rust-colored mold on it. And it was lopsided, because half of the holes for the rings had been torn out.

"Jesus, what a slob." He said it out loud. He couldn't believe he hadn't noticed this before.

He got out of the shower and toweled off. In the bedroom, he put on sweats and flopped down on the bed. He stared at his phone for a long time.

Suddenly — well, it felt that way, at least — he found himself in the car, driving. He pulled up in front of her house. His hands shook a little as he rang her doorbell. His hair was still wet, and he could feel it freezing into crunchy tendrils at the back of his neck.

She opened the door. Her eyes were still puffy from crying. The TV was on in the background, loud. She smiled when she saw who it was.

"Hi." He wasn't sure what to say.

"Hi." She waited for him. She wasn't going to make it easy, he could tell.

"I just came by to see if you wanted to go out again some time."

"We didn't go out this time." She was still smiling.

"Okay, well, to see if you wanted to go out."

"Your hair's wet. Come in. You'll freeze to death."

He stepped into the warmth of her house. It was so clean and bright and filled up.

"Sit down; I'll go get a towel."

Fender headed for the couch. The aimless feeling was gone.

Ginger came back with a towel and sat next to him on the couch. "I never made the pizza, if you're still hungry." She pulled the afghan back over her, tucked it around her legs.

"I ate when I got home." Ginger's dog came over and looked at him. Fender shifted. "Your dog's giving me the stink eye."

Ginger smiled. "That's Zoë. She's probably mad you turned down the pizza."

"It's a real similar look to the one your friend gave me." *After she tried to inhale me, or whatever the hell that was.*

She shrugged. He liked to watch her mannerisms. Every little gesture came with a light in her green eyes, or a lift of an eyebrow, or a shy smile. She was fascinating.

"I don't know what Molly's deal was. Protective or something. She left again right after you did."

The dog was still sitting in front of Fender. "Come here, pup. You want up on the couch?" Fender patted the cushion next to him. *Don't scare the dog. Women love their dogs like children.* "You can come up."

The Husky looked at him, looked at Ginger, and then jumped up, squishing herself between Fender and her owner.

Ginger laughed. "She's not just protective; she's the chaperone, apparently."

"She seems quite comfortable in her role." Fender scratched the dog behind an ear, and the dog made what sounded like a contented sigh.

Ginger looked him in the eye. "You're good. The ear scratch is always well-received."

They looked at each other for a moment. He'd kiss her, but the moment felt so peaceful, he didn't want to botch it. He was really good at that. Plus, there was a large dog in the way.

He decided to try to talk to her, despite his usual rule about not screwing things up by talking too much. "You're not from here, so where are you from?"

She frowned. "How do you know I'm not from here?"

He laughed. "I'd guess we're about the same age, and I've lived here forever. I would've run into you."

"Maybe you did, and you just don't remember."

Not a chance. "I'm positive I'd remember running into you."

Her skin went pink under her freckles. The reaction sent a rush of heat through his chest. *Did I just do that to her? I like that. I want to do that to her again. Maybe other stuff, too.*

"I'm from back East. I went to UConn and moved out here after I graduated."

"By yourself? For a job?" He watched her face. The dog snored between them.

"By myself. No job. I just didn't want to live there anymore. I wanted something new. I'd been out West skiing with my family when I was ten. I decided to pick a place out here with a good ski hill where I could actually afford to rent a place."

Fender tried to figure out how he could touch her hand. He kept talking while he tried to find a way. "I guess that eliminated Aspen."

"Not a lot of choices fit my bill. Except Boise. So, here I am." She smiled at him again, twisted a piece of her hair between two fingers.

Fender felt a wide, unstoppable grin on his face. "Here you are." He stopped before he said the rest of what he was thinking: *Here you are, in my life, and I like it.* For the first time, in a very long time, he just wanted to sit, be who he was, and drink this person in. He felt—did he dare to say it? He felt happy. Content. Even with a big dog drooling on his pant leg in her sleep.

A couple hours later, Fender drove home through empty streets, still feeling happy. At a red light, he put down the window. No cars clogged the intersection. He sat alone, waiting for the light to turn. He could hear the "Don't Walk" sign click on and off, warning away nonexistent pedestrians.

He wasn't just happy, he was euphoric. And all they'd done was talk. About nothing, really.

The cold air stung his cheeks through the open window, so he put it up and turned on the stereo. Fender recognized the song; the lyrics told of misdeeds and lies in a relationship.

God, he felt like the song was about him. He was the liar, the criminal. He turned the stereo off.

The secret was bound to come out. He should be the one to tell her.

The red light turned green. At the silent intersection, Fender sat for a moment. There weren't any other cars. He let his car idle, kept his unmoving hands on the wheel.

"Not yet. Not yet."

He said it out loud, to the cold empty street.

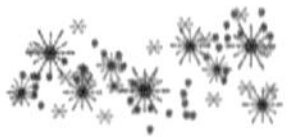

Fender had left very late, and Ginger had tried at first to go to sleep, but she gave up as the sky outside of her window began to brighten with pinks and oranges. She got up and went into the kitchen. The Husky followed her, excited about the prospect of food coming so early in the morning. Ginger put Zoë's bowl down and sat at the kitchen table.

She kept smiling. They'd talked about nothing. She'd spent a long time explaining the lesson programs up at Blackwolf. It was boring stuff, to be sure, but Fender had never stopped looking at her for a second, seeming riveted. She'd felt unsettled, with his eyes on her like that. When he'd nod or ask a question, the blood would rise in her cheeks. She hated that she was a blusher. It made her so transparent. It'd been that way all of her life. As a little girl, she could never successfully lie to her mother. As soon as the lie had sprung from her lips, she'd turn a deep beet color, and that was it. The truth was out.

The flush in her cheeks last night had been about something more, too. She wanted Fender.

Admitting it sent a delicious shiver through her.

Sex had been okay with Brad. At first, she'd been driven wild with what she thought was desire. Looking back, she thought maybe it was desperation that drove her wild. After a while, she'd been less than thrilled. Brad was fairly utilitarian about sex. It was something you needed physically; you did it, then moved on. And she didn't believe he meant to ignore her, but their lovemaking was done when he was spent. If she wasn't ready for it to be over, well, Brad never seemed to notice that.

She sipped her tea. She'd done that to herself. She went to great lengths to please him, and not just in bed. Somewhere along the way, she'd taught him that pleasing her wasn't a priority.

She sighed, and Zoë rolled over at her feet, echoing the long breath of air.

"Oh, Zoë, your poor Papa. Poor Brad." She let her mind turn over his name a few times. It didn't hurt too badly.

Then there was Fender. She didn't know much about him. He'd said before that he owned a shop. Sold jewelry. She didn't know where he lived. He talked a little about his dad, how they'd lived alone for a long time when Fender was a kid. She couldn't tell if the mom was dead or just gone. She'd been afraid to ask. Something about Fender made him seem reluctant to talk about himself last night.

But that made him all the more interesting. She closed her eyes for a second.

I want this man in my life, she thought. She stood up and went to change her clothes. *I want this man in my bed.*

She didn't have to look in the mirror above her dresser. She knew she was blushing.

Chapter Ten

It was a day of millers. Millers: ridiculous people who would wander into the shop like lost cows—cows in sneakers and puffy parkas—slurping coffee, marking up the display cases with grimy fingers, and buying nothing.

Fender stood behind a case near a hoodrat-wannabe white kid, all flat-brimmed hat and unlaced Adidas and DGK hoodie. Fender watched him so he wouldn't steal anything. The punk probably lived with his mommy and daddy on one of the boulevards in town, probably drove a nice sensible Subaru and walked the Labradoodle and did his calculus homework without being told—when he wasn't pretending to be hard.

Fender thought what it would be like to reach over the counter and punch him, but then his attention was diverted by an impossibly tiny girl with bright blue hair standing in front of him.

"Excuse me?" she peeped. She was quite possibly a baby bird in disguise.

"Huh?" Fender realized she needed his attention.

The boy standing next to her stepped up. "She said, 'Excuse me.' We need your help, if you don't mind."

Of course I mind. "Not at all. What can I help you kids with?" He gave the boy a good look. The couple hung on to each other's hands, the boy an anemic, blond, string bean in all-black: skinny jeans and a button-up shirt, plus a black trench coat for extra emo-Goth-manga-anime-I'm-so-different-I'm-exactly-the-same effect.

Good Jesus. You are twelve.

"We're buying an engagement ring." The white noodle in the black get-up puffed out his chest as he declared this.

"Uh-huh," chirped the bird girl in agreement.

Fender closed his eyes, breathed in deeply, exhaled slowly.

Then he opened his eyes.

"No, you aren't."

The pair turned their heads, looked at each other, and turned to look back at him. Bird girl tilted her head like a confused pigeon. "Huh?"

Fender shook his head. "No, you aren't buying a ring. I could offer you a promise necklace, or something horrifying like that, but instead, do this for me: Use your money to backpack across Europe together this summer. Take lots of pretentious pictures, get in a fight on the Paris Metro, realize you hate the way he chews his food in Milan, break up in front of the taxi stand at JFK, and spend a terrible connecting flight home to Boise wishing you'd never met each other."

Fender took a breath but held up a hand, preventing either from inserting themselves into his tirade.

"Then, and only then, if you still think that you'll just *die* without each other, come back and buy a ring from me. For now, good day."

Boy noodle looked shocked. "What? That's it?"

"Adieu to you, children. Have fun storming the castle!"

The impossibly young couple shrugged and walked out of the shop.

Sam strolled in. "Tell me those two didn't buy a ring."

Fender picked up his keys. "Of course not. I have my standards." He pointed to the door. "I will accompany you on your errand now."

Fender usually humored Pop with a visit to the Record Exchange. They'd look through the old LPs for jazz albums like Thelonious Monk or comb through the 45s for early rockabilly. Once they found a first pressing of The Everly Brothers' "Wake Up Little Susie," and Fender thought Pop was going to have a coronary.

Today he followed Sam into the store.

"Tell me what we're looking for again?" Fender asked with a sigh.

"I can't remember the name of the band. They were in the Gobi tent two years ago at Coachella. They had an 'I' in the beginning of their name."

Fender tried, tried very hard, not to roll his eyes. "Yep, that narrows it down. My God, we'll be here all day."

But then it didn't matter, because someone sneezed two rows of records over.

A guy spoke up. "Bless you."

"Thanks."

I know that voice! Fender's whole nervous system came to attention. *Ginger.*

He looked up, but the display was too high to see over. He elbowed Sam in the side. "Heads up. Ginger's in the store."

Sam looked at the back of a Village People record. "What?"

"Ginger's in the store."

"That girl you saw last week?"

"No, some random chick. Yes, that girl. Who else would I give a shit about?"

It was Sam's turn to roll his eyes. "Excuse me. Go say hi to her."

Suddenly Fender's hands felt clammy. "I don't know."

"Come on. Go say hi to her." Sam gave him a push down the row.

Fender put his shoulders back. *C'mon, Fender. Man up.* He took a deep breath. "Fine. I'll just go say hi."

He padded down the row and turned the corner.

Ginger thumbed through the LPs. Her hair hung long and soft and reddish-gold down her back. She was rapt, examining the back of an old record. Dust floated in the air, stirred up by her turning of the album cover. She wiggled her nose and sneezed again.

"Gesundheit." Fender walked up to her.

She looked up in surprise, and a wide grin spread over her face. Her green eyes twinkled. "Fender! What are you doing?"

"Shopping. Sam's looking for a needle in a vinyl haystack." He edged closer to her and smelled a subtle fruity scent. *God, she smells good. I never noticed that skiing.* He reminded himself he was supposed to be talking to her. "And you look like you've scored."

She held up the old R&B album. "Bell Biv DeVoe, brother. This is gold."

"You were a year old when that came out."

"So were you. Still a classic." She smiled at him.

I like it when she smiles. Fender edged a little closer to her and felt the hair on the back of his neck prickle. Ginger bit her lip and seemed to take a tiny step closer to him, too.

"Ginger, did you see this?" A guy strolled up behind her, and Ginger took an abrupt step away from Fender.

What the hell! Fender looked the guy next to Ginger over. He was a deep bronze color and had sandy blond hair. He had a Bob Marley album in his hand. *Douchebag.*

"Bode, this is my friend Fender." Ginger stepped out of the way so the men could shake hands.

I don't want to shake Malibu Ken's hand. Who the hell is he and what's he doing here and who names their kid Bode? Fender shook his hand. "Bode."

Malibu Ken looked at Fender for a second and then resumed his line of questioning. "This is, like, a really old copy of this album. I wonder if it's worth anything."

Ginger smiled again, and Fender imagined she was apologizing for her golden retriever friend. "It was good to see you, Fender. Season's over soon. Hope to see you up on the hill."

I'm going to kill this guy. We were about to have a moment, and he ruined it. "You know it. Take care, Ginger."

She held up her prize LP, gave Fender a little nod, and followed the jerk who ruined everything over to the other side of the store.

Fender stood, watching her walk, drinking it all in.

"Did you say hi or did you just stare at her like that?" Sam whispered in his ear.

Fender smacked him and pushed him away. "God almighty. Did you see that guy she was with? What the hell is up with that?"

"You mean the bro? I did. Hope that's not your competition. He looks like he does healthy things regularly. I hate guys like that."

"Yeah, Malibu Ken could be a problem."

Sam looked Fender up and down. "You could get a spray tan. That might help."

Fender threw up his hands. "Why am I friends with you? Go find your hipster album, and let's go."

It sucked to leave with Sam when Fender knew exactly who he should be leaving with. One thing was for sure, she smelled nicer than Sam ever had.

Chapter Eleven

It'd been a long time since Fender gave a crap about anybody. At least that was the articulate way Sam put it during their conversation a week or so after their record store errand (when Fender was supposed to be working). Actually, he'd put it that way several times in the conversations they'd had since his night at Ginger's house.

"Thanks a lot, Sam. What about you and Pop? I don't give a crap about you guys?" The office of the shop was quiet, as was the rest of the store, even though it was three o'clock in the afternoon.

"Pop and me, we're guys," Sam explained helpfully. "You don't have sex with us. I am stunned—*stunned*, I tell you—that you went over to her house and just talked. This is the first time I can remember when you weren't trying to crawl into a lady's underwear. Are you sure your name is Fender Barnes? And are you ever going to see her again? Ski season's just about over, so you'll have to man up."

Fender stood up and walked out of the office. This topic made him sweat, and he paced around the shop trying to get away from it. "Sam, it amazes me that you ever get laid with a mouth like that," he called over his shoulder.

"It's been a while, my brother, but I don't think my colorful vo-cabulary has anything to do with it." Sam was into one of the display cases now. He had a tray of sapphire rings out and loaded two on each stumpy finger.

"Would you stop that? You'll make the rings all clammy."

"No, really. The reason I can't get with a woman is my contentment." Sam stood a little straighter behind the counter. Whatever his "contentment" was, Fender noticed he was proud of it. Or he liked having all that jewelry on.

"Are you going to elaborate on this?"

"I'm content. I have a job, kind of. I like my life. I don't care if my breath stinks and my hair clogs up the drain in the shower. And I'm not willing to clean the shower or brush my teeth or do anything else for a woman. I don't need fixing, and I won't do it just to get some satisfaction in the equatorial region of my life. Women should dig who I am, and if they don't, I'm not going to leave the contented zone to meet 'em on anything."

"Uh-huh." Fender had lost track of what Sam was saying. He'd been, for the last few moments, watching a bubble of frosted blond-brown hair bob down the sidewalk, headed straight for the store. He did the only thing that seemed right.

"Fender, what the hell are you doing? You're sitting on my toes."

Fender replied from the floor behind the counter, indeed, from the floor at Sam's feet, on Sam's toes. "You need to hide. It's Naomi, Jimmy's wife. Hide, Sam!"

Sam sat down, Indian-style, in one fell swoop. He kind of plopped down on Fender in such a way that knees and butts and weight were not evenly distributed, and Fender yipped like a kicked poodle.

It was too late. She was in the store. The bells above the door jingled her arrival merrily. And someone was with her. And whoever it was had noticed the commotion behind the counter. Fender looked up and saw Jimmy.

"Fender?"

Sam popped up with a rapidity that seemed impossible for a man his size.

"Hello, sir, is there something I can help you with? Mr. Barnes is unavailable at the moment." Sam tugged his T-shirt down over his belly.

"He's not unavailable. He's sitting at your feet. Behind the counter." Naomi pointed an airbrushed nail tip at Sam.

Fender rose from behind the counter in surrender. "I'm right here, Naomi. Hi, Jimmy."

"Well, hi, Fender. What in the Sam Hill are you up to? Damn strange behavior." Jimmy eyed Sam.

Sam grinned from ear to ear and whacked Fender heartily on the back before retreating to the back office. Jimmy straightened his tie and put an arm around Naomi's waist.

Fender tried to recover. "Jimmy, I'm sorry about that. We were talking about…never mind. How are you? And Naomi…" Fender forced a smile, remembering her solo trip in early December to appraise the canary diamond. "How's the lovely bride?"

She giggled nervously. Jimmy leaned over to kiss her on the lips, but she grimaced and wiggled out of his embrace.

Fender resisted the urge to gag. Jimmy had no idea what a piece of work this Naomi was. Or maybe he did. "Now, Jimmy, you're going to make her blush." Fender stopped himself from sticking his tongue out at her. He settled for giving her the old squinty Clint Eastwood look instead.

Naomi gritted her teeth at him, and then turned to face Jimmy with a wide, plastered-on smile. "Jimmy says I'm hell-on-wheels. Isn't that cute?"

Hell-on-wheels, my ass. More like bitch-on-wheels. Fender couldn't believe these two were still together. Amazing. He didn't understand.

"Fender, we need a ring."

Fender almost choked. "Another one? What for?"

Jimmy frowned at him. "It's *for* our anniversary."

"But you only just got married." Fender stopped before he said anything else.

Sam was right behind him. He jabbed Fender in the ribs. "Aren't you supposed to encourage them to buy something, moron?" he whispered.

"It's the anniversary of our first date. We celebrate all of our special moments. What about this one, Jimmy?" Naomi pointed to a ring on the second shelf of the case next to them. Fender looked to see which ring the vulture had laid her eyes on. A sudden sinking feeling gripped him by the neck.

Naomi pointed to a large solitaire diamond in a platinum setting. The diamond sparkled under the case lights. Fender thought for just a second it was winking at him. *Oh shit. It isn't any diamond. It's that diamond. That ring.* The Ring.

Fender had put it out on the floor to dispose of it, but now that he was faced with the prospect of selling it, he wasn't so sure. Could he get rid of the problem by getting rid of the ring? *Sure you can. Get the ring out, let Naomi the hyena latch on to it, and sell the thing.* He opened the door to the case and fished the tray out. *Time to lay it on thick.*

"Oh, Naomi, you sure do have good taste." He looked up at her. She mouthed something at him that looked like "Bastard." He grinned even wider. "Nope, Jimmy, your girl here has an eye for the good stuff, no doubt about it. You're never gonna get a cheap piece of jewelry past those beady, er, sharp eyes of hers."

Sam coughed. He shot a glance at Fender. His ability to spot bullshit from a mile away was renowned.

Jimmy picked up the ring from the gray velveteen tray. Fender's heart started to pound. He wasn't doing anything wrong. No one probably even noticed that Dead Boyfriend's check never cleared. He was dead. A little money out of a ring D.B. couldn't use anymore wouldn't hurt anyone.

Naomi and Jimmy had taken the ring over to the store window, followed by Sam. Now he held it up for them, rotating it and tilting it in the natural light. Fender knew letting him near customers was asking for trouble. The last time Sam had "minded the store," when Fender had served jury duty (total hell and he swore he'd never do his civic duty again, but that's another story), Fender had regretted it. Sam had fashioned a crown out of coffee filters from the back office, and every time a woman purchased a ring, he'd had her don the crown and sing "It's My Special Day," while he took pictures. That'd scarred some formerly repeat customers for life.

But right now, if Sam distracted Jimmy and Naomi, that was fine by Fender. *Is this all right?* They were going to buy the ring. What if he told Ginger the truth someday, and she wanted to see the ring Brad was going to give her and he'd sold it? Would she be mad? Would she stay with him?

Now he laughed at himself. Like she was "with him" now anyway. Even if they were a couple, it was all a matter of time. That's why he didn't believe in marriage. Sooner or later, people drove each other crazy, and somebody would leave. That was always the way it went. He stared at the back of Naomi's bubble head of hair and stood a little taller. Ginger was going to figure him out soon enough, and he might as well do things the way he always did: for himself. And if he got to suck some more money out of a twisted couple like Jimmy and Naomi, then so be it.

"So, what do you think?" He needed to close this deal and get these two out of the shop.

Naomi batted her eyelashes at Jimmy. Sam, standing behind them, grimaced. Fender held back a surge of pure nausea.

"Fender, charge my card. You know the drill." Jimmy gave his wife a hug.

He didn't even ask the price. Astounding.

Over Jimmy's shoulder, Naomi sneered at Fender, like she'd won some kind of game. "Do you want to wear it home?" Jimmy talked to her in a voice reserved for small children — babyish and high. He signed the sales receipt without even looking at it, mooning over that horrible woman the whole time. Fender rolled his eyes at Sam. Sam made that grimace again.

"You two go on. I'm glad we could be of help." Fender walked them to the door of the shop. He shut and locked the door behind them.

"Well done, my friend. That was a pricey ring!" Sam slapped him on the back.

"You have anything going on?" Fender walked to the office in back, fighting the acid rising in his throat.

"Do I ever have anything going on?" Sam looked curious. "Why, what's your plan?"

From the top file cabinet drawer in the office, Fender pulled a bottle of Cuervo. "Because I'm going to drink myself blind, and I thought you might want to participate."

Sam shrugged. "Sure, I'm in. I haven't been ripping drunk in a while. And you're always good for a few laughs."

Yeah, Fender thought, *a few laughs.*

It'd been almost three weeks since Ginger had hung out with Fender, sitting in her living room and talking until late in the night. But then she'd seen him at the Record Exchange about a week after that, and Bode had been with her. Now, as time passed, she started to worry a little. Maybe Fender thought she was dating Bode? Or he was waiting for her to do something? How was this supposed to work? The ski season was winding down, and he hadn't been back, so now there'd be no more lessons. Should she call him? She always hated this part. She wanted to see him again. But she didn't know about calling. It'd been nearly seven months since Brad. But calling another man, pursuing another man—it just didn't seem right. And she hadn't even told Fender about Brad. Or about much else. They didn't know each other very well.

Of course, she told herself, *you won't know him very well if you never see him again.* Hence this afternoon's project: driving downtown. She had her phone on the seat beside her, open to Google Maps, with "Barnes and Son Jewelers" marked by a red push pin in the middle of the screen.

She parked and walked toward the block. She'd probably driven by his shop thousands of times. She jingled her keys in her right hand and felt the adrenaline rush of risk. *He's probably busy with customers. I'm going to walk in and have to stand there. I should have a reason for coming down.* But she couldn't think of any.

She walked up to the street corner. The building was across the street. The shop was the corner space, with windows facing both busy streets. She could see "Barnes and Son" stenciled on all of the windows in elaborate gold script. As she came closer, the shop door opened. She slowed down, panicked at the thought of actually seeing him.

And there he was. He was letting someone out. The person turned a bit, and Ginger noticed it was the large man who'd been skiing with Fender the first time she saw him. Sam, wasn't it? She heard him laughing, a loud wheezy sound. Then she realized Fender had seen her. *Oh boy, here we go.*

"Ginger! What're you doing?" Fender and his friend turned to face her.

"I came to see you." *So much for having a reason to be here.*

"I'm so glad! Do you remember Sam? This is Sam." Fender seemed more animated than usual. Sam reached out and took her hand, shaking it heartily.

"It's nice to see you again. What are you guys up to?" She felt her hands shaking. She clasped them together to hide it.

Sam looked at Fender. "I'm leaving, and Fender's going to have you in to show you around the shop. Bye, now! Nice to see you!" Sam shot across the street before anyone could react. His large form bobbed up and down as he made his way around a corner.

Fender seemed startled. "Okay, I guess Sam had to go. Do you want to come in? I closed early today. There's not much to see, but you can have a drink with me."

"A drink? What's the occasion?" Ginger liked the idea of being alone with him.

"There was a bitchy customer in here." Fender paused. A troubled look came into his eyes and furrowed his brows. "There was some other stuff, too, that I did. It's not worth mentioning, but it *is* worth drinking about. Sam and I were going to go down to the Rendezvous, but I sense that he's ditched us, so it's just you and me."

"And it was a bad day? You're striking out all the way around."

"Let's just say it wasn't a shining day in the life of Fender Barnes and commence with the drinking," he told her. "Do you like tequila?"

Ginger surveyed Fender, head to toe. His black hair was still a little shaggy, and it hung a bit into his blue eyes. He squinted when he looked at her, like he was asking a question. He wore a black leather jacket, cut slim and ending above a pair of dark blue jeans. Tucked into the jeans was a thin green bowling shirt, with a white tee underneath. He rounded his shoulders over a little, and Ginger could see a vulnerability to him she hadn't noticed before. As she walked in through the door, she brushed closely by him. She caught a whiff of men's cologne mixed with liquor. Something jumped inside of her.

"Yeah. I like tequila."

Fender felt the alcohol settling in his blood. Ginger brushed by him, and the hair stood up on the back of his neck. He closed the door behind them and locked it again. She stood in the center of the floor, turning around to look at all the jewelry cases.

"This is a nice place." She looked up at him.

"A nice place that you've never been in before."

She ducked her head, a little embarrassed. "Well, yeah, I guess. I don't have a big budget for jewelry."

"Don't be embarrassed. You are one of the many non-customers of Barnes and Son. So, this is the showroom, and there's a back office, and that's about it." He looked at her again. He felt brave, with the warmth of the tequila in the spaces between his bones. "Sit right here, on top of the display case." He came close to her, touched her on the elbow.

"Will I break it?" She hopped up on the counter when he shook his head no.

"I'll get the tequila. Sam and I are heathens and drink straight from the bottle, but I suppose you'll want a glass." He went to the office and grabbed the tequila and a coffee cup. *I can't believe she's here, in my shop. If she only knew what a scum I am, what I did just minutes ago.* He shook the thought off. *She's here; that's what matters. She's here, and she's the most heavenly thing I can ever hope to come close to.*

He returned to the front room. She was looking into the case she sat on. Her knees poked out from under her purple skirt. He tried not to stare at them as he handed her the coffee cup.

"Give me a little tequila first. I have to catch up," she said.

He poured a little. She downed it.

He looked at her knees again. "You've got a lot of scars."

She straightened up when he spoke to her. "I'm famous for being a klutz."

He reached out and traced a long scar that ran from her kneecap partway down her shin. "What's this?" *I can't believe I just touched her.* He panicked for a second. *God, I hope she doesn't slap me. Maybe I'm reading her wrong. Maybe she doesn't like me.*

No slap came. "That? Oh. As a new skier, maybe you shouldn't hear this one." She smiled at him.

He pretended to choke. "You? You're the expert. What happened?"

"I was skiing in a clinic, with all the big boys in the ski school. Unfortunately, I was skiing like I had something to prove. I hit a tree stump buried in the powder, and that was it. Detached a tendon and had many, many stitches I'd like to forget."

"I knew I had a reason to fear for my life. Remind me of that story when I'm thinking of going skiing next season."

She shook her head. "No, Fender, it's a reason to keep skiing. If I got back up and did it again after that, then you know skiing's fun."

Fender thought for a minute. "I usually give up on stuff if it causes me physical harm. Like girlfriends." *Now why did I just say that?* He looked at her. *Less talking, Fender. The more you talk, the less women like you.*

"You've given up on women? How sad." She smiled at him.

"How cliché, you mean. Well, okay, maybe not completely. Lately, I've been thinking maybe they're not so bad." He filled her cup with more tequila.

"I'm glad to hear that." She held up her mug. "I'm not going to drink alone. Go get another cup."

He did as he was told. When he came back out, she was looking at the jewelry in the case again. "Do you want to try stuff on?"

She raised her eyebrows. "Is that allowed?"

"I'm the owner, so I'm thinking we can do whatever we want. I'll open the case, and you go for it. Hell, Sam does it all the time. You'll look a lot better in the goods than he does."

She motioned to the bottle of Cuervo. "Load up there. We're going to do a toast."

He was intrigued. Mischief danced in her eyes.

"To Fender Barnes: skier—" he coughed in protest "—jeweler, man of many talents." They touched cups, and she drank the shot.

Fender walked around to the other side of the case and pulled out three big trays. "Okay, princess, bedeck yourself."

She crinkled her nose. "I don't usually wear any jewelry. But so much at once is kinda fun."

"You aren't a spinner." He smiled. *Maybe I shouldn't have said that.*

"What's a spinner?" She arched a brow.

Fender shrugged. "I swear I'm not a total misogynist. Spinners are girls who dress, I don't know…" He chickened out. *She has so, so many reasons to hate me.*

"Spit it out. I'm tough. I can take it, or I can punch you in the mouth if it reminds me of me." Ginger smirked.

"Now you're just teasing me. A spinner is a girl who dresses in shiny stuff to get a guy's attention, like a fishing lure—you know, a spinner." Fender took a breath. "Please don't hit me."

"Are spinners good or bad? Seems like they might be kind of essential to your business." She waited for his response, twirling a very large ring around her pinky.

Fender swallowed. "We, Sam and I, generally make fun of them. Though they *are* good for business, and I have dated some women who qualify as spinners. Can we switch the subject now? And anyway, you don't need jewelry to get someone's attention." *Why did I say that? I'm embarrassing myself. Jesus, Mary, and Joseph. I am such a total moron.*

"I don't?"

Fender spoke without thinking, and without hesitation. "Of course not. You're beautiful."

She blushed pink all the way to her ears. "Thanks."

He changed the subject before he threw up, picking up a tray of rings to show her. "Which ring would you want if you were into all the shiny stuff, though? You know, if you *did* want to give me your business?"

Fender wanted to hug her for not embarrassing him. *Hug her, kiss her…* He took a deep breath and walked back on the other side of the counter to contain himself. *Get a grip, or you'll scare her away, stalker.*

He wasn't keeping track, but as time and more Cuervo passed, and he found himself sitting up on the counter with Ginger. He sat as close as he could without sitting in her lap. She hadn't said anything about it yet, so he assumed it was okay.

"Fender?" She looked at him. He couldn't believe he had the guts to look her straight in the eye for so long.

The conversation stalled. She was going to say something, maybe, but she seemed to change her mind about it. Instead she broke the tension, wiggling the rings on her fingers at him.

The moment was killing Fender. He took her by the arms and pulled her to him. "You are so great." He leaned forward and kissed her. She kissed back, her hands running up under his leather jacket. *If I die right now, I die happy,* Fender thought. He wove his fingers through her strawberry blond hair, soft and long. She tilted her head back, and he trailed kisses from her jaw to the velvet skin of her neck. She breathed out through her lips, and he could feel it, her mouth making his skin moist. His other hand rested on her knee, with all its scars.

There was a hard pounding on the door. Ginger jumped in his arms. "What was that?"

Fender headed to the door. "Christ!" He could see a figure, silhouetted by strong afternoon sun behind.

"Fender! Open this door!" Fender wanted to puke. It was Pop.

He apologized over his shoulder to Ginger. "It's my insane father." Fender opened the door and slid outside before Pop could weasel his way into the shop. Pop's whole body was twitching.

"For the love of Mike! What are you doing in my store? The whole world can see you!" Pop's ears reddened when he was embarrassed. They were scarlet.

"I'm not doing anything, and it's not your store." Fender instinctively ducked his head, bracing for the response from Pop.

"You're making out in the showroom with some woman. On top of the display case! You'll break it!"

"Pop, it didn't break. And I wasn't making out with her."

"She's got on all the jewelry. I don't think that's right. You can't use the merchandise to…to—" Pop paused, searching for the right word "—score! It's disgraceful. This isn't how you win a lady's favor."

"I just kissed her. Besides, I can't get any farther with her if my father interrupts, can I?" Fender shook his head. "I can't believe I'm having this conversation."

Pop softened a little. "Well, you should be taking women out, not to the shop. Women like to be entertained, wined and dined. You've got to start figuring these things out on your own. I can't be here to teach you forever, you know." He composed himself, drawing his short frame to its full height. "I want to meet her."

"Pop, no!"

Pop came closer now, zeroing in on his prey. "Yes. You're doing terrible things in my store. The least you can do is introduce me to the woman."

"Yeah, Pop, we were going to sacrifice a chicken next. If you promise not to needle her with questions, you can meet her."

"I have an interest in women you kiss in front of God and everybody. Is that not normal?" Pop was already pushing past Fender, eager to get inside.

Fender hurried in behind him. The best he could do now was damage control. "Ginger? My father wants to meet you." He scanned the store.

She stepped out from behind the office door. "Of course." Her entire face was a color similar to Pop's ears. Fender smiled a little.

"Ginger? What an unusual name. Is that Dutch?" Pop had a hold of her hand and stroked it. Women were his thing. He could charm any woman. Fender had never had Pop's luck.

"I'm so sorry I didn't come out sooner. I wasn't sure who was at the door, you were banging so loud."

Pop patted her hand now, still not releasing it. "I was so pleased to see Fender at the shop, I got a little enthusiastic, I guess. I never know what's going on here anymore. Fender's the boss now."

Fender lifted one eyebrow in surprise. "Really? Well, it was sure nice of you to stop by. You said you were having dinner down the street? Your friend's probably worried. I'll walk you out." Fender had Pop by the elbow and moved out the door in one swift motion.

Pop said good-bye to Ginger in a sweet tone. Out on the sidewalk, he shot Fender a sly smile. "I can't blame you. She's cute. Nice hands. Couldn't help but notice you two had been drinking, though. Is that a good idea?"

"Pop, I swear—"

Pop scooted down the street before Fender finished his reply. He'd probably tell the whole gang at the Rendezvous in under five minutes, cackling all the while.

Fender went back in the shop. Ginger had picked up the glasses and the bottle, moving toward the office to put them away. He helped her.

"Well, that was my pop. I guess you were going to meet him at some point."

Ginger nudged him. "Oh, he's fine. He's nice. I thought he'd be mad, since I had on all the loot. That's why I hid in the office. I was taking off the rings."

Fender liked that she cared what Pop thought. "He wouldn't care. He loves women. If you're female, you can do no wrong in Pop's book." He paused for a moment. The passion had evaporated. His chance was gone. Now all he felt was awkward, the same old stupid Fender he always was. "It's just as well he came by. I should probably feed you before I get you too drunk."

She nodded. "I could eat. And I'm not a good drinker, anyway. I get weepy." She looked uncomfortable, and Fender decided to change the subject.

"Well, then, it's settled. No more debauchery for the night. Let's go to Acapulco House for tacos."

A few minutes later, they walked down to Acapulco House from the shop, and Fender spent the whole journey consumed. *I should hold her hand. Why am I not holding her hand? If I do and she doesn't want it, it'll ruin everything. But maybe she's pissed that I haven't just done it. Jesus.*

"This is a good plan. I think tequila and I need to take a break from each other."

Fender missed what she said. "What?"

She smiled at him, just a little teeth over that full bottom lip.

I should be kissing that lip. I want to kiss her again. When? After dinner?

"I just said I probably shouldn't drink any more tequila."

"I'm sorry. Can I be honest with you?" Fender scolded himself. If he was really going to be honest, it should be about the ring.

"Sure."

"I'm too busy thinking about holding you again. Maybe kissing you. I'm not listening much."

This made her blush. She smiled and looked down at her toes, biting her lip in embarrassment. "You're so…"

"So?"

She shook her head, stopped walking, and looked him in the eye. "Different."

"Thanks?" He waited to see where she was going with this.

"Yes, that was supposed to be a compliment. *Good* different. I like it. I like you." She took his hand.

He led her into Acapulco House. His heart pounded. *Be cool, Fender. Don't screw this up.* "Do you want a booth?" *I want a booth, so I can sit close to you.*

"Fender?"

"Ginger?"

"I think I'm going to be sick." She made a break for the restroom at the back of the restaurant.

"Not what I thought you were going to say." He said this to the spot where Ginger had been a minute ago.

And that was about it for the night.

Chapter Twelve

Ginger awoke the next morning to a gray spring day. Molly had texted the night before, and Ginger knew she'd expect a full report—any moment now, though it was far too early.

Ginger heard Molly let herself in the front door. "Hello?" she called from the living room.

Ginger looked at the dog at the foot of the bed. "Are you gonna get that?" Zoë lifted her muzzle in polite interest, opened one eye in the direction of the front door, and relaxed again.

"Some watchdog," Molly said as she entered the bedroom. She wore beaten-up jean shorts and a thin button-up shirt that smelled like the damp rain outside. "Aren't you a layabed. Not hung over, are you?" She offered a coffee. Molly was living clean these days, having sworn off alcohol and pot and chocolate, and talking a lot about farm to table and slow food and vegan living. Coffee she couldn't let go of, though. Molly had her limits.

Ginger crinkled her nose in distaste. "I'm not in the mood for coffee, I'll tell you that much." She sat up and took the newspaper from under Molly's arm. "I don't know. This doesn't feel like a normal hangover. My stomach is rumbly, that's it."

Molly looked dubious. "You *are* hung over. That guy tried to get you drunk."

"He's Fender, not 'that guy.' And I was the one encouraging the tequila shots, not him."

Molly straightened up, sitting tall on the bed. "He put the moves on you, didn't he? Did you punch him? You're supposed to go for the eyes. Gouge 'em good, right in the eyeballs." Molly was apparently visualizing the attack, gouging the air with enthusiasm.

"Oh, Molly. He kissed me. That was it. It was great. I had a nice time, except for the puking part." She rubbed her complaining stomach. "But I still feel crappy."

There was a silence. Molly pretended to look at the paper for a moment. Then she put a small hand on Ginger's elbow, gently. "It's guilt, isn't it? That's why you're tied in knots."

"No, it's not that. It can't be. It felt so right last night."

Molly stood and paced the bedroom in thought. She paused, facing the bed. "It's one of two things. A, you're just not ready. Or B, something about it isn't on the up and up. Is there anything about the guy that's fishy?"

Ginger combed at Zoë's tail with her fingers. "That's what it's about, I bet."

Molly brightened. "See? I knew I got a weird vibe off of him when I met him. What's the deal? What's wrong with him? Is he an ex-con? Although I think that'd be kind of cool. I once dated a guy who was supposedly a fugitive. Turns out he had a couple outstanding parking tickets, pretty boring."

Ginger broke in. "No, Molly, honey, no. I haven't been on the up and up, and I bet that's why I feel so crummy about last night."

"What?" Molly sat on the bed again.

"I haven't told him about Brad—about dating Brad, or about his death. I didn't want to seem morbid or hung up."

Molly's face clouded. "It's been less than a year. That's not hung up; that's normal. Maybe you feel like shit because it's not time to move on."

Ginger felt as if she were being scolded. "Is that how you feel? You think I'm forgetting about Brad?"

"No. I'm sorry. That's not fair."

Ginger had a pillow in her hands now, twisting it into a ball. "I'm not going to forget about him. But we weren't married. I was just a girlfriend, Molly. I didn't know any of his friends; his parents acted like I didn't exist…" There was more Ginger felt like saying. She didn't. The room was quiet. Zoë breathed in and out, sleeping witness to the tense moment between friends.

"You know what? I'm going to go. You need to sleep; I need to run errands." Molly started to leave the bedroom.

"Molly, don't. Come here and read the paper with me. Come on, let's not disagree. I don't like squabbling." Ginger grabbed Molly's hand and made her flop back down on the bed.

The two hung out for another hour, reading the paper and listening to Zoë snore. Then Ginger walked Molly to the door and said good-bye.

She sat down on the sofa and looked up at the ceiling. She wasn't even sure she knew what made her feel sick right now. It felt like something strong, stronger than she was.

She got up to go take a shower. The feeling might go away then. She hoped she could wash it off.

"Did you get any last night?" Sam practically yelled into the phone from the other end of the line.

Fender couldn't help but grin. "No. Not because she didn't want it to happen, though."

"What, you were the one to draw the line? I find that very hard to believe."

"No, it wasn't that. You know how I feel about her. One word: Pop. Okay, two words: Pop and tequila."

Sam coughed hard. "That's three words. And what the hell does your pop have to do with this? This isn't some sicko father-son thing I don't know about, is it?"

"Never mind. I have to tell you about it, and it's too complicated for the phone. Where are you?"

"How could it be complicated? You kiss, you touch, you butter her up a little—the tequila was helpful, I bet, except that you said it wasn't—you give her the old college try—"

"The old college try, Sam? Why so coy?"

"Oh, Fender, how cruel you can be to me. I'll meet you at Astro Burger in twenty minutes. I just love our little girl talks." He giggled for effect and ended the call.

Fender smiled. He liked thinking about being with Ginger. *This might just work out after all.*

Eighteen minutes later, he arrived at Astro Burger to find Sam had taken over the biggest table on the sidewalk out front. He had his shit piled on the chairs and all over the open table top. He'd already gotten himself a guacamole burger with onion rings and was proceeding to wolf it all down.

Fender approached. "Hey, don't wait for me; go ahead and order."

Sam spoke through a mouth full of food. "Are you an idiot? I was hungry. This ain't no rest home. Go get a burger."

After Sam was fed, he wanted details. "So, how did this happen—or not happen, I guess. Were you close to success? She came to see you; that had to be a good thing. What did she want? Did she want to *talk* to you?"

"I've been to her house, and I had all those lessons. I think, yes, as hard as it is for you to believe, she wanted to visit with me. She likes my company." Fender picked at the burger in front of him.

Sam chuckled.

Fender nudged his elbow. "What? What's so funny?"

"No. It's just, I was wondering what it's gonna be like now when you give her that ring that old Dead Boyfriend got for her. You'll be trying to get it on with her and then whip the ring out and be like 'Surprise! This is why I know you!' God, that'll be weird, won't it?"

Fender was never good at hiding guilt. He stared at the sign above Sam's head, the neon burger, encircled by the rings of Jupiter. *Here it comes.*

Sam tossed his napkin down in disgust. "Shit, Fender, I know that look. What did you do now?"

He could barely say it. The words kind of made Fender nauseated. "I sold it."

"What? What in the hell? You already sold it! You sold it? To who?"

"To Naomi and Jimmy. That's what they bought yesterday. But I had a good reason. And technically, it hadn't sold. I never cashed the check from Brad, so it wasn't…I had a good reason." It was too late for that. Sam was busy going off.

"That diamond you sold to the psycho woman of the year? What the hell were you thinking? And how are you going to explain this to Ginger? What the hell!"

"Yeah. Like Ginger is your best friend or something." Fender knew he sounded like a nine-year-old.

"Now look, I didn't say anything when you didn't tell her at first. But, God, what are you waiting for? When she's giving birth to your first son? 'Push, honey, and breathe, and oh yeah there's a ring, breathe…' You are seriously messed up, my friend." Sam stood and looked around for a moment. "I think I want to leave now." And he walked away.

Fender felt lost. Where was this going? Two seconds before, he'd felt full of hope and love. He stopped, panicked. The world went cold, like ice trickling down the nape of his neck. *Love. L-O-V-E.* "Shit." He said this out loud. *I don't want to be in love. This is not good. This is bad.*

Ginger made him feel fabulous. But he might have screwed it all up. Sam was right. He couldn't live his life keeping this secret from her; he was too stupid, and he'd screw it up in no time. She'd wonder, *how come you were up skiing? You don't like to ski. Was that the first time you saw me?* Or she'd tell the story of how they met, and Fender would stand there, arms wrapped around her, feeling the black center of his heart going cold because the woman he loved (he sat back; it stunned him to say that word, even in his head) was telling a lie, and she didn't even know it.

Astro Burger and the surrounding streets had turned gray. He didn't know what to do. Except he could do what he always did to women: he could leave. It's not like he and Ginger were even together. *I have to get away before I hurt her and destroy her and before she finds out what a total fraud I am. I'll leave; I'm good at that.*

He left his meal uneaten on the dirty white table and wandered off, chilled to the bone by his own deceit.

Chapter Thirteen

It was April, and the wet spring days had started to dry out. Ginger waited for Fender to call, but he didn't. It'd been a week since the afternoon at the jewelry store, and she decided whatever it was that had creeped her out must have creeped him out too. But she couldn't help but feel hurt. She'd thought things had been moving along, going pretty great. Except maybe for the puking part.

When she could think of the night without too much awkwardness, she remembered his kiss. She did a lot of quality staring at the ceiling while in bed, and the feel of his kiss often came back to her then. She'd get up, feeling his mouth on hers, missing it. She'd get a glass of water and think about the wet of his lips.

One of those sleepless interludes brought her a new idea: what was with all this waiting around? She was a bad ass — Bode told her so. He'd been a witness to her bad-assery. *Bad asses don't wait around. Bad asses go get what they want.*

And she wanted to see Fender again. She needed to see him. She would tell him about Brad soon enough. It'd all work out. All she knew was that she wanted to see him, and she'd not felt so certain about anything in a very long time.

She tried calling him the next night. His phone went straight to voice mail. She was too chicken to text.

She decided to quasi-stalk him. He'd mentioned the bar where his dad held court, the Rendezvous. *I'll check at his shop, I'll check at that bar, and then I'll try calling him one more time.*

Zoë watched her get ready, looking confused about all of the fuss. Ginger put some curls into her hair. She remembered his hand in her hair, so maybe that was something about her he liked. She wore a skirt again. He'd noticed her knees, even if it was because of the scars.

She parked downtown and walked by Barnes and Son, but the storefront was dark. She peeked in and grinned, thinking about the kiss.

Bad asses get what they want. They go get it. Go get him, Ginger. She chuckled to herself. *I've missed my calling as a motivational speaker. Maybe a life coach.*

The Rendezvous had character, that was true. It was a skinny slice out of a city block. The façade of the bar was lipstick red and shiny chrome, the same as it'd been since the fifties. It wasn't quite out of its dive-y phase, but soon enough some new owner would jump on its potential and turn it into a hipster hot spot.

Not yet, though. The smell of old grease and ancient cigarettes came to Ginger's nose when she walked in. It was dim. She stood for a minute, waiting for her eyes to adjust. *Now I just feel stupid. He better be in here.*

And then there he was. He stood tall from one of the booths and took long strides over to meet her.

"What are you doing here?" His eyes were bright blue. He looked surprised.

"Coming to get you." She smiled.

"Let's get out of here." He took her hand and led her out of the bar.

Score one for the bad ass. Ginger resisted the urge to click her heels together in celebration.

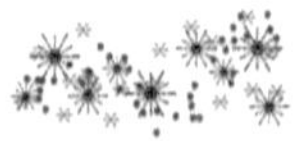

With her hand in his, Fender felt brave. And he didn't care. He didn't care if this wasn't right. He didn't care if he was a liar. *Life is too damn short. She's here, she wants to see me, and I want to see her.*

"Where are we going?" She followed close on his heels, didn't let go of his hand. He loved the feel of it.

"My place? It's not far. We can walk."

"Okay."

They walked the rest of the way in silence. From time to time, he'd look over at her, just to make sure she was still there. He didn't let go of her hand for fear that she'd evaporate into thin air. She seemed to hold tightly to his, maybe for the same reason. Something about the whole thing felt very urgent.

They came to his building. They slipped in the front door, and Fender led her up the stairs to his place.

He swung the door wide and pulled her inside. "Hi."

She smiled. "Hi." She kissed him. She leaned in, clasped both his hands with hers, and kissed him slowly and deeply.

He shut the door behind them. "I'm glad there's no tequila involved tonight."

"No throwing up, I promise." She pulled him close again, kissed him.

"I know your head is clear. I like that."

"I know what I want, Fender." She let go of his hand and walked into the condo, her boot heels ringing on the wood floors.

He kind of hated not touching her. It made it real, when he had her in his arms. She'd gone through the kitchen, was in the living room, looking out at the night.

"What's our plan, exactly?" *Shut up, Fender, you'll ruin it. Women hate you when you talk.*

She turned away from the windows to face him. "You could kiss me again."

He came to her and kissed her again. He held her close in his arms, and his hands pressed her close to him. "Like this?" He traced the line of her jaw with his fingers, feeling her delicate bones under her skin, and kissed the hollow where her collarbones met.

"Yes. I want this, Fender. I want you." She stepped back and pointed down the other hall. "Is that the way to your bedroom?"

Whatever I did to deserve this, thank God for it. Thank you, universe. He nodded and took her hand. His heart pounded, his pulse echoing in his ears. He looked at Ginger, took all of her in. *I need to remember this, memorize it.* Her face glowed with desire, and the amazing thing was, she desired him.

The fact of it was stunning.

The sun came in through the windows too soon. All night he'd held Ginger in his arms, listened as she slept, her breath soft on his chest. Morning meant waking up, and in Fender's experience, it usually meant finding some reason to make a hasty retreat. It meant reality. He hated reality.

And his reality with this gorgeous creature—the one sleeping so peacefully, her head resting on him—his reality with her was a castle built on the shifting sands of a big fat lie.

It was going to crush her. He had to get away.

But last night, it was so right. I can't even think of a time close to that. Ever. He stroked her strawberry hair, turned every detail of last night over in his head, as if he were eyeing each facet of an exquisite diamond.

And there he was, back to the problem at hand: the diamond.

Ginger stirred in his arms. She made a tiny noise, and it sounded like she was distressed. She trembled in his arms. Another whimper escaped her lips.

A nightmare. She's having a nightmare. His heart broke. *It's probably about Brad, and when I wake her, I'll lie and pretend I don't know. This has to stop.*

"Ginger? Wake up, sweet thing." He rubbed her shoulder, patted it lightly.

She sat up, eyes wide. "I'm awake. I'm awake."

He touched her on the arm. "Are you all right?"

She put her hands to her eyes, rubbing the dream out of them. "Yeah."

"Bad dream?"

She nodded, then shook her head. "Yes, I think. I don't know. It's been a long time since I've slept very well."

He sat up. *This is the last time I get to do this. I'm going to make it count.* He kissed her, ran a hand down her back, which was cold, bare and smooth in the morning sun.

She ducked her head. "I should get dressed."

"Slip something on quick. I want to show you something." He handed her the clothes piled on the floor on his side of the bed. They'd all come off in a rush last night.

She took his shirt from the pile and pulled it over her head. She still had her knee socks on, the ones she'd worn under her boots the night before.

She climbed out of bed. "What are you going to show me?"

I wish I could show you how exquisite a creature you are. He looked at her, in his Polo and her knee socks, her long hair wild and splayed out over her shoulders, the sun catching the flyaway strands in its beams. "In the kitchen."

She waited for him to pull on some pants, and then he took her hand and walked her through the condo. They were quiet. *Something is up, and it's not just my guilty conscience.* Fender searched her green eyes for a clue but couldn't find one.

"I found this when I moved in." Fender took her to the wall behind the kitchen table. It was bare brick, original to the building. He touched a finger to the old crumbly mortar. "Look here."

He pointed to the pencil marks he'd found the first night he'd been here.

The trouble in Ginger's eyes seemed to clear, and her brows knit together in curiosity. "What's it say?"

"John and Zeila. There's a heart, too, and I think this—" he traced a shape on the smooth red brick "—is supposed to be a dove."

Ginger came close to him, leaned into his shoulder, and traced the names and pencil markings with her finger, too. "I like that." She pressed her lips together in a firm line. "I think I need to go."

He felt his heart tighten. "Why?"

"I just…I think there's stuff we don't know about each other. A lot of stuff. Maybe we did this too fast." She stared at the hem of the shirt she wore, pulled absently at a loose thread.

"I think we did this exactly right. I think this is the one thing I've done right in a long time."

She smiled a little. "Inside this moment, inside last night, I think you're exactly right. But I need to get straight with a lot of other stuff."

He wanted to protest, but a voice inside spoke, cold and clear: *Whatever she thinks is wrong, she's not even got the half of how bad it is. You're a cold-blooded liar. Let her go before you crush her.* He swallowed hard. The bell that tolled was tolling for him, and maybe she could hear it ever so faintly.

"Ginger, maybe you'd better go. You may be right about us. You're better off without being involved with me. I can give you a long list of women who'll back me up on that."

She shook her head. "It's not that. It's—"

"Trust me, it's absolutely that." He pulled her close, one last time. *Make it count, remember the details.*

He stared into those green eyes. He parted his lips, just so, and kissed her slowly. She opened her lips and pressed her mouth to his. He wanted to be gentle, but she met him with raw need.

He found himself falling into the kiss, felt her hands grasping at him, slipped his hands under the mane of hair and down her delicate spine—

He stepped back. "Stop." He heard it come out of his mouth. "If we're ending this, you need to go. I can't do this." He wiped his mouth, tried to catch his breath.

She nodded. "I know." Her eyes were wet with tears, but she looked at the ceiling. "I'll go get dressed."

She disappeared into his bedroom. He paced in the kitchen, and when she emerged, he was disappointed to see she wasn't wearing his shirt anymore.

"I'll go then. Thanks, Fender, for everything." She held her hand up a little, in a halfhearted wave good-bye.

"It's best this way. You don't need to get mixed up with me, Ginger. I promise."

She turned her back on him and left.

Another Fender Barnes disaster. Typical. The day suddenly felt very long in front of him, and he was hard-pressed to find a point to it.

Chapter Fourteen

The hole in his life opened up just about then. Fender closed the shop for a week. He sat at home in the bedroom at the foot of the bed, smoking—a habit he'd given up years ago. Or he slept. He told Pop he was sick and asked him to stay away. He screened his calls and didn't answer when it was Sam.

Ginger never called. He was glad, actually. He wasn't sure what he could say to her. The truth was out of the question. It was too screwed up to explain. He'd sometimes sit in the empty bathtub in his clothes and try to come up with a solution. He always thought pretty well in the tub. He was too afraid of the mold ring to actually take a bath, but he sat there, trying to solve the situation until he felt as if drops of blood were forming on his brow.

None were, and neither were solutions. He was scared. None of the other women he'd been with were important. But it was better this way.

One night, he decided not to stay home anymore. Somehow it seemed logical to go out to the Rendezvous and see Pop. *I should get on with my life. Women are women.* Maybe if he could get one of them to wrap her legs around him, he'd feel better about everything. She wouldn't even have to have a nice name. Or be very pretty. Just some bitchy young thing who could wake up and leave him like the dog he was.

So he showered, but he didn't shave. And he went down to the Rendezvous. Pop saw him when he walked in and waved him over. It was always the same booth, the vinyl with the worn buttons.

"How are ya, Pop?" Fender waited for the tirade about the family business and the prodigal son pissing it all away. But Pop's eyes looked warm.

"I'm fine. How're you?"

Fender settled into the booth. *It could swallow me up and take me away, maybe.* He kind of hoped this. *Maybe with enough liquor, it could.* "I'm fine, Pop. I've been sick, I told you. Where's the waitress? I need to get a drink."

"She'll be over in a second. I hope you're feeling better. You look pale. Maybe you should come stay with me. I could cook for you." He seemed to be trying to look inside Fender's head. It was annoying.

"Stay at the house? With you?" Fender didn't mean to sound so rude. "I'm sorry, Pop. It's a lovely offer, really. Thanks for worrying about me. I just don't think I feel like playing bachelor with the old man right now. I'm not well."

"That's the whole point. Look, I'm not going to twist your arm. But you could come stay. Let's leave it there. An open invitation."

Fender felt like he might cry. "Thanks, Pop. I appreciate it." He sat there, quiet for a minute. Pop stared at the crack in the Formica table. When the waitress came up, tray in hand, Fender tried a brighter tone. "Okay, now we're in business." He handed her a credit card. "I'm going to need an open tab, please."

The tab had lengthened, and the evening, too, when Fender spotted Sam at the door of the bar.

"Oh shit. Pop, get the waitress. I've got to go." The last thing he needed was for Sam to bring Pop up to speed. And he wasn't going to listen to the lecture. It was all over anyway.

Pop looked puzzled, maybe afraid. "I'll go find her." He made his way through the narrow bar to the wait station. Fender noticed Sam stop and talk to Pop. Pop pointed over to Fender. *So much for avoiding the lecture.* He looked around for a waitress he could grab.

Too late. Sam stood in front of him. "Hey, Tiger. What's up? Drinking for Jesus, I see."

"Something like that. I was just going." Fender tried to stand up and leave, but he lost his balance and caught hold of the table.

Sam closed in, protectively. "Sit down, Fender. We'll get you into a cab in a minute. Let's chat."

Fender felt claustrophobic. "Don't hover! You're not my mom."

"No, I'm not, and praise heaven for that." He sat across from Fender in the booth. "What's going on, pal? Where've you been? What happened with Ginger, the night she came to the Rendezvous?"

Fender was silent. He was running away from all of this, and everyone wanted to drag him right back into it.

Sam leaned back in the booth. "Okay. No more talk about it, I promise. I think I know what's going on, so maybe I'll join you, how about that? The cab won't get here for another twenty minutes or so. That's long enough for me to try to catch up." He chuckled. "It's been a while since I've seen you like this. A real bender's what this is."

"Yeah, whatever." The room had started to pivot a little, and a sore mood settled onto Fender like a thick vapor.

Sam chuckled again. "Not a bender. It's a Fender Bender! How come I haven't thought of that before? God, that's kind of funny."

Fender didn't think it was very funny. He leaned across the booth and punched Sam straight in the mouth.

Chapter Fifteen

Leaving Fender that morning had hurt. And the weeks passing hadn't made Ginger feel better about it. But it was best this way. She'd not told him about Brad, and she didn't know how. She couldn't start something new until she made peace with all of her feelings. But it hurt, the look in Fender's eyes.

Summer's approach actually made things worse. When she'd previously been single, Ginger had worked summers as a lifeguard, teaching swimming lessons to the same little children she taught to ski in the winter. But the last few years, Brad had encouraged her to stay home, hang out with him when he got home from the clinic. He'd liked that he could pay the bills. He'd kind of bragged about "taking care of her." She hadn't really known what to think of it. Sometimes she felt safe, protected. It'd been nice to sleep in and read and do other things she was always too busy for in the winter. But she could take care of herself.

Now she had to. The prospect of marking the anniversary of Brad's death alone was unthinkable. She realized that part of her had hoped to lean on Fender when the date came. It made her even more lonely to acknowledge that.

As summer began to unfold, the days warmed. The soil dried out, and the sun shone on the foothills and turned them lush green.

Ginger tried to fight back the feeling of being swallowed up. She took Zoë on long walks and tried to savor the sun and the warmth and be grateful. She did her best to move forward, even though the point on the horizon wasn't much to look at.

Part of that moving forward had to involve a job, and it seemed easiest to go back to the pool. She'd lifeguarded for several years at Cassia Pool. She called up the City Rec director and had her old job back in fifteen minutes.

The first day of the season came quickly. They opened the pool in May before the kids were even out of school for the summer, and Ginger quickly remembered how she always enjoyed the quiet routine of the early season. She'd open the pool in the cool of the mornings, but never got in the water until later. It was frigid in the mornings, and the only ones who could ever seem to stand it were the old ladies who came every Tuesday for water aerobics.

Her first morning back, Ginger crouched by the side of the pool, taking small samples of water to check the chemicals. Sometime that morning the other lifeguard was supposed to come by to train with her. She heard the metal gate out front swing open and looked up.

It was Bode. Bode of the chewed parka. They'd worked on being friends, skiing together when they saw each other, going to lunch downtown. When he'd complained about having no luck finding work for the summer, Ginger'd suggested the city rec department. But this was a little too cozy, maybe. Of all the pools in the city…"Shit," she said under her breath. Skiing and shopping for records together was one thing. Working together for a whole summer, where there was no avoiding him, that might be another thing altogether.

He looked thrilled. "Ginger! You're the other lifeguard? Wow. I get to work with the bad-ass girl." He smacked her on the back, a big smile on his face. She almost fell over under his enthusiastic shoulder clap.

She took a step back. "Bode. You're a lifeguard?"

Maybe he heard a note of worry in her voice, or maybe he realized she wasn't as enthusiastic as he'd been, because he looked at her for a minute, his hand resting on the top of his head.

"Yeah. It's cool, you and me working together, isn't it? We're a team."

She nodded and put out a hand. "A team. Of course it's cool. You can buy me new vinyl with your paycheck." He took her hand and shook it hard.

Ginger relaxed. They spent the rest of the day going over pool rules and how to handle the chemicals, then cleaning the pool deck with bleach. The work felt really good. Bode worked hard, too. Maybe she could put up with him for a summer.

As the sun crested in the sky, they began to sweat, and Ginger felt the moisture pool between her shoulder blades and under her breasts. She and Bode had stopped talking after some pleasantries and worked side by side, quietly. Now he stood and stretched.

"Ginger, is it okay if I get in the pool?"

"Yeah. When no one else is here, it's not a big deal." She set aside the scrub brush and sat back on her butt, giving her knees a rest from the concrete.

He pulled his T-shirt over his head and dove into the deep end. She could see his shoulders and arms pull against the water. They were lean and brown.

She realized she wasn't working anymore, just watching him. Bode surfaced, and she went back to scrubbing.

Chapter Sixteen

All of life has its cycles, and even as summer swung into full effect, it was hard to ignore the upcoming anniversary of Brad's death. The Frisbee boys in the park had appeared again. Ginger tried not to look at them. Where was her head, thinking she could date before Brad was even dead a year?

It'd been too soon, and she'd been shallow and selfish to try. Brad deserved a little respect. How could she have been willing to forget about him so hurriedly? Even complain about him. And Fender didn't want her anyway.

During their days at the pool, she talked out a lot of this with Bode. He was very sweet. He understood that she hadn't been ready to date. That explained *their* disastrous date, she told him. Even her dog had known it wasn't time yet to move on. Now she and Bode were friends. She told him how scary it felt after Brad died and how nice Fender had been to her. But they also decided he must have sensed she wasn't ready and backed off.

Which was different than the theory Molly offered up to explain Fender's silence. She was less than complimentary. Fender rubbed Molly the wrong way; Ginger could see that. So, she avoided that tirade-inducing subject when Molly was around.

Sometimes, though, her attempts to live mindfully were sabo-taged. She'd be teaching a swim lesson, and Bode would jump in the pool to cool off. Or the Frisbee boys would miss a wild toss and run into the street to retrieve the disk, their bare chests coming danger-ously close to her front yard.

She didn't know what to do. Her stomach remained a quivering knot. She didn't feel back to normal yet, and she wanted to be. She still felt off her game. She wasn't at her strongest, and the anniversary was coming. It frightened her.

At home one night, she lay on the couch with the screen door open. The evening air had cooled and began to flow into the living room, bringing with it smells of cut grass and sweet hyacinth. She tried to remember the name of the neighbor who'd planted all of those hyacinth bulbs as she closed her eyes, letting the smell and the cool air settle on her eyelids.

A touch on the arm awakened her. Fender stood above her, next to the couch. She tried to sit up, but couldn't. Lying there, she felt her heart pound. He didn't speak. She looked at his eyes as he sat down on the edge of the couch. She tried to raise an arm to touch his face, but it was as though she was lead-heavy. She couldn't move a toe, much less her arm.

He rested his hand on her again. The hair on her arms prickled, charged by his touch. His hand glided up her forearm to her shoul-der. Fender stared her straight in the face as his hand slid under the material of her blouse. She felt his fingers at the strap of her bra. Ginger looked down at his hand. Her blouse was open now, and the edges of its deep purple silk made her skin look stark white. His hand rested on her breast. Every part of her blazed fire, and she felt nervous sweat on her lip. She looked up at him to plead for action, more touch, his body pressed tight to hers.

Then, standing over Fender's shoulder was Brad. He watched.

She woke up and fell off of the couch. She sat on the floor. The room was empty.

Chapter Seventeen

Fender remembered apologizing repeatedly to Sam, but not much else from that night. Someone made the decision that Fender would be staying with Pop for a while, and Fender didn't protest. The thought of going back to his very quiet condo made him nervous.

Pop, for all of his annoying habits, was a gracious guy. He didn't lecture Fender. The day after the outburst, Fender awoke on Pop's couch to rustling and bumping noises coming from his old room. He got off the couch (which took quite an effort, considering that his head was a very swollen and sore watermelon balanced on a thin toothpick) to investigate the ruckus.

When Fender had declared his independence and moved out of the house, Pop had turned his old bedroom into a study. He'd furnished it with an outdated console TV, two very comfortable La-Z-Boy recliners, and an old turntable. He liked to play old LPs and watch boxing on ESPN2 with the sound turned down.

When Fender entered the room, Pop was in the midst of dragging one of the hulking recliners into a corner. A small cot stood by the doorway and pillowcases and sheets draped the other recliner. The stack of dusty record jackets was gone — maybe Pop had hidden them in the closet. It made Fender's heart hurt. Pop was always good to him, no matter what kind of asshole behavior he exhibited.

"Pop, did you drag that cot up from the basement alone?"

Pop was busy scooting the recliner into the corner. "It's not very heavy, Fender. I didn't want to wake you."

"It wouldn't have been a big deal." He wasn't sure what else to say, and Pop was quiet. They set up the cot.

Pop never did ask what was wrong, not that week or the week after that. Fender assumed he'd pieced together the facts with Sam's help. But he didn't bring up Ginger, or the ring, or anything else. The matter seemed to just hang in the air, waiting for someone to grab it and pull it down into a conversation. It was the second houseguest at Pop's, but Pop didn't acknowledge it.

Fender tried not to think about the whole thing, but he couldn't avoid it. By day, it hovered in the corners of the room, up by the cobwebs on the ceiling, but at night, it sat on his chest like a large animal. He had trouble breathing with it crouching on him like that. He didn't really sleep with it there.

Fender tried to get better, or find a solution, but he was stuck. It was determined that he was still "sick" and that Pop and Sam could fill in for him at the store. Fender didn't talk to Pop much. He slept through the day, catching up on the sleep he missed at night. When evening came, he sat on the back stoop and smoked. If he wasn't smoking, he ate cereal and watched movies from the seventies on the TV in his room.

One night, he sat on the back porch eating a bowl of cereal in boxers and one of Pop's old bathrobes. When he finished the cereal, he sat for a moment. A cat appeared at the back of Pop's yard. It must have squeezed through the fence, behind the hydrangeas. He called it in a quiet voice. Pop had been asleep for a while, so it was probably three o'clock or so.

The cat approached Fender warily. Then it smelled or spotted food and trotted over with more purpose. Fender set the cereal bowl down at his feet, and the cat began to drink the leftover milk. It was small, with tiny paws. It had gray fur and black tabby markings. Its front feet were white and the back ones tiger-striped.

The cat lapped at the milk. Otherwise, the night was very quiet. He reached down to pet the cat, which flinched in fright, but settled back down to the milk when it realized Fender meant no harm.

Fender sat there, petting the cat and looking up into the darkness. High clouds were lit with moonlight. They glided above the earth, headed to the horizon. The sky was a strong blue, illuminated also by the reflection of the moon. The moon itself had tendrils of clouds twisted across its face. The night was so clear, Fender thought he could make out individual craters on the moon's surface. He breathed in deeply, and the cat began to purr, arching its back to get the full benefit of Fender's petting.

He started to cry. Tears fell down his cheeks, and his nose and throat clogged with phlegm. He coughed and sobbed, and everything came out. He let it. He rested his head on his arms, which he'd folded across his knees, and he cried. The cat circled at first, concerned perhaps by the noises coming from the man. When Fender quieted, it lost interest and ran across the lawn, pursuing a moth into the shadows at the corner of the yard.

Chapter Eighteen

Ginger slept with the light on and the dog next to her in bed for several nights after her dream or vision or whatever it had been on the couch.

And she didn't sleep well, so she went by Molly's house before she went to the pool for work one morning. Molly was in the bedroom, in a very uncomfortable-looking yoga pose. She was still marijuana-free and had declared yoga her "new high."

"Be careful, you might break something." Seeing Molly made Ginger feel better already.

"It's supposed to be downward-facing dog."

"It looks like maimed llama. You got a minute?"

Molly stood and gave Ginger a hug. "Anything for my favorite girlfriend. How are you?" She picked up an armful of dirty clothes from the bed and made Ginger a place to sit.

Ginger sat and started to tie and untie the fringe of the bedspread. She needed to tell Molly about her dream — about Fender, or Brad. Whatever that thing was, it'd been a thing she couldn't forget about.

Molly didn't wait for Ginger to start talking. "Uh-oh. Something nasty happened. Are you okay? What is it?"

"I'm fine. It was a nasty dream. A daydream. I don't know. A visit of conscience."

Molly sat down next to Ginger, ready to listen. "Let loose. Give me all the gory details."

Ginger related the dream. She told Molly about Brad's appearance in particular. The mental picture made her palms clammy. "It's creepy, isn't it? I can tell you it hasn't been fun being in the house alone since then. I'm glad I have Zoë to hang on to." Ginger tried to move the conversation along, afraid Molly was at a loss to contribute.

"No, you know what? I think I owe you an apology." Molly moved a pen around a note pad in the shape of big triangles.

"What do you mean?"

"Well, I got this vibe off of Fender when I met him. I don't know what it was, but I just didn't like him. So, I've been a brat about him to you. But this tells me something. One thing it tells me, it tells me you like Fender. You're really interested in him."

"I was, but it was too soon, like you said."

"No, no, let me finish, because I think we both know it wasn't." Molly could be very assertive when she wanted to be, Ginger remembered. She stayed quiet and let her talk.

"Okay, so, the first part is just about you wanting Fender. But you can't move; that's right, I forgot about that part. You want him to take the lead, make the decision to start the relationship. 'Cause you're scared, or you don't feel like you can be the one to initiate. But the bad part, the Brad part, that's pretty obvious."

"Obviously about what?"

"Well, you haven't made your peace with the whole Brad thing."

"Why do you say that?"

"He's your guilty conscience. You think you're a bad person because you found this guy you like."

"I did love Brad."

"I think we should be honest, Ging." Molly sat next to her. They both looked intently at the fringe on the bedspread for a moment. Molly continued. "Brad was a good person. But he annoyed you. You talked about that all the time when he was alive."

Ginger tried to swallow the growing lump in her throat. "But once you live with someone, they always end up annoying you a little. That's just life."

"Ginger, he was just a boyfriend. He was a good guy; don't get me wrong. But you have to make your peace with him. Let go."

"How?"

"You need to do a cleansing. Of yourself, your house. I can help you with it. We can do it after you get home from work."

"What's it about?"

"The Pueblo Indians use sage to purify stuff, people. I think we should do that for you. That's a good start."

Ginger gave Molly a big kiss on the cheek and left to go to the pool…

Where she thought about her advice the whole day at work. A fresh start. Maybe she should cleanse herself of Fender while she was at it, too. She didn't want to think about him anymore; it just made her sad.

Molly was waiting on the front stoop when Ginger got home. They went inside together. Molly unfolded a cloth she'd tied hobo-style and displayed its contents on the rug in the living room. She spread out bundles of sage, little rocks, an eagle feather, and picked up her phone.

"I made a playlist on my phone—good meditative chanting stuff. I'll put it on, Ginger, and we'll do this. You sit in the middle of the cloth. Put the chakra stones around you. Hold the feather."

"Molly?"

"Yeah, Ginger?"

"I forgot to tell you some stuff."

"About what? Fender?"

"No. It's not just Fender. I notice other guys, too. Bode, at the pool. The guys who play Ultimate Frisbee in the park. Maybe that changes things."

Molly stopped arranging the rocks and looked at Ginger for a moment. "Have you ever had dreams about these other guys?"

Ginger shook her head no.

"Did you ever sleep with these other guys? Kiss them?"

"No, of course not."

"Then the other stuff is hormones. Good Lord, girl, you *are* a human being." Molly patted her on the back. "I think we're on the right track here. Don't worry. We're going to take care of it—get your head in the right place so you can get on with getting on with your life."

Molly pushed play on her phone, and a very soothing melody of flute and chanting began. She told Ginger to close her eyes. Ginger had a hard time concentrating. She felt silly. Then she smelled the pungent odor of the sage wafting to her. Molly was circling, blowing the sage at her. Ginger relaxed a little. *Even if it doesn't help me get past the Brad stuff, it's kind of nice.* And Molly was so sweet to be concerned.

But concentration continued to elude her. Ginger felt really off track now. She kept her eyes closed as an image of Bode, swimming underwater, came to her, followed by a quick flash of the Frisbee boys, all smiles and tans. Then she remembered Fender's eyes crinkling when he smiled at her. She thought about his kiss, and warmth rushed through her. Maybe she was feeling better about all this.

The phone rang. Ginger and Molly jumped at the sound. Ginger got up and caught the phone on the fourth ring.

"Is Mrs. Janson there?" It sounded like a young girl. Ginger felt sick at the sound of Brad's last name.

"There is no Mrs. Janson, I'm sorry." She started to hang up.

"Well, ma'am, this is Natalie Higgins from Central Evergreen Bank. I have this as a number to contact regarding Mr. Janson's closed account at our branch."

"I was his girlfriend. Is there something I can help you with?"

"I'm not sure what to do in this situation. I should have waited until our manager came back, but she's in Boca Raton until Thursday, so I thought I'd better call."

Ginger felt a little dizzy. "What is it about?"

"Well, a check presented against the account. I thought I'd call someone before I sent it back; I didn't know if it was something you'd want to pay."

Now Ginger was bewildered. What could possibly be clearing now, almost a year after Brad's death? "What's the check for?"

The young voice hesitated. "Umm…Here it is. Yes, see, this is why I called. It's for quite a bit of money. And the memo is odd. It just says 'the ring.' The check is signed by Mr. Janson and made out to Barnes and Son Jewelers."

The floor spun under Ginger's feet. "Send it back unpaid." She hung up the phone and dropped to the floor.

Molly rushed to her. "What's wrong? What the hell is wrong?"

"Cleansing ceremony's off. I wasn't just a girlfriend after all. Brad bought an engagement ring. From Fender."

Ginger closed her eyes for a moment, trying to steady herself. An image popped into her brain. She stood under the green awning before Brad's grave, almost a year ago. Tears blurred her eyes. She looked up, looked across the gathering of people as the preacher talked about Brad. There was a man, a younger man, with dark hair in a somber suit. Standing across from her, he looked up at her, catching her eyes for a moment. Then he turned and walked away from the gathering. The shoulders of his dark suit glistened in the heat. She distinctly remembered watching the man stride to a car and drive off.

The man was Fender.

He was at the funeral.

Ginger went to the bathroom and threw up.

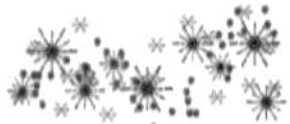

Ginger had never cried so hard. Not long after throwing up, she'd shown Molly the door and crawled straight back under her covers. When Brad died, she'd felt numb all over, and she'd shed very few tears. She'd just felt tired, empty of life. Now she was devastated. What if he'd made it home? He would've proposed. She would've said yes. She might even have been married by now. Something about that chance stripped away hurt more than knowing Brad was gone forever. It made her think about a happiness they might've found together that had evaded them as boyfriend and girlfriend.

She wouldn't hear of any of Molly's sensibilities now. Sure, she'd almost been open to the fact that she'd never really felt perfectly right dating Brad. But things were different now.

She and Molly didn't differ on their opinion of Fender at the moment. When Molly realized Fender had sold Brad the ring, she concocted a wild plan to visit revenge on the jeweler. Ginger didn't care about that; she just never wanted to see him again. She didn't understand why he'd been at the funeral. She didn't understand why he was on the mountain. But Brad had to be the link between her and Fender. Fender must have been preying upon her, after something.

She spent three days straight in bed, crying for a life she might have had.

Chapter Nineteen

Fender woke up several mornings after his cleansing late-night catharsis, and it occurred to him that he had slept well — three nights in a row of good, normal sleep. It felt liberating somehow. In the mirror, his eyes weren't puffy anymore, and he felt better. He used Pop's shaving cream and shaved.

The Morning Bird was busy this time of day. The regular breakfast customers usually lingered until nine or ten. They nursed cups of coffee and chatted long after the workers ate and rushed to jobs in nearby office buildings.

Though he hadn't been here in weeks, he recognized a few of the regulars sitting at the counter, and Sam stood behind it, talking. He was unbelievable. Somehow he managed to retain this job. Hell, how he even got himself out of bed in the mornings to cook for the breakfast rush amazed Fender. But he always seemed to do it, no matter how late Fender had kept him out the night before.

Sam noticed him, and Fender instinctively ducked his head. He was ashamed of what he'd done to his best friend. But Sam called out to him. He seemed glad to see him.

"Hey! It's Fender, everybody! Fender! Come here and get a cup of coffee!" Sam set a cup on a placemat a few seats down from the regulars. The old men leaned away from the Formica counter to get a better look at him. Satisfied, they turned back to their coffee and conversations.

Fender sat at the spot Sam had set for him. "Hi." He wasn't sure about this, still. He could see a faint mark on Sam's lower lip, maybe from the socking Fender had given him. "I'm such a total asshole."

Sam patted him on the shoulder, handed him a menu. "Yes, you are. But I am, too. And when you really get down to it, so is most everybody. All is forgiven. Now I feel it's my duty to cook you some eggs. You look better, but as the Southern womens would say, you look peaked, pal."

"No, really, I'm so sorry. You're my best friend. I'm sorry." Fender realized he had a hold on Sam's elbow, keeping him from escaping to the kitchen.

Sam leaned in, lowering his voice. "We were just worried about you. You don't have to apologize. We just want to help you out of whatever it is that has sucked you down."

Fender tried to look optimistic. He sat up a little straighter. "Well, I think I could use your support. I think I want to tell Ginger the truth. Tell her about Brad, about the ring, all of it."

Sam set down the coffeepot. "Really? You know, Fender, I think that might be a good idea. Yes, I do."

Fender felt like maybe he hadn't blown it with Sam. "Yeah. You know, I've thought about it a lot lately. I owe her the truth. I owe it to you and to Pop to tell her, too."

Sam waved this last point away. "You don't owe us anything, Fender."

"You guys helped me out. You've been taking care of the store. You had the balls to tell me what you thought of me selling the ring. I need the two of you around, and I need to do something to deserve that."

Sam's face went flat, and he shook his head. "I want you to be really clear about this. Look at me. Look me straight in the eye when I tell you this. Pop and I don't need you to do anything. You don't have to do anything to deserve us."

Sam had a toothpick in his hand and began to pick his teeth. "Despite the idiotic things you do, Fender, your heart's in the right place. I may not look like I have high standards, but I do. I wouldn't be your friend if I didn't think you were a good guy. Believe that." Sam slapped Fender on the shoulder one more time and went into the kitchen.

Fender could see Sam from the neck up now, standing at the grill behind the order window. He was preparing something. Probably Fender's eggs. Fender had to raise his voice for Sam to hear him. "So, what I want to do is tell Ginger the truth. I was hoping you could go with me, kind of for moral support."

Sam must have set the pan down on the flames. He came back out front and rested his hands on the counter in front of Fender. "I can do that. I'd be happy to do that. I just want to see you up and around again."

Fender breathed in deeply. "I think this might do it. This will fix things."

Sam pulled the dishcloth from at his waist and wiped his hands on it. "You know, Fender, she may not want to talk to you or see you again after you tell her the truth." He took a breath. "And you can't be surprised about that. She might not like you much when she hears the truth."

"I know."

"Okay, just so you're realistic. Don't expect hearts and flowers."

"I don't. I need to do this, though." Fender fiddled with the place setting in front of him.

Sam nodded. "Yeah, you do, my friend." There was a pop from the kitchen. "Oh, Christ! Your eggs." He hustled back into the kitchen and called through the window. "You'll eat, I'll finish up here, and then we'll go talk to her."

"Okay." Fender felt a little stronger than he had in a while. He hoped he could hold out.

After breakfast, Fender sat in the passenger seat of Sam's car. He gave directions to Ginger's house, and they pulled up on the street, across from her door.

Just then the door to Ginger's house swung open. Fender elbowed Sam in the side. "Here she comes! Scooch down in your seat; I don't want her to see us. We'll just follow her. She must be going to work or something. Maybe I can talk to her there."

Sam ducked his head a little in an effort to hide. "Fender, I don't 'scooch.' I'm a big man." He started the car and pulled out behind Ginger's white hatchback. "Okay, partner, let's go make things right."

Fender straightened his shoulders. "Let's go." He was a man ready to stare down his fate.

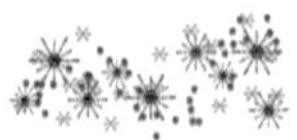

Some days after the phone call from the bank, Ginger went back to work. She needed to escape the house. She couldn't even stand to look at Zoë.

She entered the pool's enclosure and came around the fencing to see Bode skimming the surface of the pool with a long pole. His face was intent on his work. She walked to the side of the pool and stripped down to her bathing suit. She dove in, swimming down to the bottom of the pool. She touched the grate at the bottom of the deep end with her hand, like she had when she was a child. That had always been a big accomplishment. If it was possible to cry underwater, she was crying now. She felt safe under here and knew Bode couldn't hear her. She put both hands on the grate and breathed out, expelling all of the air from her lungs. How long could she stay under? She pulled her feet underneath her and stared up at the flickering surface. The light played with the water, shooting its fingers down into the blueness, mixing the elements.

Her chest hurt. She was going to have to go up. *I used to be able to stay under longer. When I was a kid, I could live down here.* She liked how quiet it was. She wished she'd taken a bigger breath.

She felt someone pull at her hair. Then the person had a hold of the straps of her bathing suit, tugging. The person slipped an arm around her neck in a tight grip and pulled her up, hard. She opened her mouth, and water rushed into her windpipe. She coughed, and her instinct took hold. She kicked for the surface, helping the rescuer who still held her tightly around the neck.

Breaking into the air, she coughed and spit up water. Bode shook his head like a dog to get the hair out of his eyes. He didn't let go of her until he'd hoisted her up onto the deck.

He stood up, running to get a towel. "What was that about?" he yelled, clearly distraught. "Are you all right? Were you caught on something?" He was by her side again, wrapping a towel around her and pounding her on the back to clear her lungs.

She waved a hand to back him off. "I'm all right. I'm okay. Nothing happened. Haven't you ever tried to see how long you could stay under?" She felt a little defensive.

She breathed in as deeply as she could. She released the breath, and it was as if she were unwinding the knots of stress in her back and neck. But letting go of the stress drew in a new feeling: fatigue. She wanted to curl up on the concrete right there and sleep everything away.

She closed her eyes and let her head rest on her knees. He was talking to her, she noticed.

"What?" Her voice was small. She felt a little better.

Bode patted her on the arm. "I said if you're going to sit at the bottom of the pool, at least use scuba gear."

"You've seen *The Graduate?*"

"The what?"

"Nothing." She laughed a little. *I need to sleep. I just need to sleep and everything will be fine.*

He leaned forward and looked into her face. "Do you want to lie down for a minute? We could pull a lounge chair around the side of the pump building. It's sunny, and no one would see you there if they came to swim."

"Yeah, that sounds good." She stood, and he put an arm around her, guiding her over to a chair.

Her body ached. She was about to close her eyes when Bode sat down on the end of the chair.

"Ginger?"

"Yeah?"

Bode looked her in the eye. He seemed older, more serious. "Was that something I need to worry about?"

Ginger sat for a moment. "I don't think so."

"Was it about Brad?" He waited for an answer.

"No. I don't want to talk about it."

"Okay." Bode unfolded a dry towel and covered her with it. "You sleep for a while, and then I'll take you home. We can lock the gates. No one comes this early anyway. I'll call Molly, and she can stay with you."

Ginger remembered talking to Molly briefly a day ago. "No, she's gone. There was a concert in Salt Lake. She's had the tickets since January."

Bode got up and looked around the pool enclosure. "Well, then I'll come by and check on you, every day. Or come cook for you after work. Unless you want me to call your mom. She could come to stay with you."

Ginger's heart jumped. *Mom would freak out about this.* "No, that's okay. It'd be good to hang out with you."

"You sleep, then, and I'll take you home in a while." He patted her again on the arm and walked around the corner. She closed her eyes and let the fatigue take her.

Voices awakened her. She was cold underneath the towel. The voices were all men's. She couldn't tell what they were saying, but she was embarrassed. What if it was J.C., their boss from City Rec? She had no idea how long she'd been sleeping. She figured she'd better emerge. Bode was probably trying to cover for her, and it'd be pretty pathetic to get fired from a lifeguarding job. She stood up and tried to smooth her hair. She wrapped the towel around her waist and walked as energetically as she could around the corner.

At the pool gate, Bode stood talking to two men. One was Fender. The other one was big. It looked like Sam, Fender's friend.

Rage rushed into her head like a hurricane. She pounded across the pool deck, driving her bare heels into the concrete beneath her.

"What are you doing here?"

All the men turned to face her, all of them looking a little scared. Fender opened his mouth to answer her, but Bode spoke first.

"They were looking for you, but I told them you didn't want to see anybody."

She pressed a finger into Fender's chest, pushing her way past Bode. "What the hell is going on? You sold Brad an engagement ring. Was it for me?"

He looked shocked. "Yes. Yes, it was."

"Where is it?" She poked him in the chest again. It felt good. She thought maybe she wanted to punch him.

"I don't have it anymore. I came here to tell you all about it."

"Did you go to the funeral?" She gritted her teeth, but she felt tears streaming from her eyes.

"I did. I was looking for you, to tell you about the ring. That's why I met you on the mountain, too. I wanted to tell you." He tried to back up, but she had him cornered against the chain-link fence. The other men stood close but looked afraid to intervene.

"You never told me. Why didn't you tell me? Why did you take all of those lessons? Why did you ask me out? How come you never told me?" She shook every time she said a word. She unleashed them, hurling them out of her body.

Fender looked like he might cry. "I should've told you. I waited for the right time. But it never happened, and by then I really liked you."

"Did he come to see you the day he died? Did he say anything about me? Tell me!"

His response to her raised voice was to speak so quietly he almost whispered. "He was really excited. Yes, it was the day he passed away. I'm so sorry."

He turned and started to leave. Ginger pushed him, hard, in the back. "I want the ring." He didn't turn around. She shoved him this time. "I want the ring, you bastard."

Sam held up a hand. "It's okay. Let him go."

Fender faced her. "I'm really sorry." Sam took him by the arm, and they turned their backs on her. Bode touched her, keeping her from following.

They left. Ginger threw her towel into the pool. Then she picked up a good number of chairs and threw them in the pool, too. It was a damn good thing the only customer was ancient Mrs. Isaacs, swimming laps on the far side of the water in her frilly green bathing cap, oblivious to the world. Rage shook Ginger's body. *This is my breaking point. I am done.* Every time she paused to breathe, images flooded her mind: The sun baking down on the shoulders of a man in a black suit, walking away from a funeral. The view outside the kitchen window as she heard an unfamiliar voice on the phone tell of an accident. Fender's lips parting as she rained hurtful words down upon him. Those shoulders, rounding in on themselves as he walked out the pool gate. She closed her eyes to all of it.

Fender lay on the couch at Pop's house with a wet washcloth over his eyes. The washcloth had been Pop's idea. *He can really act like an old lady sometimes.* Sam sat on the opposite couch. He picked at a barrette he'd found in the cushions, making a plinking sound with the metal of its clasp.

"It could've been worse."

Fender almost smiled at the absurdity of the whole situation. "Um, how?" He didn't look at Sam. He just stared into the wet of the washcloth.

"Well, you didn't have to tell her. She already knew. That saved you some time."

"Could we review again how she knew?" *The gods hate me. It's becoming painfully clear. Even a Greek hero would've gotten the message by now.*

"Like I tried to explain, I kind of had lots of money and checks and stuff spread around the shop. This was when you were at home having your moment, and Pop and I were keeping the ship afloat."

"Yes, I remember. And I'm still appreciative." Fender watched little pieces of who knows what float around in his eyes under the dark washcloth. His head hadn't really started to pound, but he was sure it was only a matter of time. "Go on."

"The check from Dead Boyfriend must have gotten mixed into the other stuff I had spread all over the desk. So, it got deposited, and she must've gotten a call about it, and you know the rest, and now can we change the subject, please."

Fender pulled the washcloth off of his eyes and turned toward Sam. He still had the barrette between his thumbs. He plucked it like it was a Jew's harp. Something odd occurred to Fender. "Hey, Sam?"

Sam looked at him. "Yes?"

"Why was there a girl's barrette in between the cushions of Pop's couch?" He chuckled and set Sam off on a spasm of giggles. It was giggles, no denying it. It didn't matter that Sam was a big man, he giggled. Sam's laughing made Fender laugh even more. Fender realized he was tired of being sad. He'd made his bed, he'd even laid in it, and he was done.

Sam's sniggling subsided. "I'm really sorry, Fender. I know how much you liked this girl."

"It's okay. I feel good that at least she knows the truth." He replayed the scene at the pool in his mind. There was still one thing nagging at him. "Things aren't totally done, though."

"What do you mean?"

"You know. It's going to be ugly, but it has to be done." Fender was trying to rally the troops for battle.

Sam flopped his body the length of the couch he had been sitting on. "It's never over with you, Fender. Like the time in biology when you stuck little Santa hats on all the dissected rats."

"That was a fine moment."

"Yeah, but the moment never lasts, and you always have to go on to something else, something more complicated."

"You thought of the yarmulke idea. I just agreed it was appropriate to recognize all faiths."

"And it was the second time that got us caught." Sam flicked the barrette at Fender on the other couch. "Well, I'm never one to miss watching you grovel. Maybe I should take pictures. I want to capture the look on Naomi's face when you try to wrench that ring off her bony little finger."

Fender smiled. He was a man with nothing to lose. "Maybe I could trade the barrette for it. What the hell is this doing here?"

Sam got up and walked to the kitchen. "Maybe it's Amy Rasmussen's. That girl was fast, even in fifth grade. You got it on with her, didn't you? Could be hers."

"I guess that beats the theory that Pop's playing with dolls." Fender followed Sam into the kitchen to make a sandwich. *Naomi.* The name chilled his blood. Oh well. He had to get that ring.

Chapter Twenty

"Let's hope all of my years as a borderline juvenile delinquent will pay off for me now." Fender paced the floor of the jewelry shop. It had been a week since the incident at the pool, and he still felt terrible. Retrieving Brad's ring from Naomi was the only thing to do to apologize to Ginger. Here he was now with Sam, trying to come up with a plan.

Sam sat in a chair he'd pulled out from the back office. "I don't see any other way to get it back than to lie, cheat, or steal. You've already tried the honesty thing with Ginger, and look where it got you. You owe it to yourself—lie like a rug on the floor. That's my advice."

I'm such a loser. How do I even function in this world? But Fender was feeling better. It now seemed okay if he never got to be with her. Just loving her was kind of different. It didn't give him hope about himself—hell, no. But maybe there was something redeeming. He could still think of her face and feel better inside.

He shook himself out of it. "Okay. Unless you have a plan, Sam, I say we just go to Jimmy and Naomi's and wing it. Maybe I'll think of something on the way there."

"Toss me the key to the display case. I think you should take another ring."

"What I really want to do is just pry the ring off the little she-devil's finger. But that isn't a bad idea, taking another ring. Grab one." He tossed Sam his keys.

Sam opened the engagement ring case. "Which one? Some of these are really spendy."

"At this point, I couldn't care less. If it was just about Naomi, I'd say something loud and obnoxious. Naomi's like a magpie. We could distract her with something big and shiny." Fender flipped through his receipt book, looking for Jimmy's current address.

Sam looked into the case. "Perhaps I should just wad up a big ball of tinfoil. I can wave it around in front of her while you grab the ring."

Fender came to the case. "But since I am trying to make things right and restore balance to the universe in the name of love, this is the one that's probably the closest in value." He plucked a ring from the tray. "And I will state for the record that I'm giving Naomi a nice swap because Ginger would want it that way—for no other reason." He paused for a moment and then handed it to Sam, who stuck it in a little red velvet box for safe-keeping. "We're ready."

Fender locked the shop, and they drove up into the foothills, following the GPS toward Jimmy's house. The homes grew larger and more decadent as they climbed. The views grew more expansive, and the houses more recently built. The yards of the homes were largely barren, homeowners trying to cultivate green grass on arid hills. A few of the lots had tiny, spindly excuses for trees. The neighborhood was a scar carved out of the side of a foothill.

"Let me guess, Naomi made Jimmy move up here after they got married?" Sam sat in the passenger seat, chewing on sunflower seeds, shells and all. Fender wouldn't let him smoke in the car, and he had to do something to keep himself occupied.

"Yeah, I'd bet." They pulled up outside a tan beast of a house. "This is it." From the street, the three-car garage dominated the front.

"I guess having money doesn't guarantee having taste." Sam spat a huge wad of sunflower shells into the gutter.

"You're disgusting." Fender punched him in the shoulder.

"Thank you." Sam picked a shell out of his front teeth as the two came to the front door.

"Follow my lead. Let's hope something comes to me. You have the other one?"

Sam patted his front right pocket. "You bet. Go get 'em, tiger. I got your back."

Fender rang the doorbell. There was immediately a flurry of frenzied, high-pitched barking. *Of course. Naomi has yippy dogs. Why am I not surprised?* He heard the click of heels on the entryway floor. He took a deep breath and tried to brace himself.

"Hush up, girls! Let's see who it is." Naomi opened the door with a wide white grin that quickly dropped into a scowl. "It's you. I'll go get Jimmy." She shut the door in Fender's face, and he heard her scream up the stairs. "Jimmy! It's that jeweler! Come see what he wants!" He heard the click of her heels again as she left the front door. He looked at Sam, who shrugged.

The door swung open again, and Jimmy stood in the foyer, dressed in a shiny navy blue jogging suit and expensive Italian loafers. He looked a little haggard. "Fender! What's up? Come in, come in. Let me show you the house." He waved Sam and Fender in with one hand, like the host he clearly felt he should be. He held a Miller Light can in the other.

"How are you, Jimmy?" Fender tried to smooth the nerves out of his voice.

"I'm good. Can't complain. Where'd Naomi go? She'll want to say hello. She loves that ring we bought the last time we were in. I think she might like it more than the yellow thing I got for the engagement."

"Actually, that ring you bought last time is why we're here. Does Naomi have it on right now?" *Please let me think of something now. Please oh please before this man kicks my ass in the front hall of his home.*

"Sure she does. I'll call her. What's this about?" Jimmy eyed Fender suspiciously.

Hiding from them behind the display cases probably didn't instill a lot of confidence, Fender thought. "Well, I'd like to talk to both of you about it, actually. And I'd like to see the ring."

"Yeah, me too." Sam let this slip.

Fender rolled his eyes. Sam had been bugging him all day to remind him what it looked like. Fender shot him a look as Naomi came back into the front hall. She stuck out her bottom lip in an effort to look unhappy. Fender laid on the saccharine. "Hello, Naomi. It's so good to see you again. How've you been?"

She ignored him, sidling up alongside Jimmy and wrapping her arms around his gut. "What does he want, sugar? My show's about to come on, and I don't want to miss it."

Jimmy patted her on the shoulder. "She loves that *Divorce Court*. I don't know why, but she does."

Sam coughed hard.

Don't look at him. He might make you laugh, and you'll blow the whole thing. Fender looked at the ring. Naomi wore it on her right ring finger. It was really large. He thought back to how Old Lady Harriman had ordered it. And forgotten about it, no matter how many times he called her. Then Brad bought it. And, well…It struck him. He bit his tongue to keep from smiling. He had her. He was going to get the ring back.

"Well, I was very concerned about the two of you. Have you been healthy? Happy? No unfortunate accidents?"

Sam looked at him out of the corner of his eye. He must have caught the new twinkle in Fender's eye because he smiled and stared at the ground.

Jimmy straightened up a little. "We've been all right. What does this have to do with the ring?"

"Perhaps we'd better sit in the living room. I think it'd be better if you were both sitting down."

At Fender's tone of voice, a look of dumb panic bloomed in Naomi's eyes. She pulled Jimmy into the living room, and they plunked down on a huge yellow sofa. Fender almost lost his train of thought as he took in the living room's decor. There were two of the poofy sofas, and flanking them were zebra-upholstered wingbacks. The walls were hung with large bearskins, dyed purple. In the corner stood an African mask at least seven feet tall. Sam also stood in the corner, poking his fingers in the mask's mouth. Fender cleared his throat, and Sam stuck his hands in his pockets.

Jimmy leaned forward on the couch. "Get to the point, Fender. What about the ring?"

Fender took a deep, loud intake of air, and then he let them have it. "Have you ever heard of the Hope Diamond?"

Naomi gasped. "Oh, it's horrible!" Then she looked puzzled. "What is it?"

This woman is as dumb as a box of rocks. But all the better for this to work. "The Hope Diamond was a beautiful blue diamond that was cursed. Everyone who purchased the diamond died before they had another birthday. It's in the Smithsonian now. No one can own it, it's so deadly."

Naomi dropped her right hand and looked at her yellow engagement ring on her left. "Is my yellow ring cursed? Are the colors bad luck? Oh, Jimmy!"

Wait a second, this train's headed down the wrong track. Detour! "No, Naomi. The curse of the Hope Diamond wasn't about the color. It was about the first person who owned it. The person…" He paused. He couldn't remember the old tale. Pop had told it to him as a kind of sick and twisted bedtime story so many times he'd had it memorized, but now he couldn't remember. There was an uncomfortable silence. Sam looked at him, nodding his head for him to continue. Then it came back to him. "The person who discovered it in India took it off of an ancient idol. It had been placed on the statue's forehead, as sort of a third eye."

"Like the 'evil eye,'" Naomi said.

Fender nodded solemnly. "The man stole it and took it to France. He fell ill, discovered he was dying, and began losing money, so he sold it to King Louis the Fourteenth. Marie Antoinette wore it often. And we all know what happened to her."

Fender paused, and Sam drew his finger across his own throat for emphasis. *God love ya, Sam. I can always count on you.* "And each owner afterward was cursed with the same bad luck. Those who wore the Hope Diamond paid for the privilege with their lives." Fender tried to really make the last word hang in the air.

Jimmy cleared his throat. "We all know this story, Fender."

"I don't, and it's making me nervous, sugar." Naomi buried her head in Jimmy's shoulder, rubbing her bouffant of hair into his shirt.

Jimmy made her sit up again. "Naomi, this has nothing to do with us. What's your point, Fender?"

Fender realized he needed to close in for the kill before Jimmy got too impatient. "I don't mean to worry either of you, but I have reason to believe the ring Naomi's wearing on her right hand is also cursed!"

Naomi gasped again and stared at her hand. Jimmy didn't look as convinced. "Why do you say that, Fender? Do you like to upset sweet pretty things?"

Fender ignored him for a moment. "Have you noticed anything strange lately, Naomi? You look a little pale. Have you been feeling well?" His question was met with a big fat tear that ran down Naomi's cheek.

Jimmy wasn't going to stand for this. "Now you've made her cry. Why do you think it's cursed, Fender? You better have a good reason."

"The ring was commissioned by Mrs. Harriman of Warm Springs Avenue. You know the family?"

"I do."

"Well, she specially ordered the diamond from Amsterdam, had me custom fit the ring to her hand, and I did quite a few designs for the setting. She was very pleased with the way it looked, the last time she tried it on."

Jimmy shifted on the sofa. "And?"

"Then she never came back to pick it up. I heard later that she'd fallen ill the day after our last fitting."

Naomi made a strange little whimper. She reached for her finger, about to take the ring off. Jimmy stopped her. "Fender, Mrs. Harriman is still alive. Did it ever occur to you that she just didn't want to buy the ring? She stiffed you. You should be glad we bought it and took it off your hands."

That would've worked if I didn't love Ginger. "Well…" He tried to sound timid. "There was actually another owner of the ring. After Harriman, and before you two bought it."

Naomi practically shrieked. "*Who?*"

"He was a nice young man. Bought it to propose to his girlfriend."

Naomi sniffled. Jimmy leaned over the poofy arm of the sofa and grabbed the Kleenex. She snatched them from his hands and held the box on her knees. "What happened to him?"

"Oh, Naomi, I'd really rather not say. Maybe we should just forget the whole thing."

"What happened to him? *Tell me!*"

Fender ducked his head and said it quickly. "He was hit by a car and killed."

A loud wailing sound filled the living room and bounced off of the purple-skinned bears' heads. Naomi was inconsolable. She flopped back on the couch, sinking into the squishy cushions. She pretended to be limp, though she managed to touch at her nose from time to time with a Kleenex.

Jimmy lifted her right hand and pulled the ring from her finger. He looked like he might eat Fender for lunch. Fender needed to finish this off and placate Jimmy in a hurry.

"Naomi! Don't cry! It tears Jimmy apart to see you unhappy. And I have a solution." Fender motioned to Sam. A step ahead, he rushed to Fender's side. He opened his palm to show the new ring, already removed from his jeans pocket. "I have brought with me today a distinguished man, who has the solution."

Jimmy was dubious. *For being so stupid that he'd marry Naomi, he's not that stupid.* "I saw this guy at your shop the last time we were there. He helped you sell this ring to us." The ring, Ginger's ring, was in Jimmy's hand, circled by the fist he shook at Sam at the moment.

Fender needed to do damage control. "Jimmy, can you and I have a private word?"

Jimmy clenched and unclenched the fist, balancing the ring on his palm. "Fine." He took a few steps into the front hall.

Fender dropped his voice to a whisper. "Please, Jimmy. I need that ring back."

"Is this a mafia thing? Do you owe the mafia? Or a cartel? Are you running drugs, because I swear to God if you get Naomi involved in some cartel shit, I'll snap your neck."

"No, Jimmy, none of that. It's about a girl. I need to give it back to a girl. She was supposed to have it. The guy really did die. He wanted to give it to her."

"And you sold it."

"I screwed up and sold it. It was a mistake. Please."

Naomi still feigned emotional distress, but Fender could see her frosted head bob over the couch cushions, spying on them.

Jimmy shook his head. "I can't believe I'm saying this, but wrap this up and get the hell out of my house."

"I am, I promise. Thank you, Jimmy."

The men walked back to Naomi. Sam fanned her with an old copy of *Us Weekly.*

Fender continued. "Yes, he consults with me from time to time. He's the one who alerted me to the curse, but it was too late — I, in my ignorance, had already sold it to you."

Jimmy snorted. "You *are* stupid, Fender. You damn well got that part right."

Sam jumped in.

It's a good thing, Fender thought, *because I'm running out of story here.*

Sam puffed out his chest. "I can cleanse your aura." He had employed a strange accent, sort of a cross between East Indian singsong and Texas drawl.

Fender backed him up. "He's an expert on the energy of crystals and gems. Very renowned cleanser."

Naomi showed some signs of life. She replied from the depth of the sofa cushions. Her voice was muffled. "Sugar, listen to them."

Jimmy rolled his eyes. "What do we do?"

Sam kicked it into high Sam-bullshit mode. "Hand me the offending ring." Jimmy obliged. Sam produced the replacement. "I believe the elders would like you to have this ring instead. That is the energy I get. But now I must bless the beautiful hand it will dwell upon."

Naomi took her cue and flung a hand from the depths of the couch. Sam held it by the pinky and the thumb and began to sing in a very painful falsetto:

"Hand of beauteeeeee...Beautiful hand on your wrissssssssst..."

"Thank you, wise one. That'll do." *It pays to have an insane friend,* Fender thought.

Two minutes later, they were out the door with the ring. They remained very quiet until the house disappeared from the rearview mirror. Then Fender felt it was safe to speak.

"We got it back."

Sam slapped the tops of his thighs. "I had no doubt. But I doubt if you'll ever have Jimmy as a customer again."

Fender held the ring up with a hand as he drove with the other. "You don't know how glad I am to have you back, you stupid thing."

Sam breathed out. "You're going to give it to Ginger?"

Fender hadn't thought this far ahead. "Yeah, I guess I am."

"And that'll be the end of it with her, huh?" Sam asked this gently.

Fender's heart dipped a little in his chest. "Yeah, I guess it will."

Chapter Twenty-One

Molly banged on the door, and Ginger could tell she was a woman on a mission. She was seriously rapping her knuckles on the screen. *Good*, Ginger thought. She didn't want to think about men, or rings, or much of anything.

"What's the plan?" She swung the door wide to let Molly in.

"Busy, busy bees we'll be, that's what. Where's your longboard?" Molly made a loop through the living room, looking behind the recliner in the corner.

"In the garage. I haven't been on it since before I moved in with Brad." She thought for a second. He didn't like her skateboarding… said it was the sport of boy band wannabes.

"I know. Which is why we're going out. Clean slates and all. Plus they paved that new subdivision road over by Alta Terra, and it's smooth and fresh and you know what it'll be like to ride that."

Ginger smiled. "Tempting. I'll go find it."

She went out to the garage and rummaged around. Some of the boxes were the ones Molly had helped her pack up after Brad died. The flap of one of them had popped up. She knelt to tuck it back in and saw the blue brim of a hat.

The Red Sox ball cap she'd gotten for Brad. He'd never worn it.

She swallowed hard. She missed him.

She pulled the hat out and yanked the tag off. She put it on and tucked her hair behind her ears. *I like it. I'll wear it. For Brad. For me.*

She found her longboard on the shelf above the lawnmower and brought it out to the driveway. Zoë perked up and started bouncing around, sensing a trip in the works.

"There you are. Nice hat." Molly put a leash on Zoë and plunked her board down. "Fresh road and then who knows? Maybe we can skate to the park and let the dog run around."

The newly paved road was a few blocks up into the hills from Ginger's house. The air was warm, and the asphalt wiggled with heat mirages as they climbed it. Zoë trotted enthusiastically next to Ginger.

"How come we haven't done this in so long?" Ginger handed Zoë's leash to Molly. "Hold her. I'm going first. She'll get tangled up and kill us both if I hang on to her."

Molly nodded. "Fine, you go first. And we haven't done this in so long because you were all about being a couple."

"Huh." Ginger hadn't thought much about that. She shifted her weight and looked down the hill, turning the idea over in her head.

"Huh, nothing. You know what I mean. You date somebody; you let all your stuff slide for his stuff. At least with Brad, you did." Molly shrugged and sat on the curb with the dog.

Ginger took a nice deep breath and centered herself on the board. Then she stood tall and picked up the foot holding her fast to the top of the hill. "Well, I'm here now. See ya at the bottom!"

She felt the smooth black ribbon of road under her board, and swiveled her hips to make big lazy curves, feeling the wheels under her feet.

"Go, Ginger!" Molly's voice shrank behind her.

She let out a whoop and heard the dog answer with an excited bark.

She reached the bottom of the hill and coasted to a gentle stop. She turned around and watched Molly let Zoë loose. Zoë bounced down the hill, barking and galloping.

Joy. That's what joy looks like. She laughed at the dog and sat on her board, arms wide to catch the big Husky.

She ducked her head to avoid the dog's sloppy tongue and heard Molly singing "Home on the Range" as she glided down the hill. "Sit, Zoë. That's enough kisses."

Molly came to a stop next to her, put a toe down, and flipped her board up on end. "That's how it's done."

"Girl, please. You wouldn't even own a skateboard if it wasn't for me."

Molly nodded. "You're right about that. And will you promise me that it won't get put up on a shelf for some guy again?"

Ginger knew she was talking about more than the skateboard. "I promise."

"To the park, and then we're going out tonight. No arguments."

Ginger nodded—in agreement or surrender, she wasn't sure. "No arguments." She straightened the brim of her cap and pushed off.

"Yes? That was a yes? I'm taking it as a yes." Molly followed her.

Ginger called out behind her as she and the dog sailed down the street. "Okay!"

But after a moment, Molly picked up the pace and passed Ginger. "Success!"

Once she had a yes, Molly seemed totally focused on fulfilling her promise. She hustled Ginger around all afternoon, not about to give her the opportunity to change her mind about the evening. They took Zoë to the park for a few hours and dropped her back by Ginger's house. Then they went to Molly's to get ready. Molly'd already decided Ginger would stay the night. They'd have a "genuine slumber party," she explained.

Molly proved to be very distracting. *Maybe I can just move in with her, and I'll never think about anything bad. She won't give me the chance; she talks so much.* Ginger smiled to herself.

The sun began its descent, and Molly flitted around the house. She lit candles and put on soft music.

"Are we on a date?" Ginger watched all of her friend's doings.

"No. Whenever I get ready to go out, I try to get in a nice, relaxed state. I even—" she had her lighter and was pulling a bundle of something out of her drawer "—like to cleanse my aura, so to speak."

Ginger felt uneasy. "The last cleanse we tried to do went very poorly, if you remember."

Molly stopped, her eyes saying she realized she'd brought up the forbidden subject. She looked at Ginger, waiting for her response.

I need to be good about this. "When you thought maybe I should wipe the slate clean. Start fresh."

"Yeah."

Ginger thought about it for a minute. "Maybe I do need to do that. Not for a guy…" She wouldn't even say his name. "Not for him, but for me. I should start with my own clean slate."

Molly looked relieved.

I've been so hard on her. Molly's been amazing to me.

"Well, I'm glad you have that outlook," her friend said. "I think you're the most resilient person I know." She took the two wine glasses from the table behind her and handed one to Ginger. It was full of a smooth-smelling red. "A toast, one worthy of my diversion from monk-ish clean living." Ginger lifted her glass. Molly smiled. "To fresh starts. And good luck this time, maybe." She took a deep swallow.

Ginger did the same. She felt the liquid warm her stomach. She could do this. "Let's go out."

The two went to a small place downtown on the mezzanine of an old department store. It looked over the ground floor, which was full of shops, a bakery, and a coffeehouse. The bar was filled with bankers from the adjacent office building, tearing it up on a Friday night. The space was warm with mahogany and gaslight. It was comforting, almost.

"Are you glad you came out with me?" Molly sat close all night, to the point of hovering.

"Yeah. I feel fine. You were right. It's healthy to be out with people."

"Girls! Hey!"

Ginger turned to see Bode. He must've seen them at the table as he rode up the escalator.

Molly smiled at him and raised an eyebrow at Ginger.

Ginger found herself happy to see him. "Come join us."

Bode sat. He and Molly launched into a lengthy discussion of the merits of yoga and quinoa and other boring but very safe topics. Bode seemed to enjoy talking about his muscles and his metabolism.

"No, seriously, if you wake up and chug a cup of hot water with lemon at, like, two in the morning, it fires up your whole body and soul when you wake up the next day. It's, like, spiritually transformational." He nodded and smiled at both ladies. Ginger was reminded of her panting, happy dog comparison again.

Molly scoffed. "If I'm awake at two in the morning, it better be because I'm getting my world rocked, not sipping lemon water."

She looked over Ginger's shoulder, down the length of the bar. "I'm going to go powder my nose."

Ginger knew the look. Molly was on the prowl. She must've spotted someone in the bar. This made Ginger feel good. Molly had relaxed enough to stop playing mother hen. *I should encourage this. It would prove I'm okay.*

"Molly, make the rounds. Don't just powder your nose; there are men out there, waiting to be met."

She looked hesitant. "Are you sure?"

"Yes. Bode can keep me company." Ginger smiled at him. He looked relaxed, too. This was working out pretty well. A fresh start.

Molly disappeared down the way, heading into the depths of the bar. "Be back in a bit," she called.

Ginger and Bode talked for a while more before she felt her eyes tiring. She spotted Molly just at that moment, making her way back through the crowd to their table.

"How's it going?" Ginger stifled a yawn.

Molly straightened up. "You're tired. We need to go, huh? I'll just tell this person I'm leaving."

Ginger had no desire to ruin Molly's night. *I've played the prima donna plenty.* "Molly! Bode can take me home. If you've met somebody, you need to hang with him."

Molly's face lit up. "You're a rock star. I have no idea if this is anything, but you never know. He's not the prettiest picture, but he sure is funny. Bigger than I usually like, but hey, that's okay. He's working for me, what can I say? I'll see you tomorrow, then." Molly leaned over and kissed Ginger on the cheek. Then she disappeared back into the crowd.

Bode was already on his feet. "You ready to go?"

Bode talked all the way home about music, and they made it back to her house before midnight. When they got inside, Ginger felt less tired. She sat on the couch.

Bode plopped down next to her. "Where's your dock for your phone? I'll play you some songs before I go. Then you'll know what I was talking about in the car."

His enthusiasm amused her. "Bode, I believe you. I've heard of Van Halen. They were big in the eighties."

Bode sat for a second. "There was another singer before Sammy Hagar."

She smiled. "Yes, I know."

They stayed up another hour, playing songs. Nothing too sad, nothing too pensive. Bode kept the tone light and the pace quick. Ginger avoided anything that might trigger a Brad flashback. After a while she admitted it: Bode was fun to be with.

It was late when he played what he promised would be the last song. He stood back from the phone in its dock and looked at her. "This one you should know. Everybody knows this."

Ginger braced, worrying it would be a song loaded with memories of Brad. The voice began tenderly: an old Elvis tune. Sentimental. Nothing that reminded her of anything painful, but a shift in the tone of the night. One look up at Bode confirmed this. His sandy blond hair hung in his eyes. He ducked his head shyly and held out a hand.

"Will you dance with me?"

Ginger sighed. "Sure."

Then she was in his arms. She felt all that tan muscle she hadn't helped but notice at the pool. Now it lay beneath a soft shirt. She felt his hand at the small of her back. Everything he did was measured, careful. He was much different than the night last winter. Now he didn't talk; he used no cheesy lines. He was just a decent person.

The song ended, and they looked at each other. A wave of gratitude washed over her, and she kissed him.

They stood together for a moment and then parted. Bode looked at her and shrugged a little. It must've been the same for him — no spark.

"What are we doing?" Bode sat down on the couch. He seemed a little disappointed.

Ginger sat down next to him. "I don't know."

"Huh."

Bode never had much to say anyway. She waited for him to continue. He put an arm around her shoulder, but the mood had changed. *His* mood had changed. It was as if the air had been let out of the room. Now it was still, calm.

He drew in a breath. "I'm glad I got to work with you this summer. I'm glad I know you better."

They'd found the place where their relationship belonged, where it was comfortable.

"You're a good friend, Bode."

He patted her on the leg, got up from the couch, and went home.

Chapter Twenty-Two

The ring again took up residence on the top of Fender's dresser, if only for a day or two. It winked at him as he passed by going to the shower that morning. But the wince with which he'd regarded it before was gone. Now the ring meant redemption—or at least seeing Ginger one more time. So what if the circumstances weren't going to be great? Fender wasn't all that surprised. Women didn't take to him. That was life.

He'd woken up earlier than usual, so he went by the cafe to catch Sam. He wanted to run a few scenarios by him and see what sounded plausible, how they could get the ring back to her. He was due to open the store later that morning, but this was more important.

At the Morning Bird, the manager told Fender Sam had called in. This was odd. Sam was never sick. He was always hung over, but rarely sick. And a hangover never stopped him from going in to work. "*Might as well get paid to feel like shit,*" Sam always told him.

Fender got in the car and drove to Sam's house. He worried a little. *God, I'm such a girl. All this softie, touchy-feely crap.*

He parked on the street. Sam's house was in the only marginal neighborhood in the entire town, adjacent to the overpass of the business loop. It seemed nobody wanted to live by the highway. The price was right enough that Sam didn't care. Fender never thought the traffic noise was a big deal, but the area *was* run down. But Sam was the antithesis of picky. He added to the allure of his abode by neglecting to water the lawn. A patch of goatheads was the only thing punctuating the dirt in front of the house.

He strolled to the front porch and tried the door. It was locked. Now Fender really was worried. Sam did not sweat security. Fender lifted the mat at the foot of the door and took the spare key.

He had the door partway open when Sam came flying into the living room — wearing a towel.

"Fender! It's early. What are you doing up?"

"I don't know. What are you doing in a towel? You're dry. You haven't been in the shower…" Fender left off there.

Sam held up the hand that wasn't binding the towel around his body. "Fender, don't. Don't open your mouth."

Fender scanned the living room. All the old magazines had been cleared off the coffee table and were stacked in a corner. The beer signs in the window were turned off. It all became crystal clear. "*You got laid!*"

Sam didn't deny it. But he waved his free arm, trying to stop Fender from hopping around in delight. "Could we please talk about this later?" He almost severed his head from his neck with a vigorous nod in the direction of the bedroom.

Fender whispered, but he'd never been very good at whispering. "She's still here? Oh, this is too sweet. I want to meet her." Fender had already moved past Sam. Sam was big, but he was slower.

"Fender, you'll ruin it. Don't scare her away; I haven't told her about my crazy friend yet."

"Please? Pleasepleasepleasepleaseplease to infinity? Come on, Sam. I won't even talk."

Sam relented. "All right. Let me bring her out. The bedroom is not a place for you to scare her. We've got a good vibe going on in there, if you know what I mean." Sam let loose with a wide grin and disappeared into the bedroom. There was bumping and rustling. Fender thought he heard a woman giggle.

Well, that's a good sign. At least it's not an imaginary woman.

The door opened a crack, and Sam came out, dressed in sweats. A woman followed closely behind him, wrapping a sweater around her slim form. She hid behind Sam.

Sam stood up a little straighter. "Fender? I'd like you to meet my friend Molly."

Ginger's friend Molly emerged from behind Sam. Fender opened his mouth in surprise. Later, Sam described the sound that emerged from Fender's mouth as:

"Bahhahhhhh!"

Everyone jumped, and Fender ran for the door. He yelled at Sam over his shoulder. "Meet me at the Rendezvous for lunch!"

By the time he'd driven from Sam's sketchy neighborhood to the fine, upstanding area where Barnes and Son was found, Fender's heart rate had returned to normal. He strolled down to the shop to open up. It probably wasn't the worst thing in the world to deal with people for a couple of hours, maybe get the image of his best friend with weird Molly in all sorts of compromising positions out of his mind. And if that didn't put him off romance for a few years at least, he still had his own predicament and the ring-returning to sort out.

After cleaning the cases, answering emails, and chasing one possible street person (or mime, he couldn't quite tell) out of the store, the bell on the door jingled again.

Two men entered and approached the case closest to the front door, browsing the Tag Heuer watches.

Hmmm. Money in the house. Fender looked at the first man, tall and slim in pegged khakis, laced-up oxfords, and a blue button-down shirt. He lingered close to the other man who wore a blue blazer and white T-shirt with jeans.

Money! These gents might actually have money—maybe I'll actually operate a business today. Fender liked the days when he could convince himself he wasn't running the shop into the ground.

The guys turned toward him. The one in the button-down looked at him, scrutinized him over tortoiseshell glasses. "What do you think, Lucas? Should we spill the beans?"

Lucas looked Fender up and down, too. "Umm…Might as well."

They crossed the store to stand in front of Fender.

"Can I help you gentlemen with something?" *Something with a lot of zeroes on the price tag?*

They smiled. Fender relaxed a little. They seemed happy. Sometimes a nice person got lost and found his way into Fender's shop. Ninety percent of the time, it was a harpy like Naomi, but you know, they couldn't all be horrible people.

"We're buying wedding rings." The unnamed buttoned-down dude gave him a big, toothy smile for two seconds, kind of the "woohoo" fake, nervous smile you give for a school picture.

"You want to check out the engagement rings? I have some nice solitaires over in this case," Fender offered.

The two men didn't move. Blazer dude elbowed button-down guy. "Tell him, Damien."

Damien cleared his throat. "We're buying wedding bands."

"Okay…" Fender tried to follow.

"For each other."

"Is it a double wedding?"

Damien rolled his eyes. "No double wedding, just a single gay wedding. Is that okay?"

I'm a moron. "Sorry, I'm on track now. I'm just really distracted today."

Lucas shifted uncomfortably. "I'd really hoped you'd be able to help us."

Nothing was clicking with Fender fast enough. Now it finally occurred to him that these two thought he was casting aspersions on the thought of a gay marriage, of selling rings to two guys in love.

"Hey, I do not care who you marry. I'm all for marrying somebody. Good luck to you. Anybody who's prepared to do that is fine by me."

Damien snorted. "Well, you're the poster boy for romance, aren't you?"

Fender's heart sunk. "Yeah, Mr. Love all the way around, right here." He thought for a second about Ginger, and the shop felt warmer. "Damien and Lucas, was it? My apologies."

They stood closer to each other, and Damien slung an arm around Lucas's shoulder. "You're fine."

"No, I'm not, actually. Just because I'm in love with someone, and just because I've completely incinerated any chance I might have with her—and by incinerated, we're talking *Hindenburg*-disaster-level incineration, total annihilation—does not mean the two of you don't deserve my congratulations. Real love is hard to come by, and it transforms the very long and sad road of life into the autobahn of love, light, and green eyes and freckles."

He swallowed hard. The two gentlemen stared at him, seeming slightly perplexed. *God, I have to fix my life.* "Let's get you the most kick-ass bands in the store, shall we? I hope you're planning on spending a ridiculous amount of money," he said, waggling his eyebrows. "I might even be able to whip up something custom for you."

Fender was pleased to see the two men smile at him, and then at each other. *No redemption for me, maybe, but at least I can try.*

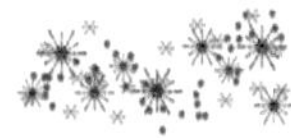

Fender had mostly recovered himself when he walked into the dimness of the Rendezvous a few hours later and looked for a spot to sit. He noticed Pop, sitting in the same booth he always did. *Why do I ever even think to look for a spot? My father, the local color of the neighborhood bar.*

Pop saw him. "Sonny! You come sit with your old man. Who's minding the store?"

"A man has to eat, Pop." Fender sat. "Besides, I'm meeting Sam in a bit."

"How's he? You're looking better, by the way. The color's back into your cheeks."

Fender ignored the attempt to discuss his life. "Sam's fine. He's great, actually. He's met a girl."

"Really? A woman for Sam." Pop thumped the vinyl seat next to him. "Well, that beats all. You know, if that clown can find a woman, so can you, Sonny."

"Thank you, Pop. Yet another reason why I hide when I see you coming down the street. Don't we have anything else to talk about?"

Pop thought for a second. "No."

"What about current events? Don't you always read the news at the library? Fill me in on the world. How are things in the Middle East?"

Pop smiled. "Sure, I read. But the ladies at the library are more engaging and so is worrying about my son. Your mother is gone; who else is supposed to look after you but me?"

"Okay. Here's the clown now." Fender waved Sam over.

"Should my ears be burning? How are you, Jerry?" Sam plopped into the booth and rattled the cutlery on the table.

Pop started in; he didn't waste time when a juicy story might be involved. "Fender tells me a lady has entered your world."

Sam dropped his head in defeat. "What a sad, sad commentary on your son's little life. Yes, I've met a lady. He just doesn't have much else to talk about, does he?"

Fender took the shot as deserved. "Yeah, but who the hell would bet that you'd hook up with such a flake? That woman is weirder than Wyoming on a Wednesday."

Sam raised an eyebrow. "Nice metaphor. How the hell would you know, anyway? You met her, like, once at Ginger's house? Boy, it took more than a minute or two for Molly to recover after you yodeled your way out of my house. But she finally explained how you knew each other." Sam took a sip out of Fender's water glass and waved at a waitress. "And how weird is that, anyway? Do you think God's trying to tell us something, or what?"

Pop looked confused. "Slow down, young men. You've lost me. To whom is God speaking? That can be a sign to seek medical help, you know. Who's the one hearing voices?"

Fender tried to minimize it. *How do I manage to have these two hash out my life for me?* "It's nothing, Pop. The girl Sam met is a friend of—" He broke off. How did he describe Ginger? It would take six years to explain it to someone.

Sam finished the sentence. "Molly is Ginger's best friend. Ginger's the girl Fender loves. You know, the one from the store. You caught them making out."

As usual, the conversation commenced as if Fender wasn't present.

Pop was clearly trying to remember. "Is this the one he got all depressed over?"

Sam unwrapped a package of saltines from the bar now. "Yeah, the one who was supposed to get the ring. Except Fender fell for her and, you know, lied to her and tried to date her."

"I did not lie. I just neglected to tell her stuff."

Sam nodded at the revision. "Whatever. He left stuff out. He almost had her, too. Oh, did we tell you we got her ring back?"

Pop wasn't following. "Back from where?"

Fender cut it short. "Never mind. We need a plan."

Sam had moved on to the salad on Pop's plate now. "Well, now that I know Molly, it's like a secret spy network."

Fender perked up. "What did she say? How's Ginger?"

"Molly doesn't like you much. But I explained how you love Ginger and all."

Fender felt a cold sweat on his upper lip. "Could we stop using the word *love*? It's making me uncomfortable."

Sam ignored him. "Uh-huh. So anyway, she doesn't think you suck so much now. Molly actually said that before Ginger found out about the ring, she was kind of warming up to you."

"Who was warming up? Molly?"

"No, Ginger."

Pop signaled that he wanted out of the booth. "This is very confusing. I'm leaving. Sam, you can have the rest of my salad. Fender, be a good son and get the bill."

Fender nodded to Pop and turned back to Sam. "How did you get hooked up with this Molly anyway? God, you have weird relationships."

"I met her at the Dubliner. She likes all the same stuff I do. It could be promising. And, excuse me, I met a girl at a bar and took her home, like normal people. You are the odd one, my friend."

Sam finished Pop's salad and waved again to the waitress. "Fries? A side order? Thank you." He looked again at Fender. "Why are you looking at me like that? Oh yes, that's right, it's a Fender-centric world. What about Fender's problem? Well, you may be in luck."

"How?" Fender felt a twitching in his stomach. Hope rearing its ugly head?

"I talked Molly into softening Ginger up. Molly's not your biggest cheerleader, but she says if you're my friend, you can't be all bad. She's going to work on Ginger to start closing some doors to unfinished business. Molly thinks Ginger was already letting go of Brad, until you mucked it up with the ring-back-from-the-dead deal."

"You, *señor*, were the one who deposited the check. What about the guy at the pool?"

"I didn't ask about everything. Molly and I have our own business to conduct, studmuffin." Sam straightened his collar conspiratorially.

"Oh, Lord. Please, I'm happy for you, but it was bad enough to see you in a towel." His mind turned back to Ginger. He could almost feel the gears turning in his head. *I'd stroke my mustache if I had one.* "That's okay. We'll find out about Malibu Ken later. This could be promising."

The waitress brought Sam's order. "Yeah, okay. My fries are here now, so I'm not listening anymore. Feel free to keep talking if you like, though."

Fender fell silent. A connection to Ginger. It had to be okay to hope a little. Maybe.

Chapter Twenty-Three

As the anniversary of Brad's death loomed, Ginger wasn't sure what to do. She'd been busy, working at the pool in the last long, hot days of summer, taking Zoë out for walks after sundown, and longboarding down the soft new asphalt by the park. She even got up the courage to take Zoë to a different vet to get her shots. It was a woman in the older section of town, in a little clinic behind a residence. The vet, Dr. Hamilton, had been very complimentary of Brad and had expressed her condolences. And Ginger had kept it together. Zoë seemed to like Dr. Hamilton, and Ginger felt as though she and the dog had made another step toward happier times.

But when she was at work, every child at the pool knew summer was ending soon, and each discussion of the coming start of school was a reminder that Labor Day would also come, and she would have to mark a very unpleasant occasion. She finally felt as though she was on an even keel, and she didn't want one day to upset her balance all over again. She'd never been much for melodrama, and she'd had her fill of it lately.

The Wednesday before Labor Day, she went to see Molly.

You've had long enough now, she told herself as she pulled into the parking lot of Molly's apartment. She hoped there was a way to go forward.

She climbed the two flights to Molly's place and knocked. The door opened and a potpourri of exotic smells drifted out. Patchouli and herbs—maybe a little onion—all touched Ginger's nose. Shortly thereafter, Molly poked her head around the door.

"Hey!" She smiled at Ginger but didn't open the door any wider.

Ginger was intrigued. Molly couldn't be smoking pot; it was too close to the ski season. Drug testing at the ski resort compelled her to be clean at least three months prior. Plus, Molly had successfully gone cold turkey all summer and seemed to be buying into the slow, local, vegan-hipster-straight-edge-whatever-it-was lifestyle. Something else was up. "What are you doing?"

Molly stalled. "I like that shirt! Is that the one we found together at The Closet? I love that store." She glanced behind her, into the apartment.

"Molly." Ginger waited for her to turn around. She gained her attention again. "What's up? Can I come in?"

"Hmm? Oh, oh, I'm terrible. Yeah." She shut the door in Ginger's face.

It must be opposite day. It was starting to feel awkward standing in the hallway.

The door swung open again. "Okay, you can come in, if you promise not to yell."

"What are you talking about?" Ginger walked into the front hall of the apartment. Molly was not usually one for housekeeping, but the place was spotless. Candles flickered everywhere, and Molly had been cooking something complicated, judging by the tower of stainless steel in her sink.

In the living room, where her dinky black and white RCA TV had been, sat a large, white metal cage with two turrets. Inside the thin bars perched two white doves. Ginger felt her eyes widen. "Molly, they're so cool! I love them. Where did you get them? Is this what you thought I'd be mad at?"

Someone answered her from the door to the bedroom. "I think she thought you might be mad about me."

Ginger turned around. It was Sam, Fender's friend. She held still for a minute. He didn't belong in this picture. Her mind couldn't figure out what to think.

Molly put herself between Sam and Ginger.

She must think I'm going into some sort of crazy fit. "I don't understand." Nothing else came to her. She waited for Molly to answer and tried not to look threatening.

"This is who I met at the Dubliner when we went out last month. This is Sam. You've already met, from what I gather."

Sam looked awkward. He stuck his hands in the pockets of his pants and smiled.

Ginger smiled as broadly as she could. "Hi. Uh, I guess I owe you an apology. I was a real bitch at the pool."

Sam walked up behind Molly and put his arms around her. "I think it was justifiable. Everybody was having a tough time." Ginger understood he was talking about her and Fender.

Molly seemed to let down her guard. She relaxed, and a toothy smile spread on her face. "We've been getting along. We like a lot of the same stuff, you know, Portland bands, nano-breweries, mustaches…I was hoping it'd be okay with you. It's been harder and harder to keep a secret."

Ginger hated being the eggshells everyone walked on so delicately. "What are the odds it'd be you guys that met? But if you're happy, I'm happy. It's not every day a man catches the eye of my Molly."

Sam glowed. He'd literally broken into a sweat, his face and neck covered with tiny moist beads. "So, it's all out now. You know, Molly and I were at three of the same Coachellas? We were even in the same tents, listening to the same bands. I mean, what are the odds of that? Good karma, I'm tellin' ya." He kissed Molly on the cheek. "I have to go. Don't gush too much about me, puddin'." He smiled warmly at Ginger as he squeezed out of the front door.

Molly looked like she wanted to gush. "He bought me the doves. Isn't that the most romantic gesture? He's not a walking gym ad, but there's more to life than six-pack abs."

Ginger smiled and was happy to find she really felt really pleased. She looked into herself, and that's what reflected back up to the surface. "Do you know that the whole time I've known you, you've never had a serious boyfriend? This is big stuff."

Molly's dark curls seemed to vibrate. "I don't want to jinx it."

"You have to dish a little, Molly."

"What's weird is that I spotted him from across the bar at the Dubliner. It's like he was putting out a vibe. Maybe it was destiny or karma or something." She caught herself. Ginger could see it. It made a little cloud that hovered in her eyebrows. Her sense of tact in regards to Ginger was very keen.

"Whatever it is, it's good." Ginger went back over to the cage. The doves nestled closely to one another. They seemed very placid. "That's what I want." Ginger pointed to the cage. "I want to be that peaceful."

Molly sat down on the couch across from the birds. She beckoned Ginger to sit with her. "You can be. You've had a lot of turmoil in the last year. Maybe you're turning a corner, with the anniversary and all."

Anniversary. *It's a happy word*, Ginger thought. *It doesn't fit this.* You don't want to celebrate the date of a death creeping back up on you. You mark it.

Molly put an arm around her. "I'm going to give you unsolicited advice. Brace yourself."

"I don't want to talk about Fender. I can't wrap my head around what he did. I can't figure it out, and it still upsets me."

"That's not what I was going to say. But you brought it up, now, so here's one thought. Forgiveness is good. It especially helps when you can't sort out why someone did a hurtful thing. But that's that. I'm not going to talk about him. And I want it to be perfectly clear that Sam doesn't expect you to go on double dates with us—you and Fender and us. Although he has said he thinks you were the first person Fender's really loved." Molly spit all this out in a great rush, lobbing it into the air before Ginger could stop her.

Ginger finally broke in. "I'll let that sink in later. What was it you were going to say? The thing you *did* want to talk about?"

"Oh. I think you should go to Brad's grave." Molly stood to move around the apartment, dousing candles.

Ginger shrugged. "I don't know."

"Yes, I think you should. I could give you a couple little Choctaw prayers to say. You could smudge a little sage. It might help you say good-bye to him. Maybe you can figure out how you really felt about him."

"You and your sage." Ginger took a deep breath. "You're probably right. Maybe I'll go this week."

"It'd be good, since it's a year exactly this week. I could go with you."

"No, I better go myself. You have someone who needs your attention."

Molly grinned. "I know. Doesn't it kick ass?"

Ginger nodded, but she couldn't say anything. She sat and looked at the doves, dozing on their perch. She wished again for peace.

Chapter Twenty-Four

Sam was over, trying to show Fender pictures of the doves he'd bought Molly. Fender tolerated that sickeningly sweet business only because he missed his friend. He was scarce lately, busy these last few weeks building a love nest with Molly—or Miss Flake, as Fender liked to call her. But it was kind of fun, because when Sam did come by, he would relay any tidbits Molly had let slip about Ginger on their last date.

Today Sam and Fender were at Pop's, cutting the lawn for him. Labor Day weekend was approaching, and it was blisteringly hot. The lawn had browned out about the middle of July, but Fender was weed-whacking a few stray blades here and there. Sam sat at the edge of Pop's yard with his feet in the neighbor kid's pool.

"The only thing I'm missing is my daiquiri. Oh, cabana boy!" He was out of reach to swat.

"I give up. The battery's dying anyway." Fender set the trimmer down and came to sit beside Sam. The grass stuck to the back of his sweaty legs.

Sam looked up into the blue sky. "Actually, what I'm missing is my woman."

"Oh, give me a break. You saw her this morning. You've been without Molly for all of three hours."

"I know, isn't it sickening? But she's the butter on my popcorn, baby, the fly in my soup." Sam splashed his toes around for a minute. "I might even be so bold as to use the—" He gasped, widened his eyes, and paused for emphasis. "L-word."

"Get the hell out." Fender smiled. Sam really was happy. It was downright surreal.

"No, really. Give me two, three weeks, a month or three, and I might say that word. To her, maybe even."

"It's about damn time, Sam. I'm glad for you." *Oh, time for an awkward, why-isn't-Fender-happy-too moment.*

"It'll happen for you." Sam looked at his toes.

"Oh, don't give me that shit. Who cares, anyway?"

"You do, 'cause you perk up every time I mention Ginger's name." Sam looked at Fender. "See? I'll be damned if you didn't twitch a little just then."

Fender lay back in the grass and looked up, over the neighbor's roof. He sighed. He felt a Sam speech coming on.

"I think I have the whole thing with her figured out, you know," Sam began.

"Oh, really." Fender noticed the peak of the roof was bowed ever so slightly.

"Yeah, I do. Now be attentive. So, here's the deal. It's like the *Jump Street* phenomenon."

Fender smiled. *Oh, Sam.* "The what?"

"*Twenty-One Jump Street.* Johnny Depp was on it, even though he pretends like he wasn't. Except for the cameo in the movie version, I think he's in denial. But he needs to 'fess up, because all of us remember when he graced the cover of *Tiger Beat.* C'mon!" Sam splashed a little, for emphasis.

Fender felt the need to redirect. "Excuse me, point?"

"The point is…Oh shit, I can't remember…No, the point is, in the show Johnny Depp had a girlfriend, and he was going to dump her. He didn't like her; she was bugging him. And then she got killed in a convenience store robbery."

"Okay." Fender felt lost. Oh well.

"This is the thing! After she died, he was all like, 'I loved her, man, we were going to get married' and everything. Until his friend, who was Dom DeLuise's son in real life, snapped him out of it."

Fender sat up on his elbows. Sam, for all of his inane theories, might have struck upon something. "So, what are you thinking?"

"Well, from what I'm getting from Molly, things weren't all peachy with D.B. and Ginger. Ginger didn't talk about it much, but Molly says D.B. told her he wanted to do something to 'shore up' his relationship with Ginger."

"Shore up? He said that?" Fender remembered why Brad had annoyed him in the store. *Now wait, Fender, that's not nice to think about. The guy's not here to defend himself. Show some respect, for Christ's sake.*

Sam was off, however; respect be damned. "Shore up. Like a brick wall or a roof. But more importantly, a roof that's leaky. A wall that's crumbling — you see where I'm going here?"

"Yeah, maybe they were having problems." Fender felt that little twitch in his stomach again. Pesky hope flipping and flopping around.

"Just like Johnny Depp! She loses him in the accident in front of the store and suddenly her brain flips off, and it's like 'Oh yeah, I loved him,' except that's why she could like you, because things when he was alive weren't all perfect!"

Sam now sat up very straight in his lounger. His point had been made, and he was clearly pleased to have garnered a favorable reaction, too. "Not a bad thing to think about, huh? Maybe it's not all over between you guys. Maybe she just needs to sort stuff out. It's coming up on a year, you know."

Fender got depressed again. "Yeah, except in the Johnny Depp thing the alive guy doesn't lie and get in trouble with her and make her feel terrible."

Sam waved him off. "There wasn't even another person Johnny was interested in. That wasn't the point of the story. The point was chinks in the armor."

"What?"

"Chinks in the armor. Ginger and Brad? That was not a match made in heaven, my friend. I'll bet you two thousand bucks she had doubts." Sam got up out of the kiddie pool, triumphant in his logic.

"Where are you going?"

"I've had enough of your company, Mr. Barnes. I'm going to go look for my woman."

Sam left, and Fender put the trimmer in the shed and stopped for a moment. Maybe the whole thing wasn't played out yet. He smiled to the empty backyard. "Thank you, Johnny Depp."

Chapter Twenty-Five

Ginger's eyes blinked open. She couldn't get back to sleep. The birds outside the house were making a racket. Magpies hassling a cat, probably, and the noise made Zoë restless. The big dog made circles around the bed, snorting loudly as she neared Ginger's pillow.

Ginger gave up. The clock said seven fifteen. Zoë must have seen Ginger's eyes open because she began to bounce up and down.

"All right, I'm getting up. For crying out loud!" Ginger swung her feet to the floor, only to have them accosted by a slobbery dog.

She let Zoë out the front door and sat on the stoop. In her bathrobe pocket she found a ponytail holder. She pulled the hair out of her eyes and fastened it on top of her head.

It was cooler this early in the morning. For the last few weeks, as school districts welcomed their children back to school and the business at the pool slowed down, Bode and Ginger had split the shifts. Bode worked early, and Ginger came in around noon. He liked finishing up early so he could go out. After his attempt at a relationship with Ginger had fizzled, Bode seemed to be enthusiastically frequenting the downtown clubs.

Ginger, on the other hand, had no interest in making the rounds. She wanted life to smooth itself out for a while. She went home to her dog and called it a good day if it had been uneventful. And she hardly ever thought about Fender.

This morning, she thought about something Molly had mentioned: going out to Brad's grave. The one-year anniversary of his death. It made her neck knot up just to consider it. Lately, she made a point of avoiding calendars.

But the air was fresh this morning. Any later in the day, and it became hot like the exhaust of a truck or a blow dryer. Maybe she should go now. If she left right now, no one else would probably be there, either. She really didn't want to run into people.

She went inside, threw on some clothes, and got her purse. She called to the dog, who was rooting around in the neighbors' flowerbeds, and put her inside, locking the house door. She was going to do this. She was going to visit Brad's grave.

She drove out the long road toward the foothills. She kept the windows down, enjoying the morning air. Ginger tried not to clutch the steering wheel too tightly.

She ascended the steep drive to the cemetery. A bright white and red sign warned, "Unlawful to remove decorations from graves. Violators will be prosecuted."

"Shit." Ginger hadn't brought anything—no flowers, nothing to leave for Brad. She felt her palms go clammy; she was already breaking etiquette and already uncomfortable in this space. She passed the gates, engraved with the words *Perpetual Care*.

The last time Ginger had been here, she'd ridden in the limousine with Brad's mother and father. It'd been kind of a surprise, riding with them. In fact, Ginger hadn't spoken to his family since they'd packed up his things and closed the door to the house a few days after the funeral. *Just a girlfriend*, they must've figured.

But they'd been wrong. Ginger had been wrong. Brad must've been thinking of her as more. He'd bought the ring, after all. Bought it from Fender.

She stopped the car to pull herself out of that particular train of thought. She was at the crest of the hill now, so she steered to the side of the drive and parked. An awning identical to the one that had shaded the mourners for Brad at the funeral stood tall in front of her. Maybe it was the same one. She hadn't noticed before that it was mounted on large black wheels. Strange vehicle.

She got out of the car and turned in a circle to get her bearings. Things looked different. At the funeral, the surroundings had been a vague background to her. She'd witnessed the service with a kind of tunnel vision. She'd noticed only a few of the odd details: the Astroturf under the chairs, the backhoe waiting not-too-subtly to the left of the site. *Fender.*

Now it was clearer. She saw much more around her. A covey of quails bobbed along between headstones in the older part of the cemetery to her right. She liked to see their lively little bodies in a place like this. They sprinted across the road like businessmen late for a train. The sun lit up their gray and brown backs and turned them lilac. The single black feather on the top of each bird's head wiggled in urgency.

She felt suddenly uncomfortable. It wasn't clear to her where she was going. Driving here, she'd thought it'd be impossible not to find Brad. Now it seemed a daunting task.

She remembered he was buried in the east section, and she remembered parking somewhere near this spot. But the graves in this part of the cemetery were marked with flat black-bronze metal markers. She had to walk up to each one to see the name of the occupant.

Maybe it was more to the left, she told herself. A Mylar balloon drifted over one of the markers. She approached it, careful to place her feet wide of the grave itself.

It was an infant's grave. So was the next one, and the one after that, and the one after that. She was lost in a heartbreaking sea of tiny crypts. Little lives, ended in one day, three weeks, a year, their markers engraved with lambs and child angels. Her head swam. She came upon a white marble bench, the headstone for Angela Rabbert. She had died the day after she was born. Under the bench someone had placed a stuffed bear, white with curly ringlets of synthetic fur. A tiny bouquet of roses lay next to the bear.

This felt peculiar. She wasn't going to find Brad. She was lost. This had been a bad idea. She stood still and looked around, looking for something familiar. She was afraid to move her feet, afraid she might tread on a child's grave. She felt sweat forming above her lip.

"Can I help you find someone?" a voice asked from behind her.

She turned around. A wiry elderly man stood on the driveway. He looked familiar. "Have we met?"

He smiled from under a thin mustache. "I believe we have. Aren't you a friend of my son's?"

It was Fender's dad. She couldn't believe it. She looked at the ground, unsure of herself.

He broke the moment's silence. "Were you looking for someone?"

"Yes, I was. His name is Brad Janson. He's supposed to be in the east section. He's buried there, I mean."

He nodded. "Oh, well, you're very close. You've just gotten too far to the left. That's the baby section. Here, come out here, and I'll show you where you need to be." He gestured to her, extending his hand.

She stepped carefully toward him. Then he took her hand, and she was out on the safe asphalt of the road.

"That's sad, isn't it?" He looked into her eyes with a large, warm smile on his face.

"Hmm?" Ginger felt lightheaded. She tried to snap herself out of it, focusing on his friendly eyes.

"The baby section. It's sad to see so many little babies." He turned her around, guiding her with a hand at her elbow. "It's easy to get lost here. Unfortunately, by the time you're my age, you'll know your way around."

He stopped in front of a granite block engraved with the words "East Section." Ginger felt her mind clear. The sun now climbed to the sky, and the air was turning warmer. "Thanks. I haven't been here since the funeral. I guess I didn't remember it very well."

Fender's father nodded. "Fender told me you had a special person in your life who you lost. I'm sorry to hear that. I'm here to see my wife."

"Fender and I aren't really in touch right now." Ginger wasn't sure why that came out of her mouth.

"I did hear that."

Ginger looked at the green lawn, marked by dips in the grass where the bronze markers lay.

Fender's father took a step onto the lawn. "If you'd like, I'll help you find his marker. Walk this way, between the rows." Ginger followed him. "My wife is over on the other side, in the older part of the cemetery. The graves all have headstones over there. It's a lot easier to find someone."

"Do you visit her a lot?" Ginger followed him, watching him look at the names on each marker.

"I try to come when I think of it. I usually end up here once a month or so. I'm embarrassed to say I like to come and talk to her. I tell her what's going on in my life, or how Fender is doing."

Ginger felt something in her chest—something melting, warming up, tightening maybe. She liked to hear Fender's father say "Fender." There was a molasses note in his voice. "Do you have other children?"

"No, we had just the one. But he was plenty—a handful, I'll tell you that. Kept my wife and me running from day one." He paused. "Did you say Brad Janson?"

Ginger's breath came up short. She hadn't been bracing herself, readying herself. "Yes."

"Here he is. Handsome marker." He stood next to her, and she hoped she wasn't leaning on him. But it did feel nice to have his shoulder next to hers. Safer. "Would you like one of my carnations?" He held up the cellophane-wrapped bundle he'd been carrying. He already had a peach carnation out of the bunch and handed it to her.

"Thank you. I didn't think to bring anything."

He chuckled. "It's another hazard of getting old. I have a little bucket of supplies I bring when I come here. Too many friends in this place now. It makes me efficient. I even have clippers to prune away the bushes if they start to overgrow someone's marker or headstone. Pathetic, I tell you."

"I think it's thoughtful. I've never been good at being thoughtful." Ginger was afraid to stop talking to him. She hadn't even looked down yet.

"Well, I'll leave you to your thoughts for a moment." He stepped lightly out of the row and walked toward the older section of the cemetery.

Without his shoulder up against hers, Ginger swayed slightly, just for a minute. Then she took a deep breath and looked down.

Set in concrete was a bronze plaque engraved with Brad's name and his birth and death dates. At the top of the marker, the words "Loving Son and Friend" curved over his name.

She let the air out of her lungs, deflated. She didn't cry, but tears clung to her eyelashes. She felt quiet inside. She'd cried about Brad so much this year. Maybe she could be quiet inside about it now. She knelt.

And waited, searching to see what emotions came. The marker had grass clippings on it, and some needles from a fir tree a few rows away. She tried to brush them off. Slivers caught in her ring finger and thumb. Fingers stinging, she sat back on her heels. "Next time

I'll bring a brush and clean those off." She said it out loud, talking to Brad. But hearing her own voice was comforting.

Ginger looked up, over his marker. At the edge of the section stood a row of fir trees. A large foothill silhouetted them. The summer sun had baked the hill for more than three months. It was almost blond now, the wild grasses bleached of all their moisture. The hill was wild, flatly contrasting the manicured green of the cemetery.

"You have a nice view." She talked to Brad again. No one was near. Fender's father was somewhere behind her now, in another section. "I'm sorry I haven't come to visit before." She put the peach carnation next to his name on the marker. *Son and Friend.* Not a husband, not a father. It made her sad to think his would be the only Janson marker in the cemetery. He wouldn't have a family plot. But he'd wanted to be in the country, in the wild state he loved. Brad wouldn't have liked being buried back east, where his family was from. She was sure they had a plot in some ancient city graveyard somewhere.

Not a father, not a husband. That was the truth of it. Brad had been a good man. A good son. A good friend to many. He'd been a good friend to her. "Anyway, next time I'll bring some other stuff for you." Something about the talking felt right. As words came from her mouth, her insides smoothed out. "Zoë's fine. She missed you a lot at the beginning. I did, too. Molly has a new boyfriend. She's nuts like always. She wants me to burn some sage for you. I forgot to bring it. I will next time."

Next time. It felt good to say that. Like she was doing the right thing for him. Doing her job.

"Well, I should go. I should go before it gets too hot." She stood up. Across the drive at the crest of the hill, the trees grew larger, and instead of flat markers, tall headstones and monuments stood in the shade. Ginger looked for Fender's father. She saw his small head, bent over the top of a headstone. She left Brad and walked to him.

He heard her and looked up. "All done?"

"Yes. Thanks for helping me find him. And for the carnation. Next time I'll bring something."

She came up next to him as he stood in front of a white marble headstone. Engraved in it were the words "Augusta Barnes." A simple stone, only the pearly white of the marble stood against the green lawn.

"This is my wife, Augusta."

Ginger nodded.

He pointed to the top of the headstone. On it were several small stones. They were perched in a row. Each looked a bit different. "That's what I really like to bring to her, if I can. She was always picking up rocks on our hikes. Used to drive me crazy because she never had pockets, so I ended up hauling the rocks around for her. Must have been what kept me so fit, all that extra poundage. If I see a neat one, I pick it up and bring it to her."

"How long has she been gone?"

"Oh, she died when Fender was little. He was six, so he and I have been alone for a long time." He stepped back from the grave, still rolling one of the rocks around in the palm of his hand. He turned and sat on a little wrought-iron bench, next to a rose bush. "Fender and I really did have a tough go of it. I did the best I could, but it wasn't easy. He never quite believed anyone else would ever stick by him. He always had one foot out of the door when he was a teenager. I got the impression he wanted to leave before I could. I don't know if he's gotten past that yet. He likes to mess things up before anyone else ruins them for him."

He stood again, walking around to the back of Augusta's grave. "But don't tell him I told you that. He'd be mad if he knew I was talking about him. Here, come look at this." He motioned for Ginger to come around to the opposite side of the headstone.

"This is my favorite part of Augusta's marker. She always teased me about my thing for music. She just about died when I told her what I wanted to name Fender. You know, after the guitar. But it amused her. She secretly liked it. I think that's what she liked about me. So, I had the marbleworks put this on the back—like I was always humming in her ear."

Ginger looked. On the back of the ivory stone were words. Again colorless, but the sun cast a shadow in their grooves.

"'Rest you easy, dream you light,'" Fender's father said. "I can't even remember what song they're from, but they just came to me when she died. Like someone wanted me to remember them."

Ginger looked at the letters. The words seemed soft, casual, spoken gently. "I like those very much."

Fender's father smiled. "I thought you might." They walked in front of the grave again. He placed the rock in his hand back on top of the gravestone. "Well, I better get going. I want to eat lunch at the Rendezvous today, and they'll be out of the bean and bacon soup if I don't hustle. It was good to see you again."

"It was very nice to see you, too." She didn't want him to leave. "Mr. Barnes?"

"Yes?"

"Tell your son hello for me."

His white smile bloomed from under the thin whiskers of his mustache. "I will." He turned around and headed for his burgundy station wagon, parked in the shade of a fir tree.

Ginger walked around to the back of Augusta's marker again. She said the words herself: "Rest you easy, dream you light."

She walked to the little bench and sat down. The needles of the trees formed a soft cushion under her feet. She felt like talking again and looked around self-consciously. No one in sight. She sat alone with the past of a thousand families. The wives of thousands of husbands, sons and daughters of thousands of mothers. But no one here was her husband. She had a good friend here. She looked at Augusta's marker. Maybe two friends here.

"I'll tell him hello for you, Augusta." The ground swallowed her words in the needles. She turned to walk back to the car.

Chapter Twenty-Six

"Fender!" Sam bellowed. Labor Day weekend was not known as a big jewelry-shopping occasion, and the shop was dead quiet.

"Back here! And stop yelling, for crying out loud!" Fender thought for a minute about hiding what he was working on, but gave up when Sam strolled in the office.

"Whatcha doin'?" Sam stood behind him.

Fender pushed away from the workbench. "Right now, trying not to smack you for breathing down my neck." He turned around to face his friend, putting himself between his project and Sam.

"Oh, now I know you're up to something. You never hide shit from me. You never work, either. What gives?" Sam tried to step to the left for a better view.

Fender scooted his chair to the left. "That's not true. And no."

"Aww, c'mon, man. Best friend here. Show me!" Sam sounded young. Like toddler-style *lemme see* young.

This is pointless. The more I resist, the bigger deal he'll make it. "Fine. Jesus, you're nosy."

Fender got up from his chair and let Sam see what was on the workbench in front of him. It was a delicate gold setting, the prongs curving up around a deep, clear emerald.

Sam nodded. "Fender, I'm impressed. When was the last time you made something custom?"

"I don't know. It's no big deal." He shrugged and shuffled some papers on the desk around.

"I'm always surprised that you've got the skills, but you've definitely got 'em. Your pop would dig this. You should show him."

Fender pushed Sam away from the bench. "Absolutely not."

"Why not?"

"He'd be mad. He wouldn't understand." Fender felt his pulse quicken, and it reminded him of a whole lot of times when he'd been in trouble.

"I don't get it. Illuminate me. He'd love to see you actually taking an interest in his trade."

"The emerald was Mom's. This is special. He wouldn't get it."

Sam tilted his head. "You're redoing an old setting of your mom's? For what?" And then, as usual, Fender saw the idea dawn on Sam—his eyes always got wide in this certain way.

Here we go. He's never going to let this one rest. Fender winced and waited for Sam to make fun of him. But he patted Fender on the back instead.

"It's for her, isn't it?" Sam said softly.

Fender felt his heart warm and expand, blooming at the thought of her. *Ginger.* "Yeah. Please don't say anything."

"I won't. Is it going to be a ring?"

"No. Mom wore it as a necklace. I'm just re-crafting it a bit. Plus the setting was loose."

Sam smiled. "I still remember your mom's chicken pot pies. Man, they were the best. If I could make them like that, I'd open my own restaurant." He edged a little closer to the bench and peeked at the emerald through the lens perched above it. "This Ginger, it's different with her, isn't it?"

Fender couldn't explain. "I think so. But she hates me."

Sam looked him in the eyes, put a hand on his shoulder. "So, make it right, then. The path of least resistance is the path with the least payback sometimes. Sometimes it's worth the struggle." He paused for a moment. "But it seems you know that, because you're here making jewelry for her."

"I just need a little time to figure it out. Just a little time."

Sam sighed. "Everybody wants more time. It's not our luxury to waste."

"Uh-huh."

"All righty, then. I need to eat. You coming?"

Fender looked back at the necklace. "Go on without me. I've got some work to do."

"Yes, my friend, that you do." Sam slapped him on the back and left.

Fender felt mired by his thoughts and his project and his problem to fix. It all hung heavy on him, an albatross on a fine golden chain. He'd returned to his work with the emerald when he heard the phone—a couple times, actually—but he let it go to voice mail.

When he finally got around to checking, the first message was from Pop, and then the second message was from Sam, calling to let him know Pop had called him, too. Pop never called around town looking for him anymore, not since high school, so this messaging worried Fender for a minute. What if Pop was sick? He could've fallen and broken something. It occurred to him that, yes, his pop was getting old, kind of.

Fender thought about this and decided to drive over to the house to check on him. *Whatever the message is must be a big deal. I can't believe it. Pop's going to get sick and die, and I've never thought about it before. I'm an evil son.* He sighed, closed up the shop, and went to the car.

"What's new, right?" he said, either to the steering wheel or to the lady in the SUV on his right at the stoplight. *Yes, ever the prodigal son. Thank God I didn't have siblings. I'm a disappointment, and my parents never even had a normal child to compare me to.*

When he pulled up to Pop's house, there was an unfamiliar car in the driveway. *That's it, now I know he's dead. Someone missed him at the Rendezvous, and they've found his poor lifeless body.* Fender felt a twinge of worry. *And he's been so nice to me lately…*

He still had the key from his temporary "vacation" at Pop's house, so he let himself in the front door. "Please let him be all right," he said to himself as he walked into the house.

Music came from the den, Fender's old room. It was one of Pop's old scratched-up records. Pop had eclectic taste in music. Jazz was his first love, all kinds. But he was also partial to the Steve Miller Band.

In fact, Fender thought he could hear Pop singing, something about peaches and shaking someone's tree.

Fender walked in the door of the den. "You're in a really good mood."

He saw why. Pop had his arms wrapped around a much younger woman. She had dyed black hair with white-platinum streaks through it. The bangs were held out of her eyes with —

"Barrettes!" Fender said loudly. He basically yelled this, and he felt his face flush crimson in embarrassment. Lo, the owner of the barrette Sam had discovered in the couch was not Amy Rasmussen from the fifth grade, but the lovely vixen currently in Pop's arms.

Who yelled, in turn, when Fender yelled at her. She and Pop turned around to face him. They untangled themselves and stood shoulder to shoulder, like elementary kids in trouble. *I can't believe it — everybody is getting laid but me. Even my ancient father is getting a piece.* Fender turned off the music and had a vision of what it would be like to be the parent of an adolescent.

Pop spoke up, regaining his composure. "Sonny! We were listening to records. This is Fiona." Pop's hand went to his chest to smooth a nonexistent tie. Old habit, probably. Nervous gesture from Pop's days as the consummate salesman.

She stepped forward and shook Fender's hand in a lively sort of way. She had a big, happy grin on her face, like a contented dog or little kid. "Jerry's told me a lot about you. It's nice to meet the man named after a guitar. Very cool."

Yay. Bonding over stories about the kid, who in this case would be me. And I appear to be older than the bonding prospect. "So, how'd you meet?" Fender tried to keep sarcasm out of his voice. *Be nice.*

Pop smiled. "Fiona works at the library. In the periodicals section."

Fender nodded. "Of course." All the time at the library made so much more sense now. Women. There was nothing Pop loved more than women.

Fiona picked up a shiny, patent leather handbag off one of the recliners. She wore those funky black cotton Mary Janes from China. *Wow. My father has a cool girlfriend. Who would've thought?*

Cool Girl spoke up. "Jerry, I'm going to go. I've got practice in an hour. Are you coming by later?" Fender detected a pinkish blush to her cheeks when she asked the last question. She gave Pop a peck on the lips and squeezed past Fender, breezing through the living room and out of the door.

Fender's curiosity was up. "Practice?"

Pop grew an inch, he was so proud. "She's in a band. Plays bass and sings backup. I'm getting them a gig at the Rendezvous. I already squared it with the owner."

"Hey, Pop?"

"Yeah?"

"We found her hair clip. In the couch. Fiona's."

Pop grinned. "Adults do things, Fender. Do we need a review of that talk? I thought that was one of the only times I really had your attention. Guess not." Pop was enjoying this and would probably milk it for eons. He'd be insufferable at the Rendezvous.

Fender slapped him on the back. "You're amazing, Pop. Really." He silently scolded himself for worrying about the old man. Pop was going to outlast him, easily.

Pop looked at Fender in surprise. "Oh! Fender, I've got news for you that you're going to love. I tried to find you. I left a message on your phone, but you didn't call back, and when I called Sam's house, I thought he was going to bite my head off."

Fender plopped down on the couch. "Don't worry about Sam. He probably hasn't paid his Sears bill again. He gets kind of testy."

Pop sat down beside him. He would get to the news, but he seemed to want to pause dramatically.

"So. Pop, you had something important to talk to me about?"

"I won't beat around the bush. This is big, Sonny. I saw her."

Fender's mind was a few steps ahead, but he didn't let the thought gel. He kept it crouched in the corner of his head, hoping. "Who? Who did you see?"

Pop readjusted on the couch. "Well, I was visiting Augusta—"

Fender panicked and broke in. "You saw Mom? You thought you saw her alive? She's been gone a long time, Pop."

This wasn't a good move. "Fender Barnes. Are you looking for a way to put me in a nursing home? No, I didn't *see* your mother. I saw your girl. Ring girl."

Fender's eyes hurt. Blood built up behind them from excitement. "Ginger? Really?"

Pop loved when people asked that. He had a stock answer: "No, not really." He slapped Fender on the thigh. "Yes, of course! She was at the cemetery."

The memory of Dead Boyfriend reared its ugly head. "She was visiting him, huh?"

Pop nodded solemnly. "Yes. This morning. She was lost, but I helped her find his grave."

Fender was mad for a second. "You're not supposed to do that, Pop. You're supposed to be helping my cause."

"Well, apparently I did something good, oh son of little faith, because she and I talked for a while."

"About what?"

"I introduced her to your mother."

Oh, Jesus. Now the crazy father-son team of Barnes and Barnes is going to steal the show. "What did she say?"

"She liked the inscription. She seemed a little unsettled or lost."

"You already said she was lost, Pop."

Pop shook his head. "No, not literally this time. When she was standing there, she just looked like she didn't know what to do next. Lost."

Fender could still see her standing on that hill in the summer sky. "She looked that way at the funeral." He sighed. "She could have been the one, Pop. The big time."

Pop looked like he was holding his breath. "She said to tell you hello."

They both were on their feet. Fender was very close to doing something that could only be described as jumping for joy. Then he suddenly saw his reflection in the sofa table and stopped before he horrified himself. Trying to regain his composure, he patted Pop on the back. Then he hugged him.

"I'm glad for you, son. Now go take care of business."

Fender felt a little scared. The proverbial door was open. She had obviously opened it. Even a social misfit like Fender could tell when a girl was giving a guy another chance. Maybe. At least he thought he could. "I'm going to find Sam. Thank you, Pop." He had his keys in his hand and flew out of the house.

Sam would know what to do. *Please, God, let Sam know what to do.* Fender tried to breathe and rushed to the car.

Sam didn't answer the door at first. He did that sometimes, especially now that he and Molly were dating. Fender knew he was home, though—he'd said as much in the message he'd left about Pop's phone call. Fender would bet money Sam just didn't want to answer the door. But he changed his mind, apparently, after Fender pounded with his fist for a full five minutes.

By the time the door finally opened, Fender was readying himself to break it in. *Kick at the lock with the heel of your foot*, he reminded himself. Sometimes a misspent youth had its advantages. He'd lifted his foot and was psyching himself up when the door flung open.

"Jesus Christ!" Sam wore a wifebeater T-shirt that didn't do a lot for his physique. "This had better be the damn Second Coming! I was sleeping." Sam surveyed Fender, whose foot was still poised for judo action. He hadn't put it down, trying to gauge whether or not he was going to have to defend himself against Sam. "And what the hell is the deal with the foot? Who the hell are you, Ralph Macchio?"

Fender put his leg down.

"Go away!" Sam slammed the door in Fender's face.

Never give up in the face of adversity. Some high school guidance counselor had said that to him a long time ago. He took the advice now and began to pound on the door again.

It opened again, slowly. Sam stood away from the door with swim goggles on his eyes and a Super Soaker in his hand, aimed at Fender. "Again, this had better be the full-on Four Horsemen, because your level of intensity is scaring me. I have taken the opportunity to arm myself, and I will fire if provoked."

Fender stayed very still. He and Sam had ruined an entire set of living room furniture in a water fight once. And while the prospect of playing with Sam was diverting, he remembered that he did have a certain life-or-death matter on his hands: Ginger was ready to speak to him again.

Sam looked like he was losing interest. "Speak, or I will again close the door, never to reopen it until I've had a good nap." He made a threatening gesture with the giant squirt gun for emphasis.

"Ginger. It's about Ginger. There's hope."

Sam pulled the goggles up onto his forehead. "Hope? For what?"

"I think she'll speak to me. Pop saw her at the cemetery, and she told him to tell me hi." Fender hopped in the air. *Try to control yourself. Hope is one thing, but it's not everything.*

Sam's eyebrows shot up in surprise. He set the Soaker down on a chair by the door and pulled Fender into the house by his shirt. "Okay, then. We have to come up with a plan, pronto. Before she thinks about it again and changes her mind. You know how chicks are. They're so flighty." His eyes lit up. "Well, you're lucky your friend is such a genius of staggering proportions. I think I already have an idea!"

Fender sat down on the couch. This could be good. Sam and he would fix it. *We'll fix it.* He let himself smile as Sam dug under the couch cushions for the phone.

Chapter Twenty-Seven

The morning Ginger and Bode were due to drain the pool, it was actually brisk outside. The long holiday weekend was over, and the heat had loosened its grip on the valley ever so slightly. She watched Bode checking the pumps and thought about the change of seasons. When fall crept in, it meant winter and skiing were not far behind. If the weather was good, she'd be teaching on the snow by Thanksgiving weekend. And it would be her *second* season without Brad. Everything would be easier.

Everything had seemed a little bit easier since the visit to the cemetery, actually. It had done something good for her soul. She didn't feel as out of sorts. In the space of just few days, she'd remembered to buy her mom a birthday card and make an appointment to get the oil changed in her car.

She hadn't taken one step that was huge, though. It still felt scary. Molly had been bugging her to go out on a date with someone ever since she'd revealed that she was dating Sam. She said it was because she wanted to double date, but Ginger knew it was just Molly trying to fix things, like she always did. Molly never pressed the issue too hard, but Ginger had the feeling she and Sam were kind of rooting for Fender. Molly mentioned his name every once in a while. It was always kind of a lightning-quick, on-the-fly mention, like "Sam and

Fender went to that restaurant together, I think," or "I think I'm free for lunch tomorrow, 'cause Sam has plans with Fender." And then she would change the subject and avoid looking Ginger in the eye for a few minutes. She could probably feel the look Ginger was always giving her.

But since she'd seen his father at the cemetery, Ginger had sort of been rooting for Fender, too. She caught herself thinking about him. She remembered his attempts at learning to ski, or just the way he looked at her when she was talking. That was the nicest feeling in the world. No one had ever looked at her like that before. Fender locked his eyes on her, and that seemed to make her beautiful. She felt like she could be something better when he looked at her that way.

She missed that. But there were still things to be considered: The ring. The lying. And it was Fender's job to fix those things, not hers. She wasn't going to go looking for him. He had to come find her and make things right.

Ginger looked out over the pool, the waterline slowly ebbing away, the water whooshing out through the hoses into the storm drains. School had started for the kids in the valley. Families were scurrying around, finishing their shopping for three-ring binders and new sneakers.

Bode scrubbed the tiles of the emptying pool with zeal. He had so much energy all the time. Ginger had read books all summer when it was slow. That drove Bode crazy. He couldn't hold still long enough to read. *It might help if he tried once in a while, though.* He was the human equivalent of a Golden Lab, she'd decided—lovable and in beautiful shape, but always in motion and, bless his heart, he just wasn't that bright. Molly had been right about him, just like she was right about every guy Ginger had ever dated.

Bode's ears must've been burning. "Do you want to go? There's no point in having us both here. We're watching water drain out of a hose. Go home."

Ginger stood up. "I think I will."

Bode shook his head, shaking droplets of water and sweat out of his hair. "Have a good one." He bent back to his task, scrubbing the steps in the empty shallow end.

Ginger headed home. It was definitely cooler today. Not cool, but not toaster-oven hot like it had been for much of the summer. She felt like doing something.

When she walked into the house, an idea came to her. The kitchen had always been in need of a fresh coat of paint, but she'd never gotten started. Sure, she'd always been busy, but standing here today, she remembered the other reason.

Brad hadn't let her choose the color. "Kitchens should be yellow or white. End of story." Those had been his words.

I'd forgotten that. What a narrow-minded ass.

She covered her mouth. Was that sacrilege? She couldn't believe she'd thought that. But it was true. *Damn it, it's the truth.* Brad, as much as she cared about him, had been a jerk a lot of times. Boy, could he be opinionated. And it was like he ruled the house. *He must have picked that up from his mom and dad, married in the* Leave It to Beaver *era.*

Ginger sat down on the floor of the kitchen and looked up at the walls. She called the dog. Zoë came trotting in from the living room and plopped down, nosing in to get a kiss.

"Hey, Zoë, what do you think of orange?" Ginger stood to get her car keys. Orange it would be.

When she started painting that afternoon, it felt almost liberating. She put on her now-favorite Red Sox hat, cranked the music, and went to work. The color was like a ripe tangerine. Ginger immediately liked the way it brightened up the kitchen.

There was a knock at the door. *No one knows I'm home.* She answered with a paintbrush in her hand.

It was Molly and Sam. Molly grinned from ear-to-ear.

"Hi, Molly. What are you guys doing?"

Sam answered. "Could you come over to the park with us? We have something we want to show you."

Now that's just odd. What are they up to? She thought about the pair in front of her for a second. *Maybe they're getting married in the park!*

She must've waited too long to say anything, because Molly started talking very quickly. "It's a beautiful day, and we were thinking about you. It's too nice to stay inside."

Ginger remembered herself. "I'm kind of in the middle of painting the kitchen."

Sam nodded. "Hence, the paintbrush." He grabbed it out of her hand and tossed it in the bushes unceremoniously. "Ditch it. Life's too short to paint on a day like this. You can finish tomorrow."

Ginger had already decided to go along with their plan, but why not give him a hard time? "I can't finish tomorrow because you just threw my paintbrush in the bushes."

Molly looked frantic. She nudged Sam in the side. "Get her the paintbrush." She smiled oddly at Ginger. "He'll get your paintbrush, and you can go wash it off and close up the paint, and then we'll all go over to the park. Okay?"

"But I'm completely messy. I have paint in my hair." Ginger had never seen Molly this rattled, and it was kind of fun.

"It doesn't matter!" Molly's ringlets shook up and down. She rushed Ginger inside and helped her wash the brush and close the can of paint. Sam stood in the front hallway, rocking back and forth on his heels, looking nervous and fiddling with the pockets of his pants.

Ginger hoped she was right about the surprise. It'd be cool if Molly got married. But why would they be so frantic for her to be there? *I mean, I'm a good friend and everything, but they could get hitched without me.*

"Okay, let's roll, people!" Molly hustled everyone out the front door. Sam kept shooting Molly looks, and Ginger started to discount the wedding theory. They weren't acting very romantic toward each other, actually.

"What's this all about?" Ginger looked at Molly.

"Let's get to the park, and I'll explain." Molly looked both ways and herded her and Sam across the street. Ginger felt like a kid in preschool.

The park across the street was busy for a change. It had been so hot lately that most people stayed out of the sun until late in the day. Today, with the weather cooling a bit, families had emerged from the air conditioning to play on the swings.

This was the park where the Ultimate Frisbee players gathered, although Ginger didn't see any of them today. She smiled, thinking of them. *The opposite of Brad, no doubt about that. But not a better alternative.*

She thought of something. "Hey, we should have brought Zoë over with us. She loves to play in the park."

Sam shook his head. "No, she'd be a problem with the—"

"Sam, shut up! You're going to ruin it, you lunk!" Molly pushed him so hard, Ginger thought he might fall over. He flinched but nodded in submission.

Amazing. Molly had this man trained, by golly. Or he really loved her, to put up with abuse like that. Or whatever was going on was really important. But what could be such a big deal?

She looked up to see the big deal standing under a tree about ten yards away.

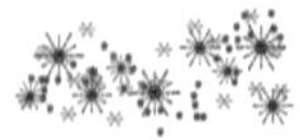

Fender watched Molly and Sam bringing Ginger across the street. His heart raced. He took two deep breaths, trying to maintain some composure. *God, I hope this works.* He tried to think of a prayer to say.

Ginger spotted him and stopped. Molly touched her between the shoulder blades. They walked a little closer, Sam tagging along behind them, and when Ginger seemed to pause again, Fender heard Molly speak to her. "Go on, honey. It's time to talk to him. You two need this."

Fender held his breath. She walked toward him.

"Hi." She looked scared.

He tried to sound normal, safe. "Hi. I'm glad you came."

"I didn't know you were here. I thought maybe Molly and Sam were getting married or something." He could tell she was holding back, waiting for something from him.

He looked over her shoulder at Sam and Molly. "They probably would get married like that. They were supposed to tell you why you were coming over here."

"They" were obviously listening. "We got her here, didn't we?" Sam called. "Don't be fussy, Fender." Molly tugged at his arm, trying to get him to be quiet. She started to lead him back to Ginger's house.

Fender called, "Thank you, again. I'll owe you for a very long time over this, I'm sure." He turned and looked at Ginger again. *If I scare her away, I'll cry. Please give me a chance.* She chewed on her lip a little. There was orange paint in her hair. She looked gorgeous.

"Why do you look at me that way?" she asked. "You did it all the time in lessons. You weren't really paying attention, were you?"

"I was paying attention to you. When I first saw you—"

"At the funeral?"

"Yeah, at the funeral. When I first saw you there, you looked lost. You looked like you needed me, maybe. You looked beautiful."

"What about Brad? Didn't you like him when you met him? Why'd you go after me?"

It was clear she was going to bring him back to this until he fixed it. *She deserves at least an explanation. She deserves a lot more than that.* "I wasn't after you. I wanted to give you the ring. But then I saw you, and I couldn't, not right away. I made a lot of attempts to give it to you, but something always stopped me. The bottom line is, I screwed up. I should have told you the truth right away. Brad wanted to propose to you. I'm sorry." He pulled his hands out of his pockets and fidgeted with a button on his shirt.

"What was he like, when he bought the ring?"

Fender leaned back against the tree's trunk. "I was in a bad mood. I was about to close, but he was very excited. He wanted to talk all about you. He mentioned your dog. Oh, and a pair of earrings you always wore, little dolphins?"

She looked up at him, and he could see tears welling in her eyes. "I don't wear them anymore. They remind me too much of him."

Fender felt the wind go out of him. *She still loves Brad. This was a bad idea.* "I'm so sorry you're alone. It never should've happened. Life can be so randomly shitty."

He was about to turn when she took a step toward him. "It can be. It can be great sometimes, too."

This is it. Put yourself out there, Fender. There's no point in not telling her all of it. He stepped forward. "I want to tell you so much. You're an incredible person — trust me, because not a lot of people impress me very much. You blow me away. I want you to know that, no matter what. You've changed me — you can even ask Sam."

He took her hand. "I have to show you something." He led her around the trunk of the tree. "Close your eyes for a second. I know, but humor me. This was all Sam's idea if you don't like it."

He let go of her hand. She stood very still. Fender hustled over to the pile of stuff Sam had prepared. Two cages sat side by side. One of Molly's doves sat in the smaller one. It blinked at him stupidly as he grabbed it. Sam had placed its cargo around its foot already. He approached Ginger again. "Okay. Open up."

She opened her eyes. He held up the white dove.

"This is from Brad, by way of an idiot, screwed-up jeweler. It's very overdue." He handed the bird to her.

The bird trembled in her hands. Ginger's brows furrowed with curiosity. "What's tied around its ankle?"

"This is the Sam part. He wanted you to see what it was and then let the bird fly away. But Molly'd kill him if we lost the dove, and you should have it, if you want it. Here, it's tied on with a ribbon. Let me help." Fender came near to her. Her eyes and lips were very close. He remembered kissing her lips.

The bird trembled again, and Ginger shivered too. Fender took a finger and pulled at the ribbon. The bird squirmed. Fender looked up into Ginger's eyes. "Hang onto him, because if we lose him, Sam's dead meat." He fumbled with the ribbon, untied it, and took the bird from her hands, turning quickly to stuff it back in the cage. "This is what you've deserved to have for a year now. I'm sorry it took so long."

He placed a ring in her palm. *The* ring. Fender was so tired of looking at it. Her hands shook.

"Don't drop it." He spoke softly to her. This was the part where she was reminded about her old love and how Fender was a big, fat liar. He tried again to think of some sort of prayer.

"It's awfully big." She didn't say anything else. Fender noticed tears falling into her hands.

"Isn't it beautiful?" He put a hand on her shoulder.

"Sure it is. There's nothing wrong with it. I'm glad I finally got to see it."

Fender felt nauseated, seeing her cry like this. "I'm sorry it makes you so sad. I wish you could've been his wife."

"You don't understand. I'm sad that Brad's gone. He was a good man." He heard the rasp of tears in her throat. "But you'll hate me for this." She took a deep breath. "I'm relieved."

"Relieved?" He tried not to sound too hopeful.

"I'm ashamed, because if he'd been all right, I'd be married to him, probably. But I didn't…We weren't…He wasn't the one for me." She paused, swallowing hard.

Fender resisted the urge to smile.

"I didn't want to marry him, Fender. I loved him, but he wasn't the right person for me."

It was all he could do not to jump up and down. *Things are still serious. Things could still go south. Focus on her!*

She continued. "The man died on the street, and all I can think is how I feel like I avoided something bad—avoided living a life that wasn't right for me. I feel relieved." She sat down on the grass, quiet.

Yes! Joy rolled through Fender. He saw hope flittering above him. Maybe this was going to work. "I have something else to give you, then. Close your eyes one more time." He hustled back to the two cages.

She spoke to him as he checked on the dove, back in its cage. "I just want to be completely honest. Please don't think I'm a bad person."

"Yeah?" The dove was trying to peck his finger. Fender tried to get back to the moment. *Focus on her, idiot!*

"If Brad picked this ring, it just tells me I was right, that he didn't really know who I was. It's very beautiful, but it's not me."

Fender wanted to cackle with glee. He'd never cackled before, but he wanted to. "Keep your eyes closed. I want to give you that other thing." Fender opened the door to the second cage. Inside was a bunny. He'd told Sam the whole plywood-rabbit-ski-lesson story, and Sam felt this was the "crowning glory" of the plan. Give her something from the heart, with its own furry accompaniment: a bunny.

Fender reached into the cage. The rabbit, probably sensing his inherent evil, shied away from him, flattening down in the back of the cage. Fender pulled the jewelry box out of his pocket. Give her another ring, one for your love, Sam had suggested. But Fender knew, as soon as Sam had said that, what was right. Fender cared about only one piece of jewelry in the whole world. One that actually had meaning—and not just as a means of buying someone off or accomplishing a goal. It sat in the box in front of him right now. According to Sam's plan, it was supposed to go around the neck of the bunny that was currently hanging on to the inside of the cage with every fiber of its bunny being.

"Stop being shy! It's time for your big number, bunny." Fender reached into the cage slowly. "You are the grand finale here, Mister Hare." The bunny skittered to the opposite corner of the cage, still out of reach. Fender lost his patience. "Let's go, Bugs." He made a swipe at the scruff of the bunny's neck.

Mister Hare was not amused. Its white head swiveled around and suddenly, the sweet-symbol-of-love bunny was the killer rabbit. It sunk its teeth into the flesh of Fender's hand.

It was everything he could do not to scream in utter agony. But somehow, he withdrew his hand from the cage and closed the door, suffering in silence.

Time for Plan B. He picked up the cage with the bunny in it, made sure the jewelry box was sitting on top, and went back to Ginger.

She sat on the grass, eyes still closed, waiting patiently. Fender touched her arm.

"Open your eyes."

She did as she was told, and Fender held up the cage.

"A rabbit?"

"It's a hare. A March hare, in fact." The little rabbit sat very still, its nose twitching. *Now* it was all sweet and demure.

"Like the one on the cat track."

"Yeah, like the one I plowed over. I hoped you'd remember. I'd take it out of the cage, but apparently it has an attitude." Fender held up his chewed-on hand as evidence.

Ginger looked curious. "What's he got?"

Fender picked up the box on the top of the cage and pulled out its contents. "Again, all of this is Sam's idea if you don't like it." He took the object out of the box. "This was supposed to be around the neck of Cujo there, but in the interest of safety, here you go."

It was a slender gold chain. At its bottom was a small emerald, suspended. It was a deep green, sparkling in its simple setting.

"It was my mother's." Fender waited for her reaction.

"What's this for? It's so beautiful." Ginger put it around her neck and touched the emerald, hanging at the hollow between her collarbones.

He sat down, close to her, taking the emerald in his hand. "That is for you. For making me notice why it's good to be here. Why I'm willing to make an ass of myself over and over again just to be with you. For the only reason life makes any sense at all. Why I don't ever want to be without you, and why I want to throw up because I'm afraid of what you might say next."

Ginger looked like she was going to say something, but she started to cry.

"Ginger Stevens, I love you." Fender took her by both shoulders and kissed her with the intensity and passion and love of an optimist. The best part was, Ginger kissed him back.

Epilogue

"We're gonna be late, and they'll kill the both of us. You can't have a wedding without the best man." Fender gripped the dash in front of him. Ginger's driving scared him.

"I'm hustling as fast as I can. We're just about at the parking lot." She pushed the little white car up the hill to the ski resort. Though spring had come to the valley again, snow lingered in the mountains.

Fender felt carsick. He tried to loosen the tie around his neck. He couldn't remember the last time he'd worn a tie. Actually, when he thought about it, it'd probably been to the funeral, on his mission to find Ginger. That was the first time he'd seen her, a year and a half ago.

The stuff I do for this girl, I swear.

Oh, but to look at her, it was a dream. It all was.

Here he sat, next to her. She was a vision. He could puke from the car ride up the mountain, but still. He couldn't believe she was his, her strawberry hair pulled up in a twisty bun in the back—a style that probably had some name he didn't know. She wore pinkish sparkly lipstick on those full, wet lips, and she had a white parka pulled tight around her slim, pale neck. Those lips, that neck, they got him thinking.

"I could kiss you right now." He said it out loud. She'd turned him into a sap.

"What?" She turned to look at him and smiled wide.

"Car!" He pushed both feet into the passenger-side floor, fake-braking with all his might.

A black SUV had come to a sudden stop in front of them, and they were about to be on the bumper, smashed to a small cube of metal and bodies.

"Oh, God!" Ginger jerked the car to the right and somehow squeezed it between the black SUV and an old Ford truck parked up tight to the guard rail. Fender jumped as the side mirror next to him snapped off.

She didn't stop until they'd threaded the needle and made it the last hundred yards into the parking lot.

"Jesus!" His hands shook.

She pulled into a spot and turned off the engine. "That was close."

Fender shook his head. "Close?" He pointed a shaky finger out his window. "You have no side mirror over here. You shaved it off. I think my sideburn on this side is shorter now."

Ginger buried her face in her hands and laughed loud. "Oh, crap! I don't know where that came from, but I didn't have time to stop. We would've smashed into the back of them."

"You're Mario Andretti all of a sudden. Stunt driver. Unbelievable, woman." He looked at her, her head back now, looking up at the ceiling of the car, laughing with an open mouth.

She was beautiful.

"C'mon, Danica, let's go to a wedding." He got out of the car.

She came around to his side, and they stood and looked at the hole where the side mirror used to go.

She took his hand and squeezed. "Looks like the stump of Luke's hand in *The Empire Strikes Back*."

"I thought that was in *Jedi*." He led her across the parking lot to the lodge, around mounds of snow pushed up to the ends of the rows of parked cars.

"Ask Sam tonight. He'll know." She clung to him. "Why didn't I just wear my snow boots? This is ridiculous."

"Because you wanted to make the bride happy, and she asked you to wear those shoes."

"Stupid heels."

"Once the reception starts in the lodge, you'll be fine." He looked forward to the part where she took off the parka.

"There they are." She squinted as the late-afternoon sun bounced off the snow. "I can't run. They're just going to have to wait for a minute."

Fender smiled. "Come here. I'll piggy back you."

Ginger shook her head. "I've got a dress on." She pointed to the silver satin poking out from the bottom of her parka.

"It's long enough. C'mon."

She obliged, and he felt her wrap his arms around his neck. "If you drop me, I'll kill you just before I die of embarrassment." The hair on his neck prickled under the warmth of her breath.

"Quiet." He hustled them over to the group of people, all clustered around an arch fashioned out of pine boughs and white flowers. He was supposed to be standing to the left of that arch with the groom. "How late are we?"

"Enough to be in trouble." They came up to the deck outside of the lodge, and Ginger slipped off his back on to the bricks.

"You two! Where have you been?" Pop hurried up to them.

"Pop, we just about died. Don't scold." Fender adjusted his tie nervously.

"This is a wedding. Everyone's waiting." Pop took a minute to smile at Ginger. "You look beautiful, darling. A vision." He turned back to Fender and snarled. "Next time I need a best man, I'm asking Sam."

"Next time?" Fender followed his father to the front.

"It's just an expression. Come meet Reverend McDaniel."

Fender shook hands with the minister and turned to look at the group of people gathered for the wedding.

Fiona and Pop, getting married. Who woulda thought it? I didn't. He fidgeted. *Where's Ginger?* He scanned the groom's side of the aisle. Sam waved from the front row, sitting next to Molly. They were bundled together in a big plaid blanket. He couldn't even tell what they were wearing. Knowing Sam, he had his Carhartts on.

There she was. His girl. Standing at the back of the gathering, by the doors to the lodge, Ginger pulled her white parka close to her in the chill of the cooling evening. The stars would be out soon. Ginger glowed — her face pink with the chill and hair up off her neck. The way she stood tall, the way her eyes shined—she stood out, a diamond sparkling in the mountain dusk.

We could get married, I guess. He laughed out loud. *That didn't take long to occur to me.*

"Fender? Can you focus, please? My bride's about to come down the aisle." Pop straightened his shoulders.

"Sorry, Pop. I'm so happy for you." Fender put an arm around him, and they watched as Ginger opened the door from the lodge for Fiona to make her entrance.

The dark-haired woman came out with a wide smile on her face. She wore a white gown with a fur cape. *Fake fur, of course. Hipster girl can't offend anyone.* Fender checked himself. *Be nice. Pop loves her; she loves him. So what if she wears red patent-leather Doc Martens?*

Fiona came down the aisle, and Pop's eyes glistened with tears. Fender couldn't help but smile at the ceremony. He really was happy for his father. Pop and Fiona exchanged vows and rings, which, incidentally, looked damned good because Fender had designed and made them himself.

The whole time, though, Fender fought to pay attention to the action in front of him, because what he really wanted to do was stare at Ginger.

The reverend presented the newlywed couple to the crowd of friends, and everyone followed Fiona and Pop into the lodge.

"Time for you to catch the garter, my friend!" Sam clapped Fender on the back. If he'd been wearing Carhartts outside, he'd peeled them off. He now wore a flannel shirt and a clean pair of pants.

"Glad you bathed for the occasion. Where's Molly?" Fender scanned the crowd, though he was really looking for Ginger.

"She's helping at the bar. Your pop practically lives in a bar, you know. There's a lot of people here with high drink expectations."

"Reception would've been better at the Rendezvous."

"Have some standards, Fender. Even Pop knows better than that."

Fender nodded absently, and then he saw her.

Ginger walked over to them. She'd shed her white parka and wore a slim slip of a silver dress. The neck was high across her collarbones.

"Hey, look at you!" Sam whistled. She dipped her head shyly.

"Don't be shy. You look gorgeous." Fender pulled her to him.

"You guys didn't see the back." Ginger twirled around for them.

The dressed dipped, hanging low off her shoulders in a drape that revealed a long length of pale, smooth back.

Fender swallowed hard. "When do we leave?"

When Ginger turned back around, her cheeks were pink, but she grinned. "I take it you like?"

He kissed her. "I like."

Sam coughed. "Still here, next to you people. Keep it PG, Fender."

He took Ginger by the hand and led her toward the dance floor. "And when do you ever follow your own advice, Sammy boy?" he called back to his friend. "We'll see you later."

Then he was on the dance floor with his girl in his arms, holding her close.

"This is much better," he whispered in her ear, keeping his lips close to her sweet skin.

"I agree."

He took a step back and held her by both hands. "Ginger Stevens?"

"Yes?"

"Can I ask you a question?"

She looked puzzled for a minute, but nodded and answered quietly. "Yes, Fender Barnes, you can."

He took a deep breath. "Can I drive home?"

She kissed him hard, grinned, and smacked his arm. "Yes. You can. Now kiss me, you goof."

Fender kissed his girl, and all was right with the world.

Acknowledgments

Many thanks go out to many people who have given me all the kinds of support I need to keep writing. To my family, especially my sons, for their patience when I'm on deadline or have a wild hair/stroke of inspiration. To my mom and dad and Aunt Joann, for taking the time to give me pep talks. To the Andersons, for being some of my first readers. To my school district family, you all are my heroes for growing the next generation of writers and readers. To my Omnific family — Elizabeth and Colleen and Cindy and especially Jessica, and to my sister authors at Omnific — what a privilege it's been to learn and work alongside such amazing talent. To wonderful readers and bloggers like Steph of Steph's Sweet Reads, Michelle and Pepper of All Romance Reviews, and Midian S. — getting to know you has been an unanticipated and wonderful bonus I'd never imagined. To RWA and the fabulous authors I met in San Antonio, what a great group of people to be associated with — I learned so much. As always to my writing group — one of these days we'll get that awesome screenplay written.

And especially to my husband, Marcus. Your unfailing support in every imaginable way is the reason I am a writer instead of a dreamer. You help me be a better person, and I love you.

Beck Anderson loves to write about love and its power to heal and grow people past their many imperfections. She is a firm believer in the phrase "mistakes are for learning" and uses it frequently to guide her in her writing life and real life.

For Beck, the path to published novelist has taken lots of twists and turns, including a degree in anthropology, a stint as a ticket seller at a ski resort, a much-loved career as a high school English teacher, and a long tenure as a member of the best writing group ever, hands down.

Beck balances (clumsily at best) writing novels and screenplays, working full-time as an educator, mothering two pre-teen males, loving one post-forty husband, and making time to walk the foothills of Boise, Idaho, with Stefano DiMera Delfino Anderson, the suavest Chihuahua north of the border.

⊷ New Adult Romance ⊶

Three Daves by Nicki Elson
Streamline by Jennifer Lane
The Shades series: *Shades of Atlantis* & *Shades of Avalon* by Carol Oates
The Heart series: *Beside Your Heart, Disclosure of the Heart* & *Forever Your Heart*
by Mary Whitney
Romancing the Bookworm by Kate Evangelista
Flirting with Chaos by Kenya Wright
The Vice, Virtue & Video series: *Revealed, Captured* & *Desired* by Bianca Giovanni
Granton University series: *Loving Lies* by Linda Kage

⊷ Paranormal Romance ⊶

The Light series: *Seers of Light, Whisper of Light* & *Circle of Light* by Jennifer DeLucy
The Hanaford Park series: *Eve of Samhain* & *Pleasures Untold* by Lisa Sanchez
Immortal Awakening by KC Randall
The Seraphim series: *Crushed Seraphim* & *Bittersweet Seraphim* by Debra Anastasia
The Guardian's Wild Child by Feather Stone
Grave Refrain by Sarah M. Glover
The Divinity series: *Divinity* by Patricia Leever
The Blood Vine series: *Blood Vine, Blood Entangled* & *Blood Reunited*
by Amber Belldene
Divine Temptation by Nicki Elson
The Dead Rapture series: *Love in the Time of the Dead* & *Love at the End of Days* by
Tera Shanley

⊷ Romantic Suspense ⊶

Whirlwind by Robin DeJarnett
The CONduct series: *With Good Behavior, Bad Behavior* & *On Best Behavior*
by Jennifer Lane
Indivisible by Jessica McQuinn
Between the Lies by Alison Oburia
Blind Man's Bargain by Tracy Winegar

⊷ Erotic Romance ⊶

The Keyhole series: *Becoming sage* (book 1) by Kasi Alexander
The Keyhole series: *Saving sunni* (book 2) by Kasi & Reggie Alexander
The Winemaker's Dinner: *Appetizers* & *Entrée* by Dr. Ivan Rusilko & Everly Drummond
The Winemaker's Dinner: *Dessert* by Dr. Ivan Rusilko
Client N° 5 by Joy Fulcher

Historical Romance

Cat O' Nine Tails by Patricia Leever
Burning Embers by Hannah Fielding
Seven for a Secret by Rumer Haven

Anthologies

A Valentine Anthology including short stories by
Alice Clayton ("With a Double Oven"),
Jennifer DeLucy ("Magnus of Pfelt, Conquering Viking Lord"),
Nicki Elson ("I Don't Do Valentine's Day"),
Jessica McQuinn ("Better Than One Dead Rose and a Monkey Card"),
Victoria Michaels ("Home to Jackson"), and
Alison Oburia ("The Bridge")

Taking Liberties including an introduction by Tiffany Reisz and short stories by
Mina Vaughn ("John Hancock-Blocked"),
Linda Cunningham ("A Boston Marriage"),
Joy Fulcher ("Tea for Two"),
KC Holly ("The British Are Coming!"),
Kimberly Jensen & Scott Stark ("E. Pluribus Threesome"), and
Vivian Rider ("M'Lady's Secret Service")

Singles, Novellas & Special Editions

It's Only Kinky the First Time (A Keyhole series single) by Kasi Alexander
Learning the Ropes (A Keyhole series single) by Kasi & Reggie Alexander
The Winemaker's Dinner: RSVP by Dr. Ivan Rusilko
The Winemaker's Dinner: No Reservations by Everly Drummond
Big Guns by Jessica McQuinn
Concessions by Robin DeJarnett
Starstruck by Lisa Sanchez
New Flame by BJ Thornton
Shackled by Debra Anastasia
Swim Recruit by Jennifer Lane
Sway by Nicki Elson
Full Speed Ahead by Susan Kaye Quinn
The Second Sunrise by Hannah Downing
The Summer Prince by Carol Oates
Whatever it Takes by Sarah M. Glover
Clarity (A *Divinity* prequel single) by Patricia Leever
A Christmas Wish (A *Cocktails & Dreams* single) by Autumn Markus
Late Night with Andres by Debra Anastasia
Poughkeepsie (enhanced iPad app collector's edition) by Debra Anastasia

Poughkeepsie (audio book edition) by Debra Anastasia
Blood Eternal (A Blood Vine series single, epilogue to series) by Amber Belldene
Carnaval de Amor (The Winemaker's Dinner, Spanish edition) by Dr. Ivan Rusilko &
Everly Drummond

Sets

The Heart Series Box Set (*Beside Your Heart, Disclosure of the Heart* &
Forever Your Heart) by Mary Whitney
The CONduct Series Box Set (*With Good Behavior, Bad Behavior* &
On Best Behavior) by Jennifer Lane
The Light Series Box Set (*Seers of Light, Whisper of Light, Circle of Light* &
Glimpse of Light) by Jennifer DeLucy
The Blood Vine Series Box Set (*Blood Vine, Blood Entangled, Blood Reunited* &
Blood Eternal) by Amber Belldene

coming soon from
OMNIFIC PUBLISHING

The Fatal series: *Brutal* (novella 1.5) by T.A. Brock
The Vice, Virtue & Video series: *Devoted* (book 4) by Bianca Giovanni
The Divinity series: *Entity* (book 2) by Patricia Leever
Let's Get Physical by Elle Fiore
The WORDS series: *The Truest of Words* (book 3) by Georgina Guthrie
The Poughkeepsie Brotherhood series: *Saving Poughkeepsie* (book 3) by Debra Anastasia
The Hidden Races series: *Incandescent* (book 1) by M.V. Freeman
The Legendary Saga: *Claiming Excalibur* (book 2) by LH Nicole

www.ingramcontent.com/pod-product-compliance
Lightning Source LLC
Chambersburg PA
CBHW020516120726
47904CB00003B/857